RISE AND FIGHT AGAIN

By Kit Hussey

This is the beginning of the Robertson family saga, time travel love stories with a rather large body count.

RISE AND FIGHT AGAIN by Kit Hussey

This book would not have been possible without the help of David Braeutigam author, friend and computer guru.

Other works by Kit Hussey
Sea of Troubles
Time Out of Season
Outride the Devil, A Morning With Doc Holliday (DVD)

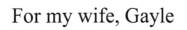

For my wife, Gayle

Table of Contents

Suspend a little disbelief so that too much science doesn't interfere with a good story.

Rise and Fight Again

I used to spend summers with my great uncle Quigley and my great aunt Marcy at their house in North Dakota. Two of the things that I remember from those visits are that the house could be really spooky for a young boy, and I remember the times when Uncle Quigley would invite me into the library where he kept a very special leather-bound book. Sometimes he would open the book, shake his head, and say, "Nothing today." And then he would put the leather-bound book back in its place and read to me from some other book. He would never show me any of the pictures in a book, "Make your own," he'd say, "up here," and he would tap his head in what I always thought was a strange way. He held his middle fingers down with his thumb and tapped his head with his extended index and small fingers. "Besides," he'd say, "without a picture, the hero always looks like you." But once in a while when he would open that special leather-bound book his eyes would light up. "Well," he'd say, "have a seat, and let's see what's been happening this time." And I would hear fantastic stories about the future, about the past, about how time was just a place. About Robertson. It was all his own invention, of course, but he swore that the stories were true, and I wanted to believe him. But I peeked at the book once. The pages were blank.

One evening Uncle Quigley opened the book and began to read.....

"Right on schedule at four o'clock in the morning the dark sky of New Mexico lit up with the successful explosion of the world's first atomic bomb. What follows is the account of why that is no longer true."

2

Why it's no longer true
----- Old Calendar, July 16, 1945 -----

The C-47 jolted east through building cumulous clouds. The general sat alone in the cabin. He was flying to Potsdam to tell the president of the United States that after years of effort by thousands of people and over two billion dollars spent, the Manhattan Project was an utter failure. He imagined the furious reaction of President Truman. "Goddamn it, Groves this country gave you a chance to win the war, and all you have done is eat a truckload of chocolate and piss away two billion dollars. Now will you explain to me why in hell the goddamn bomb did not go bang?"

A flash of light snapped his attention to the right side of the aircraft. The right engine burst into flame and then exploded. The thunderous noise came blasting through the plane's interior. The general shouted at the cockpit, "What the hell just happened?"

The co-pilot turned in his seat and gave the general a cheerful thumbs-up gesture, and the plane lurched and jostled onward.

The general tried to make himself understood, "The engine," he shouted again. The two pilots were looking straight ahead at towering black thunderheads. The general tried again. "The engine! The right engine! You've lost the right engine!" He pointed out the right window and froze in terror as a mesmerizing crack ripped slowly across the wing root toward the rear of the wing. Frantically he looked for his seat belt. It was on the floor, and the gyrations of the plane would not allow him to reach it. 'Shit,' he thought, 'I hate these goddamn machines.'

The co-pilot twisted in his seat, caught the general's eye, and shouted over the din of flight, "The weather ahead looks pretty bad, General. Better fasten your seat belt,"

"The what?" the general shouted back.

The co-pilot shouted again, "The weather, sir."

"The what?" The general couldn't hear above the engine noise. "Goddamn it son, talk up so I can make a goddamn decision."

The plane began to shake violently. "The weather." The voice echoed in his ear. A loud ripping noise. The right wing snapped off of the fuselage, and the plane rolled on its back and began to flip and dive uncontrollably into the chaotic turbulence of a thunderstorm.

"General," the voice screamed.

"What? Speak up. I've got to tell the president..."

The corporal shook General Groves' shoulder gently again and repeated, "General, wake up, sir. The weather, sir." Outside the building a tympani of thunder accentuated the corporal's prodding.

General Leslie Groves awoke and focused on reality. "Shit," he grunted.

"Dreaming again, sir?"

"Yeah. What is it?"

"Sir, Mr. Oppenheimer thinks that because of the storms, the test should be postponed."

"What storms? The sky is clear."

"Not anymore, sir."

"What are you talking about?"

"The storms, sir. They came out of nowhere, and Mr. Oppenheimer wants to postpone the test." Thunder roared again. Rain tap danced on the roof.

"The test hasn't happened yet?"

"No, sir."

Groves sat up at the edge of his cot, relieved. "It wasn't

a failure then?"

"Sir?" the confused corporal asked.

"Never mind," Groves grumbled. He got to his feet and looked out the door. "What the hell happened to the goddamn weather?"

What happened to the weather? The weather was different the second time the first atomic bomb was tested. With time travel, occasionally these subtle changes happen.

Come take my place
----- The Present, Guardian Hall -----

The upper-class cadet addressed his tour group of freshman cadets. "Okay, grubs, next stop will be The Museum. The gunnery sergeant in charge has been associated with Guardian Hall training for... well, forever. He is a kindly-looking white haired gentleman who knows all there is to know about Guardian history. He has this tame professorial manner, but be aware that on a count of two, he can down a glass of beer with one hand and kill, clean, and skin an opponent with the other. Address him as Gunnery Sergeant Takis or "Sir.""

"Welcome to Guardian Hall." The old man wore the dark uniform of the Guardians, and the thin silver arrow on his chest indicated that he was a Bowman. His white hair and his eyes inspired awe in the cadets. "This building is also known as the Museum, as the Library, as Kanagra-she (the Place Where Hell is Kept Alive). I am, then, either the guard, the curator, the librarian, or the Fiend." A murmur of uncomfortable laughter came from the assembled cadets. The old man continued, "As you approach Commitment Day in your training, it is important that you know what you will be putting at risk. And so we tour." He turned and approached the door. It was a simple wooden door with a brass knob on the left side. Originally, the knob had been decorated with a lacework of fleur-de-lis. Now the worn remains of the design glowed with the patina of many touches. To the surprise of the cadets, he actually had to touch the knob and rotate it so that the door would open. It seemed strange.

"Those who view here must desire it, and so the door is of the ancient style and must be opened by the viewer," he explained as he passed through and into the large room beyond. The cadets filed past him into the Hall. "Stay as long as it takes.

Return whenever you have the need. Commitment Day is a ceremony." His tone indicated his disgust for ceremony and pretense. "Here is where you will decide. If you choose to continue with us, those few who are able to finish the training will become Guardians. You will bring balance. For that, you will be mocked. And when doubt has taken charge of the situation, you will be able to harness powers as the Guardians maintained here have done, and for that you will be completely and utterly feared."

The cadets moved through the Hall. In enclosed exhibits throughout the room, the remains of Guardian heroes were on display -- gruesome display. Some preserved in the state of final battle. There were pieces of bodies. Sometimes just fragments. Some looked whole and were attached to life support, eternally maintained. And with each display, there was a hologram of the battle scene. Viewing helmets provided opportunities to hear the screams and confusion and smell the scene. The old Guardian continued, "Two of our exhibits need explanation. Every moment the cells of our bodies are dying and being replaced. And we continue to be the same. We occupy the same space. Memory continues. On rare occasions, one here will somehow use this to rebuild. Rebuild the body. Rebuild the brain. They sit up, take out the tubes, and climb off the shelf. This happened recently, and so you will find a vacated exhibit. There is also a space that is always empty. It is reserved for the Guardian yet to give his life." The reserved exhibit's face recognition program reacted, and as each cadet approached, he was shocked to see his name displayed as the occupant.

Many of the cadets were violently repelled by the exhibits and withdrew from the Hall. Above all else, the Guardian Force hated war and insisted that its wasteful horrors be the last resort. The cadets who remained in the Hall this day reverently continued the tour, experiencing the vicarious overload of war. They stared at the reserved exhibit. It waited like a coffin -- austere, its emptiness sneering through the clear screen. And next to it was the vacated exhibit they would never forget. The deeds had been beyond belief, and now the berth was empty, the tubing neatly coiled, the linen and kit arranged just as if it were a barracks room ready for inspection.

One of the cadets approached the Guardian and said, "Excuse me, sir."

"Yes?"

"Cadet Brock, Sir, I have a question." The old man nodded and the cadet continued, "All this seems so grotesque. This is not a museum. It is a chamber of horror."

"So it is," agreed the Guardian.

"Why? Why not let these beings go in peace to their deaths? Why keep them on display? Pieces of them on display? Growing old in comas. Fed by support systems. It disgusts me."

"Good. If you choose war, this is what you'll get. Not shiny buttons and parade bands. You'll get this. This disgusting horror. And it is our hope that if you know the cost of battle, you will desire the skill to avoid it, and you will be on the way to becoming a true Guardian."

The door to the museum opened and two figures entered. They were dressed as civilians, but their bearing indicated they were military. They were hard men, men with many scars. For most, the military is a profession of service. These men had served to kill. The cadets in the room gave way. Instinct told them, 'Do not bother these men.'

The old Guardian spoke first. His voice was level and calm, like deep water flowing over rocks. "So, Mister James, Mister Peavey, here to pay your respects?"

"We heard he's off the shelf."

"Yes, that is true."

"How long ago?"

"Two days ago," the Guardian said.

"Your grubs showing any promise?" the one called James asked, referring to the cadets.

The Guardian shrugged a silent non-committal answer.

The two surveyed the cadets in the room. Their stares withered most of the cadets, but one continued to study the two men, and that drew their attention. James came to within a few inches of the cadet's face and asked in carnivorous tones, "What's your name, Cadet?"

"Brock, sir."

"Brock, my ass." This time it was the one called Peavey who spoke, glaring into the cadet's eyes as if searching for something to kill.

The Guardian interrupted quietly, "Gentlemen, this is not a barracks."

"This is none of your business, old man." James' words were spoken too softly to carry to the rest of the room, but the whispered intensity did carry, and all the cadets knew this was not a friendly exchange.

The Guardian's bearing remained controlled and calm, "What is old on one world is not old on another. Many have not understood this. I am still here. They are not. It is something to consider, especially since there are only two of you."

Peavey chuckled, "That's good, Gunny. That's real good. Nice level tone. Good intensity, eye contact, all that shit. I know I'm scared. How 'bout you, Chris?"

"Forget it, Peavey."

"Okay." Peavey's remark was jovial, flippant. He turned and moved toward the vacated exhibit.

James followed and the two of them stood for a long time staring in silence at the coiled tubing and neat emptiness.

"Well, shit," Peavey finally said.

"We missed him by two days. Two stinking days."

"At least he wrote us a little note, ain't that thoughtful."

On the wall beside the exhibit were the handwritten words, "Come take my place."

"So much for our walk in the park."

"Yeah. Now what?"

"A-hunting we will go." James said and headed for the door. Peavey followed and the ancient door closed behind them with a sound of distant thunder.

The Guardian spoke deliberately into the silence that hung in the room, "Some rebuild for the better. Some do not. It doesn't happen often, but the ones that come down off the shelf, who rebuild, they can be awesome sons of bitches. You have just met two."

"They're Guardians?" Brock asked.

"Once they were. It would seem they have lost the balance now."

"I did not like them," Brock said softly.

"They did not like you, Mister Brock."

"Why did they come here?"

The Guardian indicated the vacated exhibit, "Apparently they were looking for him."

The cadets never returned to Guardian Hall as a group. They came singly, and as the days passed, fewer and fewer were left to come. Two thirds withdrew. Half of those remaining did not pass the training. Those who did, spent a lot of time standing before the vacated exhibit, contemplating the handwritten note, and wondering if they had what it took. The note, 'Come take my place,' was a reference to words from the *Rhyme of Pierceling Heights*. There was a signature with the note that matched the name of the Bowman in the deed record above. The name was Robertson.

The Book
----- Old Calendar 1944, Killdeer, North Dakota -----

Grass. Heat. Wind. As far as you could see -- grass. Not quite green and not yet dead, it undulated in tawny transition. Shadows passed through it in waves, the accidental creations of the sun, a few transient clouds and the motion of the grass yielding to the wind, and the shadows gave it the likeness of the long fur of the hunting wolf.

The cool of morning long gone, the air quivered upward over the grass, bending and twisting reality as it rose. Not so very long from now, there would be no grass, no heat; there would be snow, and then there might be a day when the temperature could go up one hundred degrees and ice would not melt. But there would always be the wind. For this is a land of extremes and expansive beauty -- North Dakota. But for the insects of the prairie afternoon that flicked and jumped and buzzed and for the antelope that grazed, this was all there was, and so their distinctions were simpler: there was food or there wasn't, there was water or there wasn't, there was life or there wasn't.

The antelope raised his head from grazing. His ears twitched and rotated slightly and his breathing searched the air. The right ear flinched to remove a fly. Everything around him was of the prairie. Prairie movements. Prairie scent. Prairie sound. As he grazed at angles into the wind, the antelope would pause, head up, searching. All normal. The antelope began to raise its head at more frequent intervals. Head up, black horns arching inward, and black eyes, black nose, ears searching in the prairie wind for hints of danger. All normal still. Ten thousand feet above the antelope, clouds eased scattered shadows over the plain, interrupting the sunshine and giving the brief solace of shade. One shadow's edge reached the antelope, and he raised his head as it arrived. Water was close. A distant crow called. The cloud's shadow moved on. All the antelope's alertness, his lookings, his smellings, his listenings, all reaffirmed -- normal prairie, no danger. And yet, something was not normal, something beyond sensing.

It was another shadow. Out of place. Not normal. And it crept slowly over the hindquarters of the antelope. It was the shadow of a man's right hand, index and small fingers extended, the rest held down by the thumb. The index finger and the small finger were abnormally shortened and their shadow was that much more jagged.

The antelope grazed. The hand paused. A small spark, a miniature bolt of doll's lightning flashed from the fingers. A sharp sting. The antelope leaped straight upward and flashed his hooves rearward. It landed and ran tearing through the prairie grass into the distance.

The sudden flurry of motion after a three-hour stalk startled the man, and his arm would be sore for two days where the antelope's hoof had bruised it. It had been worth the effort, even in the heat, to teach a lazy antelope his vigilance lesson. The man rubbed his arm, thankful that the hoof hadn't hit between his eyes. A lesson for both. The man smiled and watched the fleeing antelope float on a silver pool of prairie mirage. Its wavy image grew thinner and thinner until it vanished. In its place a spectral manor house slowly materialized and hovered over the silver pool. Details supplanted distortions. The silver pool sank into the grass, and the mansion joined the reality of a nearby hill.

The mansion had stood there since 1863 when it was built in isolation by a French family for reasons unknown. Now it was the destination of a lonely figure slowly approaching, rubbing his arm -- pilgrim and destination materializing for one another out of the grass, the heat, and the wind.

Inside the mansion, in the library, a small feather circled in the air, its recurring path imposed upon it by the invitations of gravity and the countering push of rising air created by the electric fan that hung from the ceiling. The blades of the fan interrupted the view, giving an old-time movie look to the movements of the man below. He was dusting. The bouquet of feathers he used passed lightly over the furniture and over the books, hundreds of books, exquisitely bound and dusty. Dust was the calling card of the ever-present wind, and in the heat of the day, any wind was welcome for the illusion of lower temperature it brought. Like the ceiling fans in the house that turned in slow motion above, humming their electric promise to move the air and cool the rooms -- illusion.

The curtains edging the open windows arched slightly into the southern rooms and pressed into the screens at the opposite end of the house as summer flowed through the rooms. The man paused as the library grew darker. It actually did feel cooler. The curtains swelled and pressed with new emphasis, and the back screen door began to give an occasional muffled bang. Some of the clouds had changed their temperament and tired of paralleling the grassland, began to roll upward away from its flatness. Their undercarriages darkened and vertical currents bent the south wind toward the sun. Moisture that had traveled that wind northward for twelve hundred miles would soon be thrown from the sky and imbedded in the prairie dust.

The caretaker quit his dusting and went upstairs to begin selectively closing windows. The newly channeled currents brought relief to the sweltering rooms, and as they swirled through the house, a small feather was jarred from its ceiling refuge and bobbed and turned its see-saw way downward.

The cooler breeze was welcomed on the road as well. There a sore-armed traveler once more took off his hat and passed his finger across his forehead, temporarily interrupting the flow of sweat. He shook off the perspiration and ran his fingers through his hair, plowing up damp furrows. His features and clothes were marked by dark lines of dust. He looked very much like a model soldier painted for a museum, with all of its details edged with fine black lines. Occasional drops of rain began to fall, hitting the road and creating miniature craters in the dust. The man shifted his coat to his other arm and scratched the crook of his elbow, where the bend required to carry the coat had harbored a chaffing mixture of sweat and dirt.

He had been occupying his thoughts with mock laws of science: the distance between a man and his destination varies directly with temperature and inversely with comfort; time is slowed by thirst; average temperature and average incomes are useless computations; the number of mosquitoes killed equals the number of mosquitoes yet to kill. Now he set science aside, took off his small knapsack, flicked his suspenders off of his shoulders, and let the new wind play through his shirt. He secured his coat between the knapsack straps and carried the bundle in his left hand. He resumed his pace toward the mansion where he already could make out the figure of someone in an upper story window.

The view southward from that window usually consisted of rolling prairie hills etched with a road, a pinstripe of dust that joined the main road to Killdeer, but now the view was dramatic. The afternoon sun and the building thunderstorm combined to introduce a solitary figure walking toward the old French mansion. The caretaker moved slightly, consciously composing the view of the storm, the road, and the lone figure within the confines of the window frame. The dark-bottomed storm accentuated the sunlight as it flashed off of the figure's white shirt and straw skimmer hat. Slightly off-center in the window, the road ended at the feet of the traveler as he crested a hill on his approach to the house. There, for an instant, he gave the impression of an arrowhead on the shaft of the road, and then the whole effect was gone. The approaching figure lowered into the downhill shadows of the road and blended almost out of sight. The sun angle changed, and the caretaker's composition faded. A few drops of rain spattered on the porch roof below the window.

The caretaker remembered something from one of the books below, 'The creations of time and light are fascinating, but perishable. . .' "I should have been an artist," he mused to himself as he closed the window to half-mast to keep the breeze and hold out the rain. "Probably pass to the south anyway," he said to the room as he turned and headed downstairs.

At the foot of the stairs the caretaker paused and then turned toward the kitchen. He opened the refrigerator door and selected two beers from the shelf. The open door of the refrigerator allowed a wave of cool air to surround him momentarily. He took two more beers from the shelf. Well, it had been hot all day, hadn't it? On the front porch the caretaker seated himself and rocked slowly, waiting for his anticipated guest. "Damn!" he said, got up and returned to the kitchen for a bottle opener. In addition, he brought a bowl of ice and returned to his rocking on the front porch. The beers fanned out in the bowl. The ice only hinted at covering them, but it was the image that counted.

The porch faced south, and the afternoon sun dictated shade to the left. And it was to the left of the porch steps that Mose, a mixture of many but a Setter by preference, had chosen to spend the afternoon. Mose had two depressions crafted in the earth -- one for the morning shade and one for the afternoon shade. He was in his afternoon diggings, dozing the half-sleep that dogs use to avoid being disturbed, when the sound of a distant storm's indigestion caused him to raise his head. He became interested, then transfixed. He rose haltingly from his earth-bed and studied the approaching figure. He felt his duty was to bark and he did so, but the sound came out more like a greeting, for there was something about the newcomer that warranted a hello. He went forward to the edge of the yard, sat, and waited. An old dog, a middle-aged man, and four beers.

The traveler completed the final steps to arrive at the mansion yard. He bent slightly and scratched the dog under its chin with a certain familiarity. "You're getting old, dog," he said softly. "Welcome to the club." Then he straightened and addressed the caretaker, "Good afternoon, sir." As he spoke, Mose rose and put his front paws on the man's chest. The man slowly scratched the dog's ears.

The caretaker whistled and called out "Down Fang! Come here and leave that man alone." Mose turned his head, and then reluctantly headed for the porch. He climbed the steps and began drinking the cool water from the ice melting around the beer bottles in the bowl at the caretaker's feet.

"Get out of that, dog. Go on. Go lie down somewhere." And then, switching to a thick western accent, he addressed the visitor. "Howdy, stranger. Come on up and set a spell. Take a load off your feet. Dadburn hot today, but the storm cooled it off a mite." The words came running one on top of the other like a badly acted 'B' western being shown too fast. "What are they giving for wheat down at the mill, and who was that masked man? Well, that about covers it."

As he spoke, the caretaker's hands moved, punctuating, emphasizing, carving the conversation into the air. He noticed the look of confusion in his guest's eyes. 'Perfect,' he thought to himself. He loved being able to create that look in the eyes of newcomers at the mansion. "Sirrah, forgive my bumpkin speech, the practice of which is for Eastern folk and pilgraming tourists. They expect it so, and on hearing what's expected, are moved to generosity such as I am come to be dependent on. Want a beer?"

"Yes, thank you, I would."

"Want two beers?"

"Even better."

"Hot damn! I could tell you weren't the lemonade and iced tea type when I saw you walking up the road. The caretaker opened two beers and handed one to his guest who sat on the porch rail and took a long drink. "Fang, go and get your dish. We've got company. His name is really Mose, but 'Fang' makes him feel young."

Mose went down the steps to his afternoon hole, picked up the old tin pie plate that was his supper dish, and brought it back up on the porch. He put down the dish and sat expectantly, wagging his tail. The caretaker scooped an ice cube out of the beer bowl and let it clank into Mose's dish. Mose lay down beside the dish to lick the ice.

"Name's Quigley Bates, mansion caretaker, tour guide, librarian, and prairie curmudgeon. We have rabbit for dinner. Want to stay?"

"Yes, thank you. I'm Paul Jones."

"Mud in your eye, Mr. Jones."

There was a pause as the two men studied each other -- just the briefest moment of awkward silence -- then Mose rattled his dish. Quigley dropped another cube of ice for the dog. "I suppose I should have turned in that dish for the metal drive so it could be made into a bayonet or a tank or something, but ol'

Mose has had it for so long . . . ever since he stole the pie out of it, as a matter of fact. Blueberry, it was. My wife was furious. She threw that plate at Mose as hard as she could. It just sailed across the room pretty as you please, went into the next room, and knocked Aunt Sophie's china cat off the mantle. That really made her mad. She did have a temper. Me laughin' didn't help, I might add. Well, Mose thought it was a game, so he went and got the dish and brought it back to her and sat there with the pie tin in his mouth, looking up at her with his face all purple from the pie, wagging his tail. She melted. Mose has been eating out of that dish or playing fetch with it ever since. He catches it out of the air sometimes. Anyway, I don't think that old pie tin would make a very good bayonet. How's the beer?"

"Best I've had in a long time."

"What can I do for you?"

"I beg your pardon."

"Mr...Jones..., with the war and all, not many people walk all the way out here, especially in August."

"Well, I understand you have a very interesting library here. I'm thinking of doing a paper on frontier family life. Maybe trace one family . . . I don't know, I haven't worked it out completely yet."

"Well, this calls for a tour." The caretaker finished his beer, opened the remaining two, and handed one to his guest. "This will be only a one-beer tour. I've got to fix dinner," he said and emptied the last of the ice into Mose's dish. He opened the screen door and the two men went inside, leaving Mose to eat his ice among the shadow stripes of the porch railing.

As they walked through the downstairs of the mansion, Quigley pointed out some of the finer architectural details. Of special interest was the walnut staircase that had been shipped from France in 1863 to grace a mansion built in the middle of Indian country thirteen years before the Battle of Little Bighorn.

"The Indians never bothered this place. 'Big Medicine' . . . something about it being guarded by warriors who lived in storms, walked with bears, that sort of thing . . . all legends, probably started by the French who built the place. Pretty clever, I think. So here it is . . . fine old Victorian mansion, middle of nowhere, don't really know why, probably never will."

"Fascinating," returned Jones.

"Intriguing, yes. Wish it were Georgian, though. Victorian is a little overdone for my taste." He paused in front of the door to the next room and rested his hand on the doorknob -- a lacework of fleur-de-lis decorated its surface. "And here," said Quigley, opening the door with a dramatic flair, "are the 'quaint and curious volumes of forgotten lore'."

The library was impressive, an exhibit hall of finely joined walnut furniture and shelving accented by the random patchwork pattern of colors, shapes, and sizes that was the floor-to-ceiling collection of books.

"Have you read all of these?"

"All of these? Good Lord no. It would take a lifetime. Sometimes it takes me hours to find one I've read before. I've been trying to organize the shelves for years actually. There I'll be, Mister Library of Congress, sorting through the shelves for a subject group to collect . . . American History maybe, Civil War stuff, or maybe adventure stories . . . and a book will get into my hand. Next thing I know, I've got the thing half read, I'm hungry as hell, and it's dark out.

Well, look around. You remember where the washroom is. You can leave your knapsack up in the guestroom. I'll be in the kitchen making magic things happen to dead rabbits. It'll take about an hour and a half. That'll make dinner about seven."

The rabbit was browned in bacon fat and then steamed in beer. The gravy had a dusting of tarragon added to it. String beans and fresh corn-on-the-cob from the Victory Garden went with it. During the meal, Quigley talked. He had been hired in response to an ad in the St. Louis newspaper. He never met his employer, but the checks came regularly, and he was free to do as he pleased at the mansion. "I read a good deal. Walk the prairie with Mose. Garden in the summer, freeze in the winter."

Quigley had actually done more than just read. Since childhood, he had lived in the worlds presented on the pages of books, retreating there, hiding from the taunts of schoolmates, the pressures of teenage parties, then from the drudgery of clerical jobs and the emptiness of unfruitful romances.

"I'll bet I could show you around in Sherwood Forest like I was a native. Did you know there was a 12th-century tourist attraction at Abergavenny Castle where the arrows of Welsh longbowmen had gone through the door of the castle? Two-inch-thick oak door. Arrows went right through and stuck out an inch on the other side. People speak of bows and arrows like they were toys. Toys, huh! Sioux warriors could drive an arrow completely through a buffalo. They could take ten arrows in the left hand and begin firing them off one after the other, and the first one wouldn't have hit the ground yet when the last one was fired. May as well have had a machine gun. And the Zen bowmen in China and Japan . . . awesome stuff! The only reason bowmen aren't used in this war is it takes too long to train them. You can teach a monkey to pull a trigger. No style left in war."

"War is only stylish in books."

"Well, of course. I was merely speaking historically. You involved in this one?"

"No, I'm going to get to sit this one out."

"Me, too. Too young for the last one. Too old for this one, dammit. You out of this one because of your hand? My apologies if it's a touchy subject, but I noticed it when you were drinking your beer this afternoon."

Jones' index and small finger on his right hand seemed shorter than normal and they had no fingernails.

"Frostbite."

"Oh. Yeah, I frostbit my toes once. Didn't lose them or anything, but they sure get cold easily. Don't know why I stay on anyway. Winters are something else up here, you know. I should go to Florida, maybe."

Quigley had always loved the beach. His sandcastles were always modeled after ones he had read about, and great battles were fought long and hard until the tide sucked away the sands and shut up the battling heroes in a young boy's memory.

"I should have been a pirate captain. I would have made a damned scary pirate captain since I know nothing about sailing." Quigley chuckled at himself. "Photography! Now there's a curse from modern science. I listen to the radio and hear what Patton has been doing, then you see a newsreel and there he is. Disgusting. You know what Robin Hood looked like? Caesar? Well, Caesar doesn't count. There are statues of him . . . but King Arthur? I'll tell you what King Arthur looked like. He was five foot eight with big ears. Robin Hood too. Patton could be five-foot-eight with big ears. But no! There are actual pictures of Patton. There he is. Tall son-of-a-bitch. Doesn't look anything like me. Damned shame, too. I would have loved to have fought in North Africa."

"You should let your hair grow."

"Why?"

"Pirates all had long hair. Covered up their ears."

"Good idea. If you would like dessert, I think it only fair to tell you that the word 'dessert' comes from a French word meaning 'to clear the table'."

"Dessert seems only fair after such a delicious meal."

"Guests aren't allowed to be laborers. You could feed Mose though, maybe take him for a walk while I make coffee. You like coffee?" Jones nodded. "Mose! Dinner's over!" Quigley called out. There was a bang from the front screen door, and Mose appeared at the edge of the dining room with his dish in his mouth. "In the kitchen, Mose," said Quigley, and Mose trotted through the dining room to wait for scraps while the two men cleared the table.

"Don't you want to know how he got in?"

"He pawed open the door and came in."

"Yes, but how did you know? Most people are pretty surprised when Mose shows up like that. Impressed anyway."

"Oh, I'm impressed. There isn't much paint left in the lower right corner of the door, the wood's grooved by his claws, and he is a pretty smart dog."

"You don't miss much, do you?"

Jones only smiled.

Mose licked plates and bowls and then went out the back door with Jones who carried the pie tin full of dry dog food. Quigley did the dishes and caught glimpses of Jones from the kitchen window. He and Mose were slowly circling the mansion. At regular intervals, Jones would pause. Mose would sniff the ground at these stops, and then the two would continue the circle until they were out of sight of the window.

Quigley placed a dish towel over the stacked dishes and said, "Dry yourselves." Then he took two cups, the coffeepot and several oatmeal cookies and left the kitchen. En route to the front of the house, he stopped in the library and took a small, leather-bound book from a shelf, put it under his arm, and headed for the evening breezes of the front lawn.

There was a semicircle of metal lawn chairs in front of the mansion facing the road to Killdeer. Quigley sat in one of the chairs and poured coffee. Jones was throwing the gray remains of a tennis ball for the dog. He noticed Quigley and stopped the game. Mose went to the side of the mansion where a well pipe and faucet stuck out of the ground. Under the faucet was an old five-gallon paint bucket that served to hold Mose's water supply. Mose made loud lapping sounds for a while and then joined the two men seated on the lawn.

"That would be a hard way to drink coffee," said Jones as the slurpings subsided. Quigley chuckled in agreement. "Mose's ball has seen better days," Jones noted.

"Yep. That's the last of them. I used to play tennis. Pretty good, too. I'll get him some more after the war, when rubber goes back to recreational uses."

The two sat in silence for a while ate the cookies and sipped coffee. Candlelight memories of lightning flickered in the distance as the storms of afternoon came down from their former heights to spread out over the evening sky and fade away. Pigeons on the mansion roof joined the crickets and frogs in the gentle requiem for the day.

"Peaceful, don't you think?"

"Balanced."

"I beg your pardon," Quigley asked.

"Peace is a false friend. We look into the embers of the day and listen to the night sounds, feel the light breeze and stroke the dog's head, sip coffee and watch the stars come out. It feels good, but it's a fool's peace, a mixture of distance, attitude, and delusion that keeps us sane. What you sense is the violence in balance, and the balance is good. Frogs are eating mosquitoes, snakes are eating frogs, owls are eating snakes. But there are enough of each that escape the violence so that tomorrow there will still be balance."

"That's depressing as hell. Kind of poetic, but still depressing."

"Not at all. It is the way it is. The sunset can still seem beautiful even though it is the product of a nuclear fiery hell. This dog is a treasure, you are good company, and the meal was superb."

"Thank you."

"Lovers pause below to kiss and join the twinkling dots of light with thoughts and wild imaginings into beasts and giants' themes..." Jones' voice trailed off, as the sun, a small star in a galaxy's corner regions, faded from the sky, and the vast starry universe put the fading light in perspective.

"You can see a whole lot of stars out here," said Quigley. "I was in New York City once. You couldn't hardly see any at all. But out here the sky is so dusted with them that I wonder why they call it space. Hardly any space up there. Just millions . . . billions of stars. Billions. That's the new word now. Billions. Ever since the budget went to a billion dollars. Billion-dollar budgets. Staggers a taxpayer's mind. The Big Dipper. Always liked that one. Probably because it's the only one I can recognize. Well, Orion . . . I can find Orion."

"Charles' Wagon," returned Jones.

"Which one is that?" asked Quigley.

"You're looking at it now. You see the Big Dipper? Other folks in other times connected up those same dots and came up with a horse pulling a wagon, Charles' Wagon."

"Charles' Wagon. The four stars in the dipper part, that's the wagon?"

"Could be. The ancient Egyptians saw a bull, a god, and a hippopotamus with a crocodile on its back. Same dots, different picture."

"Who's Charles?"

"I don't know."

"Interesting," said Quigley.

Jones spoke:

> "You know Orion always comes up sideways.
> Throwing a leg up over our fence of mountains,
> And rising on his hands, he looks in on me . . .
> So Brad McLaughlin mingled reckless talk
> Of heavenly stars with talk of hugger-mugger farming,
> Till having failed at hugger-mugger farming,
> He burned his house down for the fire insurance
> And spent the proceeds on a telescope
> To satisfy a life-long curiosity
> About our place among the infinities."

Quigley asked, "What was all of that about?"

"That is from a poem by Robert Frost."

"Ah, poetry. I prefer Kipling. Adventure, glory, stirring stuff:

> If I had raised my bridle-hand, as I have held it low,
> The little jackals that flee so fast were feasting all in a row;
> If I had bowed my head on my breast, as I have held it high,
> The kite that whistles above us now were gorged till she could not fly.
> Lightly answered the Colonel's son: Do good to bird and beast,

But count who come for the broken meats before thou makest a feast.

If there should follow a thousand swords to carry my bones away

Belike the price of a jackal's meal were more than a thief could pay.

That's good stuff. Frost is like reading a landscape," said Quigley.

His guest returned:

"The best way to hate is the worst.

'Tis to find what the hated need.

Never mind of what actual worth,

And wipe that out of the earth.

 Let them suffer starvation and die

Of being brought down to the real."

"So," said Quigley, "you like Kipling, too."

"That was Frost," said his guest, and then continued:

"Lost souls revisiting the earth

To see old loves that they be well

And find their hold upon the heart,

In life so strong, in death depart;

Therefore with peals of soundless mirth

Goes each one to his place in hell."

"Not bad for Frost," said Quigley.

"That was Kipling," and he finished his coffee.

"Ah," said Quigley, "reminds me of 'I am hurt but am not slain. I will lay me down and bleed awhile, then I'll rise and fight again'."

"I like that," said Jones. "Who wrote it?"

"I'm not sure. It was a song that my mother used to sing. Some sort of English folk ballad, I think." Quigley leaned back and looked up at the night sky. "Do you think we'll ever travel to the stars? See other worlds? Maybe other life somewhere up there?"

Jones rubbed his knees and did not respond.

"You okay?" Quigley asked.

"Just getting old. I guess I should have had them replaced."

"Replaced?" Quigley was mildly astonished at the thought.

Jones did not comment. He scratched the dog's ears, "Mose, how are your knees doing?"

"Replaced. Yeah, that's a good one. It's my back, though. That's my complaint," Quigley said, and then continued to rattle on about the sky and all the possibilities that were in it. His guest let his mind wander and a sad, far away look crept onto his face. Quigley noticed and stopped speaking.

"I'm sorry," Jones said, "you were saying?"

"Light years."

"What?"

"Light years," Quigley began again. "They are the wrong measurement, don't you think? I mean, it's like measuring the pints of water in the world's oceans. There is such a quantity, of course, but what good is it? The number of miles light travels in a year, now I ask you. Useless, that's what it is, a useless measurement. You can't possibly hope to have enough time to travel such a distance as the light-years to the nearest star, let alone really get around in the universe."

"It's a good concept," Jones said. "It's just backward."

"Backward?"

"Backward, yes."

"What do you mean?"

"Don't use time to travel distance, reverse it. Use distance to travel time.'

"You mean use miles to travel years?"

"Miles, meters, whatever."

"You're serious, aren't you?"

"Of course. For example, I've traveled a lot of miles to get to 1944 and my knees will swear to it. And looking back, it hasn't seemed to have taken that long. So maybe you could get to that nearest star, if your knees hold out."

"So, you aren't serious," Quigley said, but the thought of walking a few steps and being in another century filled his mind. Suddenly it made sense to him. "You think it would be possible, then?"

"What?"

"Really traveling in time like in the H.G. Wells story."

"The one about the doctor or somebody who invented a time machine?"

"Yes."

"A machine seems cumbersome," Jones said.

Quigley agreed, "Exactly! And limiting, cumbersome, a machine is definitely not the way."

"So, how are you going to do it?"

"Oh, not me. I mean, I can't really travel in time personally. It must be like a sculptor who can see a statue in a solid block of stone. Everybody else just sees a block of stone, but the sculptor sees the hidden possibilities. You ask him how he does it, and he'll say he just does it. That's why he is a sculptor. Now if you consider that time is a river, most of us are stuck on that river, going downstream one day at a time. But what if you could go from bank to bank? Get off the river, cut across to anywhere you wanted, like you said . . . a mile, a meter, whatever. You'd have to be able to see the possibility, to see the route as it were. Like the sculptor sees the hidden statue in the stone. A time traveler would just do it, you see, with no more difficulty than you had walking on the road to get here this afternoon."

"But if you got off the river, you'd be outside of time. You'd no longer exist."

"Yes, perhaps. I never thought of that. What if time is more complex, like the statue, three-dimensional? A three-dimensional river, or maybe several rivers?"

"Like a den of snakes." The words came quietly.

"That's an unsettling image, but yes, like that, I suppose. And if there are junctures at specific times where the rivers meet, it's possible to . . . well, this is all science fiction, of course. But what if it were possible . . . God, what an adventure! Think of the people you could meet."

"Robin Hood."

"Robin Hood, exactly."

"You'd have a hell of a Christmas card list."

Quigley laughed.

"There is something else to consider."

"What's that?" asked Quigley.

"Robin Hood would no longer be skinny, and have big ears. He'd be real, like Patton. And smelly. No showers in Sherwood Forest, you know. And you'd need to have a costumer and a dialect coach, and even then you'd stand a good chance of being burned alive for being in league with the devil."

"I wouldn't go backward."

"So you don't really want to be a pirate?"

"Pirate? No. Well, there are pirates and then there are pirates, if you know what I mean."

"Then you want to go forward."

"Yes."

"Then you'll need to be careful. Here and now might be as far as the future goes. Go any farther and there would be nothing there."

"What do you mean?"

"Well, certainly not all time has happened yet. You could go off scale, and there you'd be, all alone by yourself -- one very lonely time traveler."

"I would go to see Guardian Hall." As Quigley said this, he subtly watched his guest for a reaction. There was none he could notice. Even the level tones of his response revealed nothing.

"Guardian Hall?"

"Yes. The training ground and museum of the Guardian Forces. I want to see that. I want to visit the Museum, a heroes' ward. Read the plaques. Tour the campus. See the Bowmen train."

"Bowmen?"

"Yes. The Fifth Level Guards . . . Bowmen. They control segments of Time, travel in it, through it. They focus mentally and project weapons." Quigley glanced at his guest, studied his hand as he held his coffee cup, not by the handle but with his hand surrounding the cup, the fingers halfway through the handle. He continued hesitantly, "Their title, Bowmen, comes from the ceremonial use of arrows, projected arrows . . . loosed from the right hand, projected, fired, whatever." Quigley stopped and then cautiously, like a boy asking for permission, he shared his dream. "I want to meet Robertson."

"Robertson?" And the tone in the voice hoped that Quigley Bates was not serious.

"Robertson! Warrior. Leader. Legend. Hero."

"Quigley, a lot of times a hero is just a guy who was looking for a hole to hide in and found they were all already taken. I think I would rather meet Huckleberry Finn."

Quigley paused. He realized how much he had been rattling on, the thoughts and hopes raving into words. The conversation had not gone the way Quigley had hoped. He felt uncomfortable, as though he had just met King Arthur and he really was short, skinny, with ears too big and teeth too many. Time was not a pile of snakes. Robertson was not just a guy looking for a hole. He was a hero, not for one country, not for one battle, not for one war, not for only a few years. Not Robertson. He was a hero in Time. A hero of worlds. He was Robertson!

"I talk too much," said Quigley quietly, "Sorry."

"Where are you getting all of this stuff, Quigley?"

Quigley Bates had a secret treasure, as dear to him as anything he had imagined on the sandcastle beaches of his life. And it was a treasure that seemed custom-crafted just for him. It was a book.

"When I first came out here to take over the care of this place . . . it was a bad time for me. My wife had . . . well, it was a bad time. I had Mose . . . thank God for Mose . . . and I had this giant empty house and a room full of books." Quigley paused. The house and he had been the same. The thought made him smile. "Well," he continued, "I was dusting the books and the duster came apart. It was old, I guess, and feathers went everywhere. The ceiling fan was on and they just stirred all over the library. I was getting frustrated, then angry. Pretty soon, I was screaming at the feathers. Swearing. Ever try to collect a bunch of feathers? A flock of feathers? Wing of feathers? Well, whatever you call a lot of feathers, they are hard to gather. You have to sort of sneak up on them. And I wasn't in a sneaking mood. The more I raved, the more the damned things flew around. It's very humiliating to be mocked by feathers.

That was when Mose first opened the screen door. I guess he thought I needed rescuing or something. So Mose started to help with the feathers, biting at them as they floated about. He got one stuck to the inside of his jowl and couldn't get it loose. He started woofing and shaking, trying to get this feather out of his face. I got to laughing so hard. I wound up on the rug, laughing so hard. And Mose came over, 'old feather face,' and I laughed even harder. It was wonderful. Everything left, all the problems, the bad time attitude. Just laughed away.

And as I laughed, a book caught my attention -- I don't know why – leather-bound, but no title. It is the strangest adventure story I have ever read. In the back, there are reference sections: one on the nature of Time, one on the history of the Guardian Forces, a description of Guardian Hall, and a glossary of terms which is especially odd because all of the terms that are explained are modern terms like 'jake,' 'cat's meow,' 'Charleston,' 'swing,' stuff like that. Anyway, that's where I got all of 'that stuff' as you call it."

"So, it's a science fiction book."

"Yes, sort of. It starts out describing a family, a rural, average family. The first time I read it, I put it aside. The second time I picked it up, I noticed the reference sections and read the one about Time, but couldn't understand very much of it. It has a lot of stuff in there about the speed of light and not being able to synchronize watches. I understood some of it, but the section on Laws of Chaos I didn't understand at all. The third time I picked it up, I opened it to the middle and got caught in the damndest adventure story I had ever read, so I started over at the beginning with the average rural family and went straight through. Wonderful tale.

A year or so later, I re-read it and it seemed different. There were passages I hadn't remembered, and some of the ones I remembered had different outcomes. So I figured I was becoming inattentive. The next time I read it there were several parts that were completely different. I thought I was losing my mind. So I re-read *Treasure Island*. Long John Silver still sailed away at the end and everything else was the same, so I went back to the leather-bound book. It was different. The book is different every time you read it."

Quigley's guest was staring at the night, not saying a word.

"I know what you might be thinking. So I'm a little crazy, I cook pretty good rabbit, and I'm harmless. Painfully harmless. I wish I could do the things the characters in that book do, go where they go. God, what an adventure! I'd give anything to see Guardian Hall. You think I'm crazy?"

"I think you should be careful what you wish for. Quigley, this encounter has been delightful. And I must say you are a very good cook. I have never had rabbit cooked so well."

"Have you ever had rabbit at all?" Quigley asked.

"Actually, no," Jones said, and the two of them shared a moment of gentle laughter. "But it is very like a chicken dish my mother cooked. Your rabbit haunted me back to the years of my youth, and that made the meal very special. Thank you."

"You're quite welcome. More than welcome. A toast, if you will, in black coffee -- To the Future."

"To the future," Jones said, "and delicious rabbit. And now, I think I shall lay me down and sleep awhile, then I'll rise and eat breakfast. It's not poetic, but it is practical."

"Oatmeal," said Quigley.

"Sounds good," Jones said, rising from his chair.

The two men headed toward the mansion door. Mose accompanied them with his ball in his mouth, inviting another game of fetch, even in the darkness. The porch light, surrounded by insects, seemed extraordinarily bright to eyes adjusted to the starlight.

"I'd like to read that book sometime."

"That's what I figured," said Quigley, as he took the small leather-bound book he had brought and handed it to his guest. "That's why you're here, isn't it? You came to read that book. You're not writing any paper, you didn't frostbite your fingers, and your name's not Jones. You're him. You're Robertson, Guardian Bowman. And as we talk, you are having one hell of an adventure thousands of years from now. I've read your book."

Without a sign of recognition, his guest took the book and continued up the porch steps. Now he had done it -- Quigley had put all of his hopes in the last few sentences, hopes that he had had since he first opened the book and started to disappear into its ever-changing pages, hopes that had roared again into his mind this afternoon as he had watched this man walk toward the mansion with sun on his shoulders, darkness and lightning at his back.

"Please."

His guest turned.

"Please," Quigley repeated with his heart, "I've got to know. Is it true?"

Quigley watched as his guest bent slowly toward Mose. He extended his hand below the dog's mouth. Mose placed the old gray tennis ball in the palm, gently, as if to say goodbye to it. The hand with the shortened fingers closed around the ball, and as it did, the name and attitudes of Paul Jones slipped into the night air. The man was turned away from Quigley, and still bent slightly at the waist, Quigley saw him move. A quick move. Hard to see. Just a flick of the arm. The ball was thrown. It sped into the night toward the far end of the porch. There may have been a flash, a spark. Quigley wasn't sure. It was too fast. The ball was headed off into the night.

Mose, feet slipping on the porch deck paint, was trying to start after it, his claws rattling as he tried. And then a solid sound. Something had hit. The man was turned in the direction of the thrown ball. His right arm had straightened with the throw, and now his hand, formed in a strange position with the inner fingers locked down by the thumb, the shortened index and small fingers extended, pointing, focused toward the far end of the porch. There, hard to make out in the darkness, was the tennis ball, impaled to the corner post by an arrow. The feathers just touching the surface of the ball, the shaft went through the six-inch post and extended two inches into the night.

"Thanks for the book," said the man as he opened the screen door and went inside. The door closed with a soft double thump. Mose was at the end of the porch, standing on his hind legs pulling at the tennis ball.

"Son-of-a-bitch," Quigley breathed, his eyes wide.

Robertson draped his clothes over the back of the chair in the corner of the room. His knapsack was on the bureau. He arranged the two pillows against the headboard and glanced over the bed at the Currier and Ives print of a sleigh and ice skaters. The pillows were feather and would condense too easily to make for a comfortable support of any duration. He climbed into the bed and bent the lampshade toward him to glean more light from the dim bulb. The light attracted a moth whose shadow roamed the ceiling and walls, appearing and vanishing and appearing on the surfaces without warning.

The evening with Quigley had been delightful -- a good start, a hopeful start, as he remembered the implacable way the Guardian Force had done its recruiting and the nightmare choices that had led to his sudden departure from his home, from his time. Now he would find his way back home and to Katherine. The dagger thought that she might have married another had interrupted his sleep for nearly twenty years, and he knew the answer lay in the pages of a small book. Robertson began to read.

The first page changed everything -- Katherine had born his son.

He continued to read. As the pages read piled against the left cover, and those yet to read dwindled to a precious few, Robertson paused, closed his eyes, and recalled the tale's events and moods that had become his favorites, recalled them to be sure. Recalled them before turning the last of the pages into view, because he knew what would happen when the last page was turned to face the cover and he would close the book.

He rested his hand on the pages that had described the countryside with its gently overlapping hills. He saw again the lane, the barn, the house.

----- O. C. Robertson farm, the recent past -----

From the small screened porch at the back door of the farmhouse to the steps on the right that gave side access to the main covered porch in the front, the scarlet sage was in regimental formation in the bed of earth. Two British Squares at the ends, connected by a skirmish line in front. The small plants were to rise to crimson glory and beckon the marigolds to follow if they dared. It would be a wonderful splash of color in front of the eggshell and grey of the stone foundation. Two cellar windows peeked half of their glass above the level of the ground and eyed the spring plantings with the dusty doubt of a winter's worth of cobwebs.

To the right, just beyond the front porch steps, in the lacy shade of new leaves, a man sat in a yellow metal lawn chair and smiled, smiled at a chubby infant patriot who was gleefully uprooting the redcoats. The child sat and unconsciously shook his latest prize up and down. It seemed haphazard that his arm was moving up and down, and attached to the hand was a plant. The arm stopped. The child absently brought the plant upward and tasted the gritty dirt. He made a face, and, still holding the plant, crawled away toward a particularly fascinating butterfly.

The screen door opened and the child's mother stepped onto the front porch. "How's it going, Grandpa?"

"Oh, we're having a wonderful time out here."

"What have you two been doing?"

"Gardening, mostly. A little butterfly chasing."

The child came toward the porch steps. When he wanted to go faster, he altered his crawl by straightening his knees and moving on all fours like a bear cub. His mother laughed as he approached.

"He's filthy. How could you let him get so dirty?" She wasn't angry, rather almost appreciative of the tender sight of her son being so at home with his surroundings. 'After all,' she thought, 'children do wash off.'

The man ran his index finger under his gray mustache. "It's not a matter of letting him get dirty. He just does it. Gifted at it, you might say. Why, just before you came out, a swirl of dust down by the barn altered its course and came right up here and attached itself to that child's left knee."

Grandpa was warming to the tale when he was interrupted by the mother's scream. The child began to cry in reaction to the emotional outburst. The grandfather was briefly startled, but then connected the mother's wide-eyed stare and the scattered scarlet sage lying limp on the grass. She was crying as she knelt beside the flower bed. After a time, the older man came and stood beside her.

"You should have seen him. He was having such a great time; I couldn't bear to stop him. Pulling and shaking those plants and getting in the dirt. It was . . . ," his voice trailed off.

----- Years Later -----

The sun was brushing the first rose-colored wash of light along the horizon, and morning blue was starting to creep upward into the black sky. The moon, high and pale, begrudgingly surrendered its sky. The doves, the pigeons, the starlings and sparrows began their subtle waking sounds, punctuated periodically by the overbearing call of the rooster. Now and then there was a complaint from a calf or cow. Pigs grunted their requests for morning feed. The farm was coming to life as day and darkness fought to control the land and establish where would be the light and where would be the secret shadow remains of night.

Deuce Robertson, now in his teens, walked with his grandfather down the lane from the farmhouse toward the barn. The elder Robertson carried two stainless steel milk buckets that softly added a dull clanking noise to the morning. Deuce paused and watched his grandfather continue, crunching the gravel under his shoes as he walked. Then Deuce started down the slight hill to the hog house to feed the pigs. He heard the milk buckets clang together in the distance as Grandpa Robertson put them both into the same hand and opened the door to the lower barn where the cows were already nosing their stanchions in anticipation of the morning milking.

'It is an absolutely beautiful morning,' Deuce thought to himself, and then he turned slowly toward the hog house. Its black silhouette loomed up from its hollow and ate away a portion of the morning sky like acid. Deuce hated the hog house when it was dark. The pigs were wonderful. He liked them. But the ominous place where they came in to feed -- that dark, sick-sweet-smelling hog house -- was a den of demons in his mind.

And there was a snake, always somewhere in and around the hog house, a giant snake. Black. Silent. Waiting. No . . . lurking. Always lurking. Even when it wasn't there, it was still there.

Deuce paused in front of the hog house door. It was held shut by a rectangular block of wood with a screw through its middle. The block was polished smooth like soft cream by the thousands of touches, turning, opening, and closing. Deuce liked that block of wood and the stir stick for the slop. It had that same polish. Deuce wondered how many people had been there to touch and polish these simple wooden items. What were their names? Had there been Indians then?

The door opened with its usual creak. In the daylight of evening feeding time, Deuce would sometimes attempt to play tunes with the creak of the door hinges, but in the morning darkness, he opened the door, endured its scream, and reached into the damp grass for the stick that propped the door open. Deuce hesitated. The snake liked long grass.

There was no light in the hog house except the light of whatever was shining in the sky at the time. And that light made the most violent shadows out of the mundane sacks and ropes, beams, fence slats, and buckets. Giant pig shadows undulated on the walls as the pigs came to feed. Deuce scooped the feed from its sack and dumped the grainy stuff into a bucket. He put the bucket under the well pipe and pulled the handle toward him, judging by the sound of the filling water when the bucket was full enough. Then he stirred the slop and poured it into the trough.

   There was a sudden, piercing squeal as one pig stepped on another pig. Deuce whirled. The slop bucket hit the floor and the remainder of its gooey contents splattered onto the floor and oozed under Deuce's feet. He slipped. The bucket launched toward the feeding pigs and hit one in the snout. The pigs ran in confusion and panic in the dark confines of the pen. Squealing and snorting, they fought to escape through the two low openings at the back of the hog house. As Deuce flailed, trying to get off of the floor, his hand grabbed the water faucet handle, and ice-cold water ran down his arm. He rolled the other direction and dumped the feed sack under him. He screamed, slipped again, and crashed into the wall. The vibration jarred the door prop. It fell and the door shut with a wail of hinges and a coffin-lid slam. Darkness.

   Only the small window now let in light, and its cobwebs and frame added to the eerie patterns inside the room. The rope fell. It brushed Deuce's hand like a snake. It was a snake. Deuce screamed again. His hand flew back and cracked into the fence slat. The snake was coiling around his feet now. He kicked. It didn't go away. He kicked and screamed. Tears and screams. He couldn't get free of the shadows, of the rope that paralyzed his mind with snakes. Then something large and solid nudged his arm. He struck out. Wildly. Blindly. Struck again and again. Across his chest, something moved. Long . . . black . . . fast. It moved quickly and by mistake slipped inside Deuce's shirt. The snake reeled and twisted, trying to escape. It flew out of the shirt neck and by Deuce's ear and disappeared down a hole in the floor, leaving its squirms and ripples tattooed on the young boy's mind. Piercing light filled Deuce's world of terror.

Out of the light came a giant, surrounded by darkness, formed out of darkness, firing light into the eyes of the boy.

"Floor looks slippery."

Grandpa Robertson stood in the hog house doorway with his whip in one hand and a flashlight in the other, shining it at Deuce and then slowly around the room. The sun was a little higher now, and with the door open, its light crept into the shadowy corners and erased their terror. Grandpa turned off the flashlight, placed it on the floor beside the door, and went off to finish milking.

Deuce was breathing hard and fast, but even so managed, "Oh, shut up, pig!" as the last of the hogs squirmed noisily out of the building. He tore open his shirt and checked to make sure it was empty. The spilled feed had found its way inside the shirt, and now the individual grains moved and tickled, and horror flashed back to Deuce. The writhing snake moved again and again inside his shirt with every repositioning of the itchy feed. Deuce took off his shirt and threw it out the door.

He kicked at the slop bucket and ran outside into the morning air. He ran up the hill and climbed immediately into one of the plum trees that lined the lane. He was there when Grandpa came up the lane from the barn with the two buckets of milk. The milk was placed on the porch for Deuce's mother to retrieve, and then Grandpa returned. He stopped under Deuce's tree and spoke slowly and deliberately, "You know, I do not believe I have ever seen a snake as scared as the one that came out of the hog house this morning. Yes sir, that was one scared snake. It's gonna be years before he gets up nerve enough to hunt mice in that hog house again. Might never get the nerve at all. We are probably going to be up to our belt buckles in mice." And then he looked up at Deuce and smiled. Deuce came down from the tree and the two started toward the house.

"Better get your shirt. You can tidy up the hog house after breakfast," Grandpa said.

After breakfast, Grandpa helped deuce clean up in the hog house. "That snake," grandpa began, "he's just another life trying to get by, just looking for breakfast. A nice mouse. Maybe even a rat. Good snake. Non-poisonous."

"How can you tell the difference?"

"Oh, color. Shape of the head. With snakes it's easy. With people it's hard. Deuce, it's natural to be afraid of some things. It helps you survive long enough to understand them. Now, when I was about your age, I was afraid of bears."

"Bears, Grandpa?"

"Yep. You see, I was camping once with your great-grandfather, and one night this bear came into camp. It was huge . . . the biggest bear you can imagine. 'Course I was pretty small at the time, so most any bear would have been huge to me, but even so, this was a giant mother bear right enough. Anyway, this bear came and shredded my tent. I heard this ripping noise and woke up. And there it was, where my tent should have been. God, it was big! One paw would cover your whole chest. Had claws as long as my fingers. The bear sniffed me all over and then began sort of flipping me back and forth between her paws, rolling me from side to side like a rubber ball. Then she got real close to me and let out a sound from way down deep inside wherever it is bears come from. That sound shook the ground under me, actually made the earth under me quiver. And the smell! I have never smelled anything as horrible as the breath of that bear. It was the rotten smell of something that has been dead for a long time, and she growled that smell of death right into my face. Right into my brain."

"What did you do, Grandpa?"

"I wet my pants."

"Grandpa, no!"

"Yes, I truly did. I was that scared. Too scared to move, too scared to scream, too scared to think."

"What happened, Grandpa?"

"Why the bear killed me, of course."

"Grandpa, there wasn't any bear. You made that all up."

There was a thoughtful sincerity in Grandpa's voice now. "Deuce, we went camping. There was a bear. Every hairy, smelly, giant bit of mother bear. I had bear nightmares every night for a long time. I saw paws, and teeth, and smelled that dead breath until I thought I would never close my eyes again." They finished the clean-up and Grandpa and Deuce left the hog house and headed to the barn.

"Do you still have nightmares?"

"Not about bears."

"How come?"

"Well, your great-grandfather who, by the way, was a really smart fellow, told some whopping lies I will admit, but when it counted, he was the wisest man I ever met. He told me to make friends with my fear."

"What did he mean?'

"I had no idea, and that's all he would say."

"How do you make friends with a bear?"

"How do you make friends in school?"

"I don't know. . . you're in class together, and you get to know each other, and after a while you just wind up friends."

"That's the answer then. Of course, if you want to make friends with that snake, you'll have to go to his school."

"What do you mean?"

"Make friends with your fear, Deuce."

Grandpa had a way of saying something in a certain tone of voice that signaled the end to his answer. That was what Deuce heard now, and he knew from experience that no matter how much he might try to get his grandfather to elaborate, there would be no more information given about how to make friends with fear.

Deuce accepted his new puzzle and changed the subject, "So, Grandpa, how did you get away from that bear?"

"Well, the noise the bear was making woke up my father, and he came out of his tent and walked right up to that bear. It turned out that the bear was a friend of his, so the two of them went to town drinking and left me to tidy up the camp."

"Grandpa, come on, tell the truth."

"Now, I'm not making this up, Deuce. Honest. See, what I did was, when I tidied up the camp, I hid the honey. That bear has been following me ever since. Wants that honey, don't you know. And over the years, we've gotten to be pretty good friends. She still smells like rotten meat, though." And with that, Grandpa chuckled and headed into the barn. Deuce followed right behind his grandfather, and when he entered the barn, the door closed behind him. The change from bright sunlight to the half-light of the barn's interior was more than Deuce expected and he lost sight of his grandfather. In fact, it seemed to Deuce that he had disappeared. It seemed strange to have happened so fast, but maybe he had just stepped into the grain bin or gone down the ladder to the lower barn.

Deuce liked the inside of the barn. It always smelled wonderful, a combination of hay and feed smells and straw dust and animals. But as he stood by the hammer mill adjusting to the low light, he smelled something else, something dead. A rat maybe. The smell seemed to get stronger. Maybe one of the barn cats had died. And then the smell surrounded Deuce like hot breath, and he heard a low growling rumble that penetrated his whole body. He felt the floor vibrate under his feet. He wheeled around. There was a shape in the darkness behind him. Huge. Standing. Giant paws. Claws the length of carving knives. Deuce's heart stopped.

The giant bear faded into the shadows, and in its place stood Grandpa with a sack of grain on his shoulder and a pitchfork in his hand. "Give me a hand, will you?" he asked in a quiet voice. "We need to open the main doors and get this hammer mill going."

Deuce wanted nothing more than to open the main doors. Light would flood the barn then. He heaved on the first door and opened it easily. Usually he needed help. Not this time. The second door slid open quickly, then the rest of them. Deuce moved the six large doors as if they were weightless.

His grandfather noticed. "You're getting to be pretty strong there, Deuce. It is truly amazing what you can accomplish when you really focus on doing something."

Deuce went over to his grandfather and helped him unroll the long belt that would power the hammer mill. "Grandpa, how do I make friends with the dark?"

Grandpa paused and straightened up. He looked at Deuce with a great feeling of pride. The boy was going to be just fine, he thought. "Well," Grandpa began, "this afternoon why don't you give your mom a hand and take one of those pies she's fixed over to Mamma Chambeau ."

Deuce agreed to do that. He would be getting out of having to help sack barley which was the most miserably itchy stuff. Its dust got into any place on your body that could be itched, and there it did its scratchy work. Deuce hated barley. But he knew that he was never lightly excused from work to deliver pies. And then he remembered that his grandfather often answered questions in peculiar ways. Mamma Chambeau was blind.

"Grandpa, is your bear friendly?" Deuce asked.

Grandpa looked the boy straight in the eyes and smiled. "She's friendly to some folks. Others find her to be particularly unpleasant."

Grandpa was pleased with the awareness of Deuce's question, and Deuce was pleased with the direct answer he received. And both the boy and the older man knew that they had just exchanged facts.

Deuce carried a newly baked blueberry pie. He walked past the pond and on up the lane toward Herbert Road. Old man Herbert had been the friend and drinking buddy of the county road commissioner, and as a result of that coincidence, the road that now bore his name was blacktopped from the main county road until it reached the entry to the Herbert farm. There it resumed its original one-lane gravel existence and disappeared into and through a wooded area for some five miles. Just before entering the woods, the road bent toward a small one-story frame house. Old-timers said the road had bent to avoid a giant tree where a thief had been hanged many years ago, and though tree and thief had passed into memory, Thief's Bend was the only address needed to locate the house where Sienna Chambeau lived.

Sienna May Kitty Ellen Mary Paul William Chambeau had been born late to her parents, and debts and favors from many a relative were paid off at the child's christening. It served as a rite of passage in the local area when a child could recite the whole name which was usually shortened to Sienna or, more often, to Momma Chambeau. Her father had been Cajun and her mother had been Irish. Her accent and phrasing were unique, entertaining, and frequently vulgar. "Did you hear what Momma Chambeau said the other day?" was a signal to cover the ears of children. This tactic was seldom successful and the schoolyard grapevine spread the latest phrase as quickly as the hushed whispers at the church bazaar and the raucous talk at O'Malley's Bar.

When she was fourteen, Sienna Chambeau married Paul Louise Reynard, a worker in the bayou oil fields of Louisiana. Reynard, himself only seventeen, had a taste for gin and would come home drunk and beat his new wife. Following one such beating, Sienna's world began to grow progressively darker until her torn retinas failed completely. But Sienna was well-liked, and shortly after her blindness and its cause became known to the bayou, Paul Louise Reynard, two sacks of cement, and a length of chain disappeared from the drill rig and were never found. A company lawyer, new to the area, was quite obstinately insisting that no insurance monies would be paid without a body or proof of death, but some of the oil drill workers took him for a ride in the bayou, and in the damp hushed depths of the swamp, the lawyer had a change of heart, withdrew his objections, and the life insurance check was duly paid to the widow Reynard. Sienna promptly cashed the check and never used the name Reynard again.

In her fifties now, Momma Chambeau was a fine looking woman. Local women envied her this fact, and more than one secretly wished to look half so fine when she turned fifty. She sat on her porch shelling peas as Deuce approached.

"Dat be Deuce-Bobby Robertson comin', yes by damn. And hello to you and your pie."

"Hello, Momma Chambeau."

"I am happy for you to see me."

"Momma, how can you always tell it's me that's coming?"

"I can't tell it's you all de time. Times are some dat it is some other body altogether, not you at all, and den I sing out 'Hello' to de other body."

"But you can't see any of us coming. How can you tell who it is?"

"Well now, maybe if a young scamp short-pisser I know of, he sings out a proper 'Hello' to ol' Momma, den I will tell him a ting or two."

"Hello Momma, I am happy for you to see me."

"Much better. Now you threw a stone into de pond and dat made the frogs quiet and de birds quiet. So I hear 'guh-sploosh' . . . quiet, and I know somebody with nothin' better to do den throw stones into ponds is coming up de lane, and dat is most likely Deuce-Bobby. Den, you sneak funny up here when you get close. You go from crunching along to real slow being, and I know dat Deuce-Bobby is trying to put a 'Boo' into ol' Momma. And de wind is at your back, Deuce-Bobby, and your pie arrived long before you did. Put dat pie on de table right in de middle."

"Can I help with the peas?" Deuce asked when he returned.

"Well now, by damn, dat is a right fine offer you make to an ol' female lady woman, and I take you up on it." And Momma Chambeau held out the pan in which she had been putting the shelled peas. Deuce took it from her and sat down by her rocking chair to finish the shelling. Momma took out her pipe, packed and lit it, and began rocking slowly while she smoked. "You know 'bout dem peas, dey are one fine wonderful ting to eat by bears in Alaska and places like dat. Did you know dat, Deuce-Bobby?"

"No, Momma."

"Well, by damn, dat is a true ting dat polar bears dearly love green peas, and the Eskimo seal people hunt dem bears and make white fur tings out of dem bears. But it is a dangerous ting to do because dem bears are one big creature by damn, and dey do not part with their fur easily." And Momma rocked and waited.

Deuce could not stand the delay and asked, "So, how do the Eskimos hunt the bears?"

"I thought you would never ask. Well, de Eskimo seal people dig a big hole in de ice, and all around de hole dey put peas. Usually dey only have canned peas, you know, but de bears like dem peas too. So dey put out de peas and den dey go and hide. Now when a bear come along, he stop to take a pea, and de Eskimos kick him in de ice hole," and Momma Chambeau laughed and rubbed Deuce's hair and laughed some more.

"Between you and Grandpa I think I've learned enough tall tales to make a flag pole."

"Tall tales? No dat is a true ting I have told you. I know because I heard it from de same snake dat tells me when de moon is full, and he is always very honest about de moon."

"What do you want me to do with the pea pods?"

"Save dem and I will boil dem up wit some nice piece of fatback and pepper sauce and have dem with rice. Ummm-ummm."

"Momma, may I ask you a personal question?"

"Well, you can ask. We see how personal before we answer."

"You weren't always blind, were you?"

"No."

"How did you get used to the darkness?"

"Ah, well for some many months, I was one pity-bound young female lady woman and dat is a fact. I tink dat all de world is ended for me and dat's a fact. But den I start to hear tings dat I never hear before ever. And den I start to feel tings, feel dem like dey were coming, like a somebody is coming to visit, and I feel him before he gets to my porch and tings like dat. And pretty soon, I am so full of curious about all dis new stuff dat I forget to be a pity person anymore."

"You mean you could . . . you can . . . sense things that you can't see? How?"

"Easy. You just gotta pay attention. You live in de air, yes? Air is all around you but you can't see it, and so everybody tink dat air is just for breathing and dey forget about it. But dat air is full up with tings, dat air will talk to you plain as I am talking to you now and dat's a fact. He bring you sights and smells, and he bring the voodoo feelin' when another somethin' is in the same air as you. And night air is de absolute best, cause it is not all cluttered up wit de light, and so it comes to you pure and talks de clearest."

"The air talks? Momma, I was serious. I really wanted to know."

"I know, Deuce-Bobby. I have a listen to de serious in your voice. Dis dat I am telling you is not about bears and ice holes. Dis is part of de magic. But you gotta pay attention. Now close your eyes and breathe through your mouth."

"Why breathe through my mouth?"

"Cause dat is de way you can breathe de quietest. And do not ask any more questions for again till I tell you. Now you have your eyes closed, yes?"

"Yes."

"Tell me everyting you hear."

"I hear birds."

"Ahh!" Momma said in disgust, "You are not paying attention. Listen and tell again."

"Well, I hear your rocking chair."

Momma Chambeau said nothing, but her silence said 'What else?' and Deuce began to concentrate.

"I hear the flies on the porch. I hear the leaves moving in the breeze."

Silence.

"I hear a scratching or a grinding."

"Mouse."

"I hear a woodpecker. I hear you breathing. I hear a bee passing."

"Wasp, not a bee."

"I hear the frogs way off."

Silence.

"I smell things too. Is that all right to say?"

Silence.

"I smell your pipe . . . the pea pods. I smell you, Momma," Deuce added self-consciously because Momma Chambeau smelled of strange herbs that she wore in a small bag around her neck. "Is there something behind us, Momma?"

"Yes."

"What is it?"

"What you tink it is?"

"I don't know."

Silence.

"I don't know what it is, Momma."

"Cat. Cat he lives by sneaking up. But you got de voodoo feeling dat he is around and dat is not for everybody to have not at all sometimes never. So you open your eyes now and say a hello to de cat. Call him 'Walker' and see if he come over to you."

"Here, Walker, here kitty-kitty. He went away."

"Yes, he do de same ting to me when I call him Walker. His name is Susie," she chuckled. "Now you go home and listen to de air there. I am goin' inside to cut your Momma's special fine pie into four pieces to eat it. You come back in four days for de pan, and I will have someting for you by damn."

"Can I help you?"

"No thank you, Deuce-Bobby. I like to tink I am an independent female lady woman, so you leave now so you can come back." And Momma Chambeau felt low with her hand and located the pot of peas and the pot of pods, picked them up, and went inside her house. As she passed through the doorway, the handle of one of the pots struck the door frame and surprised her. "Shit and go blind! You snake fucker goddamn door, when did you move? I will curse you and you will spit blood and die!"

It sounded like Momma Chambeau's curse might actually happen, and Deuce left the porch. "Goodbye, Momma. Thank you."

Deuce always enjoyed talking with Momma Chambeau. She seemed to think differently from so many other people, and he remembered one of her favorite sayings that seemed backward. 'When you believe it, you will see it.' Most folks made light of Momma's sayings, but if you thought about them, they held a great deal of common sense wisdom, and the imagery of her curses was the stuff of nightmares.

Deuce stopped at the top of the lane to get the mail. He pulled the newspaper from its yellow tube. As he opened the mailbox, it reminded him of Momma's house. Her curse flew from its dark interior and imbedded its vision in his mind. For a frozen instant the mailbox was Momma's house, the front door spit blood from its seams and cracks. It slammed open. Thick lumps of blood flew and hit. Flew and hit again with the loud cracking splat of impacts. The whole room splattered. The mantel dripped onto the hearth. Sticky crimson horror oozed down the walls and flowed onto the floor. The vivid reality that attacked so suddenly from the peaceful mailbox shocked Deuce. His hand jerked back. His mind whirled. It was like some macabre paint fight between fiends. That struck him funny. Two diminutive devils throwing handfuls of red paint at each other, and the terror wisped away like smoke. He laughed out loud. He wondered if Laurel and Hardy had ever performed a paint fight -- starting slowly, accidentally, with an errant brushstroke, the deliberate retaliation, the deadpan counter as Stan slowly painted his partner's necktie, the belt pulled out and paint poured down the trouser front. He laughed again. Then he thought of the facial expression a passerby might have as he watched a boy laughing into a mailbox. This made Deuce laugh harder.

He was still chuckling about the whole thing halfway down the lane. And then his pace slowed, and he stopped and stood in the middle of the lane. All of the terror and shock had been in his mind. So had the humor. The blood spitting door. The devils. Laurel and Hardy. As he thought about it, he realized he had been controlling the action of the vision, forming the portions of blood and projecting their impacts on the walls, just as he had mentally poured paint down the front of Stan Laurel's pants. Deuce smiled. He had made a friend of fear.

Farther down the lane a crow alighted on a fence post, cockily surveyed the area, and then lowered himself the last four feet to the ground where something shiny had caught his eye. He nudged a white piece of stone and then looked up. He hopped around to poke at the stone from a different angle and then flew off as Deuce approached.

Deuce bent down and picked up the stone the crow had been interested in. It was surrounded by dried mud. He put the mail and paper under his arm, and as he picked the bits of mud from the stone, its shape took on definition. He had found an arrowhead. A treasure. He wondered how long it had been there beside the lane. Had he walked by it all those countless times, or had the crow brought it with him? Indians filled his thoughts for the rest of the walk to the farmhouse.

Deuce's mother called from the kitchen to ask if Momma Chambeau liked the pie. He put the paper and mail on the table beside Grandpa's chair and went into the kitchen to tell his mother about his visit.

"Spit blood and die," his mother repeated, "Momma is colorful," and then imitating Momma Chambeau's dialect she said, "and dat's a fact. I would prefer if you did not use those other phrases though. Your grandfather will hear of them, and he doesn't need any new oaths."

"Okay, Mom." Deuce said. "Oh, look what I found." And he showed her the arrowhead.

"It's hard to imagine that a piece of rock tied to the end of a stick would do much damage," she said, "but I saw an arrowhead in a museum once. Not a real museum. Just a roadside exhibit and a souvenir shop. But the arrowhead was stuck into the leg bone of a buffalo. Stuck right into the bone. Anyway, be sure to show it to Grandpa. He likes things like that."

"You bet, Mom," and Deuce went upstairs to his room to put the arrowhead in his treasure box along with the Civil War bullets, the shark's tooth, and the special marble. As he was just starting up the stairs, he heard his mother in the kitchen, chuckling and repeating Momma Chambeau's speech to the door. He knew that he would hear the oaths again. Mom had a temper, and some of Grandpa's most beloved phrases had originated in the kitchen.

The arrowhead secure, Deuce headed to the barn for milking time. As he passed the main barn doors and walked down the incline by the corn crib, he heard a rustling noise. Deuce peered into the shadows under the corn crib. The corn crib sat on a platform of oak two-by-twelves, and the oak platform sat on concrete block walls that formed an equipment shelter. The rear concrete block wall was embedded in the incline of earth that sloped up to the barn doors, two sides were also concrete blocks, and the east side was open. A hay rake was the only piece of equipment currently under the shelter, and the rake's multiple heavy wire teeth pointed at the ground like some instrument of torture lurking in the afternoon darkness. A blade of light sneaked through a gap in the oak ceiling and slashed diagonally on the rake. Just for an instant, three of the upheld teeth glowed in the light and then faded into the shadow-on-shadow seclusion as the sun withdrew its foil.

Behind the rake, life and death were locked in the far corner. On a small scale to be sure, but for the participants it was a world at war. A farm cat, known at milking time as Mueller, controlled all the angles of escape from the shed. Mueller was a skillful hunter, and he understood how to maneuver his prey. He was a very large cat that had been around and had the scars to prove it. His dilemma at the moment was that his prey was a rat almost as big as Mueller himself. Its back was wedged in the corner and this rat had nowhere to run. The cat was low to the ground, one foreleg slightly forward; the rat had his back arched, his neck tilted upward, and his teeth bared. There was going to be a lot of pain unleashed in this conflict. A lot of pain.

Mueller eased closer, focusing on the rat's neck just below the chisel teeth. The rat compressed further into the corner. He looked even bigger as his body was pushed up by the concrete blocks. And those teeth. Mueller watched the lips of the rat ripple above those teeth. Slowly the cat inched backward. Inch by inch. Then as the distance increased, death and pain left the space between the two animals. The rat relaxed and moved along the wall and disappeared into a space in the foundation. The cat turned and trotted into the sunlight toward the entrance to the lower barn. He entered and joined a growing number of farm cats who were assembling for milking time.

Deuce followed the cat into the lower barn. The two cows were already inside the stall with their heads through their stanchions, munching on some hay. Grandpa appeared with two freshly washed stainless steel milking buckets, selected his stool, and closed the stanchion around Beatrice's neck. He sat down and began the rhythmical process of milking. The stream of milk hit the empty bucket and made a loud ringing noise that was the dinner bell for all of the farm cats. They arrived from several directions and began to nudge their way into their dinnertime spots. Deuce got his stool and bucket, closed the stanchion around Matty, and began his milking. Periodically, Grandpa would angle one of Beatrice's teats and squirt a cat. The cats loved it, even though being covered in warm milk did detract from the natural dignity of cats. The doused mouser would then lick himself far past the point of cleaning, enjoying the memory of the unexpected treat.

Sometimes the milking went on in silence with only the sound of the filling buckets slowly changing pitch. Sometimes Deuce and his grandfather would talk; sometimes they would exchange stories; often Grandpa would softly muse through snatches of songs he knew, repeating a verse or phrase that was especially to his liking, as if meditating on the memories associated with the words and the tunes.

"Ol' Miss Murphy, where's your daughter?" Grandpa sang quietly. Deuce had never heard any more of that particular song, and whenever he had asked about the rest, Grandpa would say, "There isn't any more," but the corner of his mouth would curve up slightly when he said it, and Deuce knew that there really was more.

"Grandpa . . ."

"Ol' Miss Murphy, where's your daughter?"

"Grandpa, there was this giant rat under the corn crib, and Mueller had it cornered, and it didn't have anywhere to run or anything."

"What's this about a rat?" Grandpa asked, returning from wherever it was Miss Murphy and her daughter took him, and Deuce told about the duel he had watched earlier.

"Wasn't that something . . . that rat just backing down the cat like that?" Deuce said at the end of his story.

"Yep."

"Did you ever see anything like that, Grandpa?"

"Yes, I have," Grandpa said. He said it in a low tone that was filled with memories. The memories hung in a pause over the rhythms of the milking for a while, and then Grandpa continued. "There are times when you have to reach way down inside and commit your entire being to saying, 'No, by damn, this is not going to happen this way.' Do you remember how Ethel Murray hurt her back?"

"Sure, everybody knows about that."

"She just reached under that creek water and pulled that tractor off of Wallace's chest, didn't she? He wound up with a lot of broken ribs, and she hurt her back. Every once in a while, someone will tap into some incredible capability, and it just explodes out of them. They didn't know they had it, so they don't really know how they did whatever it was they did. Like Ethel Murray and the tractor. She doesn't even remember doing it. Didn't think about it. Just did it. Saved her husband's life. And she doesn't let ol' Wally forget about it either. That woman's got more jewelry than Carter's got pills. Anyway, here's the thing of it. If you know you've got this potential, and you learn how to call on it, and you train to use it, well, you can summon up some powerful 'no's' that way. Some powerful 'yes's' too. 'Course you have to be a pretty tough rat to pull it off. And you don't want to go around making a habit out of backing down cats if you're a rat."

"Why not, Grandpa? I mean, if it works like you say it does?"

"Well, first off, it's very tiring to always have your ass on the line, always looking over your shoulder for the next cat. And second, while it's all well and good for the old rat to reach way down inside and commit, there is nothing to keep the cat from doing the same thing, and then you get rat for dinner. And lastly, because of the Whim of the Universe . . ."

"What's the 'Whim of the Universe'?" asked Deuce.

"It seems to be the Whim of the Universe that just as soon as you get to where you think there isn't a cat in the world that you can't handle, along comes a bear. You understand?"

"Sort of," Deuce said.

Grandpa began to chuckle. Something funny shook his shoulders up and down. "Ethel, one Sunday after church it was, she took Wally aside and she poked her finger in his tractor ribs, and she told him if he didn't quit giving Sally Pool the eye, she was going to put that tractor back on his chest."

Grandpa had stopped milking, and Beatrice bent her neck around in the stanchion, her mouth full of hay. She looked at Grandpa and chewed in that circular motion that cows use to eat hay, snorted subtly, and turned back for more. Grandpa nudged her udder and resumed milking.

"Your great-grandfather," he began, and then interrupted himself, "God, that sounds like some ancient person, and I still remember him like he was standing right there in the doorway. Not an especially big man, but strong, and really good with animals . . . I've told you this before?"

"Yes, you have."

"Well, when he was a young man in Taos learning this and that, he was chasing after a Spanish girl named Madrigal. He always got real wistful when he mentioned her. Not as far-off wistful sounding as when he thought of this other girl – he called her Colores -- but I'm sure that wasn't her real name. Still Madrigal must have been something special. I never did find out exactly what happened with Madrigal, but there he was in Taos trying to impress her when a sort of rendezvous broke out. Mostly it was traders and locals, but a few mountain men and trappers were there. It wasn't an all-out, kicking, roaring rendezvous like some others he went to later, but it had its moments. Well, Grandpa was still young, not filled out yet, and I don't think Madrigal was too interested in him. Probably she was a good bit older. But to impress her, Grandpa was showing off with his knife. Four or five others and Grandpa were throwing knives at a tree section. In the center of the tree section the jack of spades was tacked up for a target. Closest throw to the card won, losers drank a shot of a local beverage called Taos Lightning and paid the winner a peso. Now, Grandpa always had a sort of an understanding with a knife. When he showed me how to use one, he threw it like it had eyes. So he did not have to drink too often, and being sober, more or less, was making a tidy sum of money. He was hitting some part of the card pretty frequently, and after a time they had to replace the card with the queen of hearts. Apparently from the distance of the throws, he was being pretty impressive 'cause quite a crowd had gathered to watch the contest.

Grandpa was walking back from sticking the old queen one more time when he noticed two riders slowly moving their horses toward the knife throw. The reason he noticed them was they were riding huge California Spanish horses, and Grandpa had never seen horses that big before. He was used to Indian ponies and burros and runty, tough horses like that. These California horses were like locomotives in comparison, and on one of them was a very large man. It looked like horse and rider would blot out the sun. The man had long black hair and a full black beard. He was dressed in buckskin. He wore a sombrero and Blackfoot moccasins. And the Blackfeet did not go around donating moccasins, so somebody had bled a little when they changed owners. The other rider was smaller, had a mustache, and wore pretty much the same sort of outfit except he had Apache-style, high-wrapped moccasins. Grandpa remembered the moccasins because he said they were about level with his chest.

Now, Grandpa did exaggerate a bit from time to time, but even so, it must have been an impressive sight to see these two mountain men come riding through the crowd. Up they rode and just sat there watching the knife throw for awhile. Grandpa said they made him nervous, and he didn't do as well as before, but still he hit the queen once in a while and got to feeling invincible again.

The big fellow asked if they could join the contest.

There was a fellow keeping score named Limpy Jack, and Limpy said that would be fine since the contest was open to all comers. 'What's the target?' asked the big fellow. Now that seemed strange to Grandpa because they had been throwing at the queen of hearts the whole time the two mountain men had been watching. Limpy said, 'Why, we're throwing at the queen of hearts.' 'Yes, but what part of the card are you aiming for?' the big man asked. 'Just any part at all,' said Limpy. The big man grunted and turned to his friend, and they spoke briefly to one another. Then the big man told Limpy to replace the card with a fresh one, and he flipped Limpy a peso coin and asked him to take it to the tree section and draw four circles around it with a pencil."

"Grandpa, they didn't have pencils back then," Deuce said, trying to trap Grandpa in his tall tale.

"Yes, they did too have pencils. Heck, George Washington had pencils with him at Valley Forge, but that's another story."

"Really?"

"Yep. So Limpy replaced the queen with the ace of spades and drew the circles. Everybody expected the two men would get down and throw knives at the target. But you know what? They didn't. They sat right there on their horses. The big man said, 'I am El Cuchillo, and this is my friend Jose de la Riata, and we will now throw things. And with that, Cuchillo pulled out two knives and his partner took a horsehair rope from the horn of his saddle. The big man threw the first knife so smoothly that Grandpa said it looked like he was only pointing toward the target. But he wasn't just pointing because right there in the middle of the first peso circle was sticking the knife. And as soon as the knife stuck . . . just when you heard it go 'thunk' . . . the other man threw his riata, and it wrapped around the knife handle. He gave a flick, and that knife came out of the wood and flew back to the Cuchillo's hand. And while the first knife was returning, the big man had already thrown the second knife. And so, in a nonstop blur of knife and riata, they did the same thing again and again until each of the four peso circles was struck by a knife, and all that from a good five yards further than anybody had been throwing and while sitting on top of their horses. As the last knife was returning in its riata noose, the big man threw a tomahawk which split the ace of spades in half. The riata returned the tomahawk as well. Cuchillo put his knives and tomahawk away, and Jose picked up the entire jug of liquor with the riata, and they rode off into the mountains. And that is when your great-grandfather learned about the Whim of the Universe, and he never forgot it."

Deuce and his grandfather had finished milking during the story and were letting the two cows out of the barn. "That was a whopper, Grandpa," Deuce said as he closed the bottom half of the stall door.

"Now Deuce, my father was never one to tell a lie or exaggerate the truth," Grandpa chuckled, "unless of course his lips were moving. But everything he ever told me surely started out somewhere as a true statement. Well, look at that damn cat!"

Grandpa had left his whip on the counter by the door, and one of the cats had curled up inside its coil. Grandpa was tolerant of almost all creatures and most all things, but about his whip he was not. His eyes flashed and he addressed the cat. Deuce understood some of the sounds. Grandpa was informing the cat that the whip was not cat territory and that the point was not debatable. The cat ignored Grandpa. There was a brief pause as Grandpa glared at the cat which simply adjusted its body as if to say 'This is my territory now,' and that did it. Grandpa made a frightening room-filling noise as if suddenly the lower barn was the den of a bear. Pigeons and barn swallows took off from their unseen perches in the lower barn and flew in a rattle of wings out the open doors. In the pasture a hundred yards away, Beatrice and Matty jerked their heads toward the barn. Up at the big house, Deuce's mother dropped the lid of a pot and instinctively reached for a kitchen knife. And cats left. Left in terror. Left in undignified pell-mell panic. Screamed as they left.

The cat that had violated Grandpa's whip shot straight into the air and tried to leap out of the window behind the counter. The window was closed and he flailed in cobwebs briefly and then leaped for the ground and headed for the half-door of the stall. He hit the floor once and was in the air again, framed by the opening above the half-door, when Grandpa's hand wrapped around the whip's handle. The whip coil extended, reaching for the fleeing cat. It blurred into a straight line and continued to lengthen. Deuce had never known the whip was that long. On and on it flashed, and then a cannon shot fired from its tip. There was a deafening silence, and Deuce could see a puff of fur floating in the air where the cat had cleared the half-door.

Deuce realized his mouth was open. He had never really seen his grandfather use the whip on anything but candle flames or dry leaves in the fall. He had never realized, until that moment, that his grandfather had been carrying a weapon all these years. He closed his mouth and looked at the distance from where Grandpa had unleashed the whip to the door opening. It was surely farther than the whip could reach. It was. It was twice as far as the whip could reach. No, three times as far. And now as he turned toward Grandpa, Deuce saw him coil the whip into its three rings, and he realized that the six feet of Grandpa's whip had somehow just clipped some fur from a cat twenty feet away. Grandpa stooped and poured a portion of milk in the big dish. He made a friendly sound and cats began to return cautiously, unable to resist the lure of the fresh milk even though a bear might be around somewhere. Soon they were back, lapping milk from the dish. A few swallows darted through the stall and things seemed normal again.

"Yep," Grandpa said as if nothing had happened, "your great-grandfather could tell some tales, and that is a fact. Now, let's see," he continued, "If I'm not mistaken, this would be your birthday." He smiled a big warm smile. "Happy birthday," he said and reached behind his back and pulled out a beautiful hunting knife with the lines of a Bowie knife but more subtle and graceful. "I figured it was time you had a proper knife." And he handed the knife, hilt first, to Deuce.

"Oh, Grandpa, it's beautiful! Where did you get it?"

"Oh, I had it made some time ago. It's got a bit of meteor in the steel just for old times sake. Here, let me show you how it works. Now this is what your great-grandfather showed me." He took the knife back from Deuce and in a smooth pointing motion threw it into the dimness of the rear stall. It stuck in one of the massive posts that supported the upper barn. As it hit -- as the 'thunk' was still in the air -- the whip once again flashed in Grandpa's hand. It coiled around the knife hilt, pulled it from the wood, and returned it in the air to Grandpa's hand. In the fraction of time that had elapsed while the knife was in the air arching toward Grandpa's hand, the whip had re-coiled, and Grandpa caught both knife and whip together.

He handed the knife to his grandson. "Pretty good trick, huh? Happy birthday, Robert." And with that, he picked up both milk buckets and headed toward the big house singing, "Oh, a capital ship for an ocean trip was the Walloping Window Blind. No wind that blew dismayed her crew nor troubled the captain's mind."

Deuce went to get the pitchfork to clean out the soiled straw that was the inevitable result of milking cows. The pitchfork was not in its usual place but was leaning against the post that Grandpa had used for his knife target. There in the dim light, Deuce saw where the knife had hit. Its point scar was in the center of a small pencil circle.

The summer sounds of evening blended well with the feeling of calm and satisfaction that came with the closing of a farm day. The trees in front of the porch began to fill with sparrows and starlings. They would come in from the sky and disappear into the leaves -- one minute flying and obvious, the next invisible. Invisible, but not quite. To the clatter of bird voices was added the occasional low tone of a distant cow, and now from behind the house and down a bit in the hog lot, two pigs sent their grunting dispute to join the evening chorus. Before the sun vanished in yet some two hours, all these sounds would give way to the medley of frogs and crickets.

Deuce finished drying dishes and joined his grandfather on the porch. His mother would come out soon also. Some nights they would just sit and listen. Some nights they would visit about nothing in particular -- the price of wheat this year; 'Got the mower blade welded' . . . 'Good'; 'The Hickersons asked for some help day after tomorrow' -- lots of nothing in particular. Some nights Grandpa would tell stories, or the talk would be philosophy, religion, politics -- fire and opinion. Those were the fun nights for Deuce.

"So where is this arrowhead you talked so much about at dinner?" Grandpa asked.

"I'll go get it," and Deuce hurried inside and up to his room. When he returned, his mother was sitting on the porch. She had brought out a birthday cake that had been hidden in the cupboard. Grandpa was lighting the candles. The cake had caramel icing, Deuce's favorite.

"Happy birthday," his mother said. And then she and Grandpa sang 'Happy Birthday' in the family's odd traditional way. Deuce's mother sang the usual song while simultaneously Grandpa sang a modified version to the tune of 'Frere Jacques.'

Deuce blew out all of the candles except one and nudged the cake toward his mother. Kate blew out the remaining candle. None of Deuce's friends did it that way, but like Grandpa said, 'It's your birthday, but your mother was there too.' Grandpa always left one candle on his cake until it melted down and flickered out. "Mom would come out of her grave and slap me down for being uppity if I blew out her candle," he would say. And from what Deuce had heard of Big Momma, he did not doubt that she might do just that.

Grandpa ate his cake and between bites examined the arrowhead. He turned it in his fingers, examined the edge, the hilt, the chipped surface, all the while 'hmmming' and 'uh-huhing' in a knowing way. "Well," he finally began, "this is a rare thing indeed. I make it to be Anasazi, about 600 years old. Ceremonial arrow, it was. See here, the way the chip marks are so symmetrical? Took a lot of extra care to do that. So you didn't want to go sticking it into some mangy old bison and have it bust off its point. But look here at this little nick. Probably used in battle anyway. Some kind of emergency last-stand use, I reckon. See the dried blood here in the crevices around the hilt? Some old Anasazi stuck this deep into something or somebody. And you said a crow gave it to you?"

"Yes."

"Well now," Grandpa said slowly, dragging out the words in a thoughtful way, "probably the soul of the Anasazi himself come back as a crow just to give you this here arrowhead for your birthday."

"Grandpa, about how much of all that was true?"

"Well now, Deuce, truth is something of a variable, especially when estimating the mystical events of the past. But I would be willing to say that as estimations go, that was as good as anybody else's estimation and probably a damn sight more entertaining."

"Well, I was thinking of trading it at school, and I was just wondering."

Grandpa drew a slow breath and looked Deuce straight in the eye, "I'd keep that arrowhead if I were you," and he continued to look at Deuce until Deuce became uncomfortable and looked away.

That night Deuce slept with his new birthday knife tucked between the mattress and the box springs. Just in case. The last thing he remembered before he fell asleep was the image of Momma Chambeau smoking her pipe and humming a tune.

Time for the sleeper is a seldom remembered assortment of bits and pieces, like the lengths of a string ball. A chance collection of ends and beginnings, where a thesaurus of dream events flicker to completion in an instant. For sleepers and for lovers, time drags on or races by with a whimsy all its own.

And so Deuce had no idea how long he had slept when he heard his grandfather, "Get up, Deuce. Deuce, this is important, get up."

Deuce sat up sleepily and tried to focus the shapes and shadows into the reality of his room.

"Bring that arrowhead and come with me."

Deuce followed his grandfather down the back stairway all the way to the cellar. Moonlight crept in through the small windows at the top of the stone foundation walls, but even so, Deuce bumped into the table saw. He seemed unable to get around it. Its dimensions expanded to block his progress. He dropped the arrowhead and was forced to grope on the floor to find it. Something moved on the floor near his hand as he tried and tried to locate the arrowhead. He pulled back his hand and hit it on the table saw.

Deuce's mind filled with snakes as his hand glanced under the saw and wedged in the rubber belt that waited to transfer the motion of the electric motor to the saw blade. The musty smell of the cellar seemed like a tomb's smell -- still and old and rotten. Deuce gasped and tried to free his hand from the motor's belt. His grandfather's hand touched his shoulder and startled him. His hand yanked free, and the force sent him onto the floor. The moving thing slithered away into the darkness.

"Come on, Deuce."

Deuce got up quickly and tried once again to get past the table saw. His hand, formed into a fist, rested on the saw table as he traced along the cold steel table edge. The table edge went on and on. The corner of the groove that guided the miter gauge caught his palm, and Deuce opened his fist. The arrowhead fell from his hand and made a faint clicking noise as it came to rest on the steel tabletop. He must never have dropped it at all.

"Come on, Deuce."

Grandpa was calling from the shadows at the far end of the room. He stood in front of a door and motioned for Deuce to follow him as he passed through the doorway. Past the doorway was a long corridor. At the end of the corridor was a dim glow of light. But the floor -- the floor of the corridor -- the floor moved. The backlight from the end of the corridor caught and glanced, flickered, and revealed the undulating forms of the multi-colored snakes that covered the floor like a carpet. Deuce froze in his tracks.

"Come on, Deuce."

"Grandpa, come back!" he screamed as loudly as he could. No sound came out. Deuce looked down at the floor. The light on the bodies of the snakes looked like moonlight reflecting on a choppy sea. Waves began to lap toward Deuce as he stood in the doorway. He stepped forward. The surf blocked his path. All along the corridor the surf lapped up the walls and formed again into snakes. Their mouths opened and their tongues flicked out at Deuce. He could see the light glinting on their fangs. He squeezed his arrowhead tightly in his hand. Tighter. The edges pressed sharply into his palm. The snakes beside him raised vertically and stared at Deuce, motionless.

In his palm, Deuce felt the arrowhead move. It twisted in his hand. It turned over. Deuce opened his palm and stared into his hand. The stone slowly changed, curving and transforming into a snake that wrapped around Deuce's wrist, and then in a flick, the snake's body extended and wrapped upward around his arm. It was like Grandpa's whip, extending and extending. The snake tightened its grip. Squeezing. Deuce's fingers started to go numb. The body of the snake began to fade. Deuce could see his arm through the snake's shape. The shape faded and descended into Deuce's flesh, sinking deeper and disappearing slowly into his arm.

Deuce's fingers were tingling, and their color turned slowly darker. His hand seemed heavy. Very heavy. It pulled him down toward the sea of snakes that formed the barrier surf before him. As his hand pulled downward, five snakes formed where his fingers had been. His hand splashed seawater as it hit the surf line, and the snakes released from his hand and launched forward into the moving darkness before them. As the snakes released, Deuce's hand restored, but the center two fingers closed inward and were held down by the thumb. The index and small fingers straightened and pointed down the corridor. The corridor cleared as the five snakes flashed forward. The ominous surf retreated faster and faster, and Deuce followed down the corridor toward the dim glow at the end. At the light's edge, the five snakes paused, turned toward Deuce, and waited for his approach as if awaiting further commands from him.

Deuce found himself at the entrance of a room carved from sandstone rock. A glow of light entered from a square hole in the ceiling at the far end of the room, and a crude ladder made of slender tree trunks and lashed rungs descended from the hole. The ladder was worn and polished from the use of many touches over the years. Standing beside the ladder was a man. Of the man, Deuce would remember only two things -- his long white hair and his eyes, dark, haunting focal points for a remarkable soul. He ran his eyes over Deuce from head to toe to head, there to hold Deuce spellbound as his eyes searched Deuce's own.

The man smiled and then looked at the five snakes arched before Deuce. He looked at them without sound or gesture, but the snakes came slowly toward him as if by command. The man stooped and the snakes joined in his hand, coiling and changing to reproduce the arrowhead. Deuce was standing before him now, drawn as the snakes had been. The man extended his hand and placed the arrowhead in Deuce's palm where it glowed softly.

Deuce looked down at his palm, at the arrowhead. The glowing arrowhead became a shaped opening in his hand, and through the opening, Deuce began to see threads of many colors weaving at random, as if blown by some gentle breeze into changing patterns. The threads withdrew into themselves to form points of color that flashed into dots of light against a background of dense blackness. Deuce was staring at a starry night sky. He felt himself begin to pass through the opening. He was falling through his own hand. It made no sense as he joined in among the stars.

Deuce awoke. His arm was cramped under his pillow and was numb. The dream was still vivid in his mind as he sat up in bed and rubbed feeling back into his arm. Deuce had really enjoyed his dream, even the snakes. He felt a great sense of loss that he could not explain, and he desperately wanted to meet the man with the long white hair and the eyes as dark and deep as the night sky. But what branded the whole thing into his memory was the arrowhead, now beside him resting on the bed, still glowing faintly.

Deuce dressed in the pre-dawn darkness, went down the back stairs, and out the kitchen door toward the hog house without knowing why. As he walked, he remembered his dream. He remembered the man saying to him, "You must go with me. There is a great evil coming, and you are the only one." "A war is coming?" Deuce had asked, but the man only laughed and said, "War is such a little evil." His eyes had flashed then and he said again, "You must go with me." Those eyes. There had been all of life in those eyes. Deuce stopped at the entry of the hog house and froze with realization. "Jesus God," he whispered, "the eyes were my own."

Grandpa hated mornings; he also loved them. Just as he was apt to say, "If God had meant Man to see the sunrise, He would have scheduled it later in the day," he would also pause to savor the morning sounds and the unique glow of each dawn. But he also seemed to take pleasure in growling about in the morning, 'humphing' and sniffing to 'get his nose started.'

He also had a running battle with the alarm clock. Grandpa hated the thing with its obnoxious double bells 'like bug eyes in the top of its head,' he would say in disgust. It no longer rang. Grandpa so disliked the jolting noise it made that he had tried a number of modifications. He taped the bells with electrician's tape, but the noise it then made was a 'thub-thub-thub' that annoyed him just as much as the bells. "Sounds like an idiot with the stammers," he said and carved two wooden bells. That lasted only one night. The violent knocking was 'worse than sleeping with a woodpecker.' He had stuffed cotton in the bells but was not satisfied. He tried rubber bands and putting baby socks over the bells. 'Clock tuning' became a humorous obsession that he gleefully pursued with imagination, perseverance, and a colorful vocabulary.

This morning's clock had the bells removed entirely, and the clapper vibrated with a buzzing tick noise. "Goddamn thing, sounds like it's choking. Gag, you wart, you stench-toad, you bell-less, tick-eating, son-of-a-bitch, DIE," and he reached over and silenced the clock, lay back briefly, and then gave a grunt of resignation and headed for the bathroom.

Kate was cooking bacon when Grandpa came into the kitchen and poured himself a cup of coffee. "How was it?" she asked.

"Sounded like it was gagging to death like this," and Grandpa made a guttural imitation of the clock. "But I've got a plan. Have you seen Deuce?"

"No," Kate answered and slapped the back of Grandpa's hand as he tried to take a piece of bacon.

"There are four pieces for each of us."

"We've got enough bacon to feed the Third Army."

"But I am only cooking four pieces for each of us."

"Well then, you better make sure you count them real close," Grandpa said as he ran his finger through the mixing bowl and stuck a big gob of raw pancake batter in his mouth.

"How can you stand raw batter?"

"Kills the taste of the coffee."

Grandpa went into the milk separating room and got the milking buckets and returned. He put his coffee cup on the counter near where the cooked bacon was draining and, in almost the same motion, picked up a piece and went out the door. As he walked toward the barn, he noticed the door to the hog house was propped open, and he assumed that Deuce was already feeding the pigs.

In fact, Deuce had been in the hog house for almost an hour, adjusting his eyes and his mind to the darkness inside the building. Grandpa peered in the doorway. It was too dark to see inside at first, but slowly his eyes began to pick out shapes and details.

"You learn fast," Grandpa said.

"Yes," was Deuce's reply.

There was a touch of sadness in both of their voices.

Leaving Killdeer
----- O. C. 1944, Killdeer, North Dakota-----

Robertson held the image of this encounter in his mind -- his father in a rude doorway and his son leaning against a grain sack, stroking the head of a long black snake. Nearby, scarcely visible, a knife with a modified Bowie blade with a bit of meteor in the steel impaled the body of a large rat to the wooden floor.

Robertson turned the final page of the little book and read, "Now it was the destination of a lonely figure slowly approaching, rubbing his arm -- pilgrim and destination materializing for one another out of the grass, the heat, and the wind."

He turned to the front of the book and then fanned through the pages. All were the same. They were now all blank. He put the book on the table beside the bed and turned out the light and went to sleep.

Quigley Bates poured a cup of coffee and went upstairs to wake his guest. But at the turn from the hallway to the stairs, he noticed Robertson was already awake and outside with Mose, so Quigley went out on the front porch and was about to call out a morning greeting when he noticed what Robertson was doing. There, in the soft light of a hazy morning, the man was juggling silver balls. The pattern of the balls in the air fascinated Quigley. The pattern disintegrated, and the balls began landing in the soft earth. Mose looked at one of the fallen balls and then back at Robertson.

"Humph," and Robertson picked up the balls and began again. Again the pattern of balls traced through the air. Again they fell.

"Humph."

Quigley sat on the porch rail and watched. He glanced at the end of the porch to the post where Mose's tennis ball had been impaled. The ball was gone, and so was the arrow. Only a hole remained where the arrow had been. He looked back at the flashing balls and sipped his coffee. The balls hit the ground again. There were five of them. Robertson picked them up and put them into a bag and walked to the porch.

"Is that coffee?"

"Yes. Want some?"

"You bet."

And the two men went inside.

"What happened to the arrow?"

"Oh, they disappear after a while. I guess they are a form of energy, like lightning. After a time, they're gone."

"You mean, you don't know?"

"No."

Quigley poured coffee. "You dropped the juggling balls a lot."

"Yep."

"Why?"

"Gravity."

"You know what I mean. Why don't you just, you know, keep them in the air?"

"Five is hard."

"So is sticking an arrow through a tennis ball," Quigley said, pushing for an answer.

"Quigley, I do some things, that's true, but not to those balls. They keep reality for me. When they hit the ground, I know that's real. And that's important. To know what's real. To be able to come back. I've known some who could do amazing things, who got to where they couldn't *not* do amazing things, and then they weren't there anymore. I don't want to get that way. Does that answer it for you?"

"I suppose. Did you finish reading the book?"

"Yes, I did. Thank you."

"What happens this time?"

"The wicked witch gets killed, and everybody lives happily ever after. I put it back on one of the shelves, so after I leave, you can keep up with things if you want to."

"Which shelf?"

"I forget."

"I understand," said Quigley, "but I am going to miss that book."

"Oh, you'll find it again."

And Quigley realized that he might indeed find the book, but it would always be history, never current events, and therein was the security for Robertson and his family. The two men spent the morning talking on the porch about recipes and beer, and in the afternoon Quigley drove Robertson into town to catch the train. Mose sat in the back and sniffed the passing air. It was a quiet ride, and Quigley wished he could get a conversation going, but like so often happens when time is short and the parting will be significant, the moments pass in silence. Life doesn't have a Pulitzer script, and a lot of it passes with only a look or a touch, a sigh, and a 'Well...' to mark the moment.

As they neared the town, Robertson asked, "Quigley, what's a goodly sum of money?"

"For what?"

"Well, how much would it cost to eat three meals?"

"Depends on what you ate."

"For example..."

"Well, here in town it would probably cost you three dollars. Maybe up to four or five if you wanted steak, and they had any to sell. In New York City it would be more. I got a tailor-made suit when I was there. Vest. Two pairs of pants. Nothing fancy. No tie, no shirt, no shoes, and they charged me $37.50. But that's the big city, and everything costs more there."

"Have you got a twenty-dollar bill I could borrow for a little bit?"

"Hell, I've got a twenty you can keep."

"No, I just want it for a little while."

Quigley gave Robertson a twenty-dollar bill and noticed that he put it into his backpack and rummaged around in there for a while. Then Robertson asked where he could purchase some cloth and some printer's ink. Robertson used the bill to make the purchases. He put the cloth and ink into his backpack but said nothing more. After they parked at the train station, Robertson again rummaged in his backpack and then handed Quigley two twenty-dollar bills. "Thank you," he said, and then in response to Quigley's puzzled look, he added, "Don't ask."

The town was a turn around stop for the Northern Pacific Railroad. Robertson purchased a ticket and found that he was the only passenger for the southbound train. One of the most haunting sounds on earth is the call of a distant train -- the loon of the industrial age. The hissing and huffing and screeching of a train at hand are always a bit frightening. From inside the train, the passing over the rail joints is hypnotic. But that distant call touches a very ancient part of the human soul. Strange, that the modern sound of steam passing through a slotted pipe would seem a call to stir dinosaurs.

The two men had sat in silence since they first heard the distant whistle. Finally, in answer to the conductor's cry, Robertson stood and shook Quigley's hand, "Thank you for the hospitality, Quigley."

Mose scratched Robertson's pants leg. He bent down, took the upheld paw and stroked it fondly. It can be easier to send a son off to war than to look into the eyes of a dog if it cocks its head slightly to say goodbye.

"Come again, anytime." And then Quigley smiled through a short embarrassed chuckle as he realized how unlikely that would be. "Don't worry. I won't tell anyone about your visit. Even if I did tell folks around here, they'd just figure I was crazy. They wouldn't pay any attention."

"It won't be people from around here that will be asking," Robertson said, and then he turned and climbed aboard through a haze of steam and disappeared onto the train. He waved to Quigley and Mose from inside, and then the train left. A simple thing, really. A train leaving. A man and a dog alone on a platform.

A stranger comes to the farm
----- O. C. 1944, Robertson farm -----

Concrete roads last a long time, but they are boring and
sterile. Asphalt cracks in winter, turns to goo in summer, and
smells medicinal. But gravel -- now there's a road with
character. It talks its raspy talk with all who pass, with a
separate dialect for every wheel and every foot. It gives itself up
to friends and strangers in pearl-like layers. It drinks the rain
and lets the weeds and grasses come and rent some middle-room
between the ruts. It provides children with kick things. It uses
its impermanence as a weapon to guard its freedom. There will
be no citified gravel thoroughfares, for gravel loves the country
peace of its lonely ways.

The mail truck came to a stop on the gravel with the
sound of a fading drum roll, and Robertson got out and thanked
the driver for the lift. Although he had given very few details of
his background to the driver, Robertson knew the small-town
way of things and how quickly the news of his arrival would
spread. The type would probably be set for the next local edition
before he could walk the last several hundred yards of the lane to
the farmhouse. 'A stranger Comes to the Robertson Farm' it
would read, and then he amended his headline to 'A handsome
Stranger' and smiled.

Robertson took the paper and mail with him down the
lane past a small pond. Two letters and a world at war, summed
in newsprint and made painful by the list of casualties from the
county. He reached the bottom of the lane where it divided. He
turned right and continued uphill toward the farmhouse. He
quietly crossed the back porch and looked inside the house. He
saw a large comfortable room, with a fireplace, a couch, a piano,
and two overstuffed chairs. At the far end of the room was a

door into the kitchen where a woman was working at the sink with her back turned toward him. The shape of her body, her hair, her persistent manner as she worked brought back a warm rush of memories. He quietly opened the screen door and went inside. Silently he crossed the room and stood in the kitchen entrance, remembering.

The woman was trying to reclaim a pot she had forgotten on the stove. What had been beans now remained lumpy, black, and welded to the bottom. The pot was slightly too big for the sink, and it rattled and banged about as she worked with steel wool, soap, and pumice. Her concentration and the dinging noises of the pot kept her from noticing the porch screen door open and close behind a dusty 'handsome stranger' with a knapsack -- a stranger who now stood in the kitchen doorway, looking at her back and hoping it was the same girl he had known so long ago.

Some subtle change in the breeze or the shadows, or maybe the sense of another breathing, set her heart to pounding as her mind filled the room with marauding army deserters. Her right hand grasped the pot lid, her left hand grasped the pot handle. She whirled. The lid sailed at the figure behind her. Robertson ducked to his right and slammed his head into the door jam. He felt a push backward and her foot sweeping his legs from under him. He crashed to the floor with the fingers of his right hand instinctively formed and pointed at the mid-section of a banshee with a lethal-looking pot who sat on his chest and screamed, "Who the hell are you?"

"Katherine?"

There was a long silence. "Bobby?"

"Yeah."

"You look different." She relaxed.

"So do you, a little."

She became fully alert again. "What's my mother's middle name?"

"Shit, Katy, I forget."

"You better start remembering, goddammit!"

"What was my mother's middle name then?" he returned.

"I don't know."

"Well then, now what?"

"Don't you move, you bastard, that's what! Or I'll beat your face in!" And tears began to fill her eyes.

"I'm glad to see you too, Katy."

"Oh, Bobby," and tears ran down her cheeks. She swung her leg from over his chest and sat beside him on the floor in a puddle of soapy water that had been in the pot. "I . . .you just disappeared. We watched the dawn. Everything was so wonderful . . . perfect . . . whatever, and it was going to last forever." She wiped her nose on her sleeve, noticed what she had done and said, "Well, that's romantic as hell," and she rolled her eyes in self-mockery and grew silent. Robertson ran his fingers down her arm and took her hand in his. Her mind whirled with thoughts and memories. She continued softly, "I was in a dream, an absolute dream, and then your dad came to me and said you had gone, and everything got so confusing. I don't even remember getting here . . . just blocked it out . . . it's not there. Danger . . . he said I was in danger, and . . . do you remember that little ring you gave me on our last night . . . the two golden hearts?" Robertson nodded. "I wore it until it got too thin to wear. My dawn ring." Her eyes filled again, and through the halting voice of tears, she managed a slight smile. "We had a pretty productive night. It was so beautiful. And your son . . ." Her mood changed, she released his hand, wiped her cheeks with her palms, sniffled in, and thrust out a breath. "Where the hell have you been?"

Robertson was taken aback by her challenge and by the blur of motives that had filled his life and now brought the question once again to his mind, 'Just exactly where have I been?' His response was his final analysis, "Truth to tell, Katy, I've been trying to get back to you."

"For eighteen years? You've been pretty goddamn methodical!"

"Could we start this conversation over?"

It had not been for a long time now, but Katy had spent many hours phrasing her love into wonderful speeches that she was going to present him with when he returned. She wished that she could remember some of the phrases. She wished she could be sure that she really wanted to say them now. She put her hand on his cheek and then lightly touched the bruise on his head. "Sorry about that. You are a filthy mess, you know." She stood up. "You gonna stay for dinner?"

"I would like to, yes."

"Want to help with the snap beans?"

"Yes."

"Go upstairs and wash up in the hall bathroom. I'll go pick the beans and meet you on the front porch, and we can start this conversation over. Okay?"

"Sounds good."

She took a basket and went out the kitchen door to the garden. "Shave!" she called over her shoulder, and the door slapped shut behind her.

The front porch faced north and was shaded by four old oak trees. An overhanging roof was supported by simple square columns painted white. The floor was covered with grey deck paint that had weathered and chipped and been repainted over the years. It was a moonscape of depressions where coats of new paint had filled and softened the chipped-out vacancies of bygone layers.

Katy and Robertson sat on the east stairs snapping green beans and talking in the thrust and parry discomfort of re-acquaintance.

What Katy wanted to know was everything; what she said was, "Nice shirt."

"Thank you."

"Why didn't you let me know you were leaving?"

"There wasn't time."

Katy looked hard at him. "A message? A letter? It didn't have to be Shakespeare or anything. Phone call? Postcard maybe?"

Robertson smiled.

"What?"

"I'm just smiling at the idea of a postcard."

"Why?"

"Did my father tell you what I've been doing?"

"No. Well, your father tells the tallest tales sometimes-- all the time, actually. And he filled Deuce's head with a bunch of stories . . . but good God, I mean . . . they were entertaining, I'll give him that. And . . ."

"And?"

"And he said you would be coming back someday. He said it was as sure as if he'd 'read it on the next page.' He has this little leather-bound book, and he would read from it to Deuce. Well, he would pretend to read from it. I've seen it and the pages are perfectly blank. There's nothing in it. But, he would tell some fanciful swashbuckling tale, all the while pretending to be reading. I think it was just his way of hoping. He really missed you, too."

"I'm back."

"Yes. That's true. But any of the rest of it . . ." Her voice trailed off and she looked at Robertson. "It's not any of it true, is it?"

"I don't know what he told you, but I have always thought of my father as a man of great truth. Some of his truths are greater than others. Whoppers, you might say. But, as I recall, my father was highly esteemed in some very reputable bars as a veritable prevaricator of truth."

Katy laughed in agreement.

"One of my dad's stories is like a pearl . . . a thing of rare and lustrous beauty, painstakingly and instinctively crafted. And somewhere deep within, there is a small grit of truth."

"Well, he told of you far in the future, fighting some sort of fights and things, and that you would come back, but that you must cross time and all the stars to return," she said with over-dramatic humor.

"Cross time and all the stars. He told you that?"

"Yes. Your dad is a storyteller, and that's for sure. But he can turn out a phrase now and then. I'll give him that."

"Cross time and all the stars. If it were true, it would be pretty romantic."

"Yes, it would," she said softly.

"Well then, I declare it 'True'."

Katy looked up from her work. "Is it?" she asked with a mocking lilt in her voice.

Robertson turned his head toward her. His eyes ran over the features of her hair and face and came to rest, staring deeply into her eyes. "It's true." Then a smile hinted across his face, and he looked away.

The tone in his voice had said that he had traveled time. His eyes had said it. But then there was that disarming smile.

And the very thought of it -- time travel. Katy returned to snapping beans, finally voting for disbelief. But there had been that moment, that instant, when she had believed it, and the thought of it had thrilled her soul.

"I haven't seen a shirt quite like that for some time."

"Oh?"

"Yeah. Shirts without collars aren't being sold much now."

"Oh, well, I'll get one with a collar then. I'll look ten years younger. Hell, I'll get one with two collars and look twenty years younger."

"Easy for you. What about me?"

"You don't need a new shirt. You look great."

"That's sweet. Even though it's just that your eyes are going bad."

"No, I mean it. You look great. A lot older but still great."

In his eyes there was that 'let's play' twinkle that she had fallen in love with twenty years earlier. Katy flicked the bean she was holding. It hit him in the ear. Robertson threw one at her. She at him. Another. Another. She put one down Robertson's back. He responded by reaching to put a bean down her shirt front. She grabbed his hand. The play stopped and their eyes asked each other 'who were they now and where were they headed.' It was *the* question for them, and it was asked with the eyes, not words, and there was no answer given.

"Is this my son coming?"

"Yes."

Deuce was coming home from school. At the top of the lane he gave a kick to his rock of the day, a brownish one that had caught his eye that morning. He had kicked it up the lane and left it by the mailbox. Now he kicked it until he got to the culvert that brought the creek under the roadway. There he stopped and threw the rock into the pond where it dutifully splashed its message that all was right with the world. Throwing rocks into ponds is one of the ways boys check on this.

Deuce approached the porch where his mother was snapping beans with a stranger. He paused, shifted his books to his other arm, and quietly looked at them. Katy was trying to find the words for an introduction. She had gone through this moment in her mind and dreams many times, but now she could only look at her son in silence.

Deuce asked, "You're him, aren't you?"

"I'm him."

"So, what should I call you?"

"My name's Bob Robertson, and I'm your father. Pick out something."

"I'll think on it," Deuce said. "Hi, Mom." He headed inside, and Katy lightly touched his hand as he passed.

"Looks like I missed a lot," Robertson said.

"Yes, you have."

Robertson felt uncomfortable. He stared at the green bean he held and began to turn it between his fingers. He tried to think of something to start the conversation going again but could not. He felt Katy nudge his arm, and he looked at her. She said nothing but gestured with her eyes and a nod of her head toward the barn.

"Is that my dad?" Robertson asked.

"Yes."

Grandpa had returned from mowing hay. He sat on the tractor seat and looked toward the house. The man sitting on the porch next to Katy rose and came in his direction, walking out of memory to fulfill the hopes of many years. 'He looks like Deuce,' Grandpa thought to himself.

Katy watched the two men embrace. From a distance it was hard for her to tell them apart. She remembered something Grandpa had told her so often, "He'll be back. He'll be some the same and some different, but he'll be back."

Deuce came out onto the porch and sat beside his mother. "He looks like Grandpa, doesn't he?"

"Yes."

"What's he like?"

"We'll see, I guess." And Katy went inside to set out the good silver.

The dinner table conversation started and stalled and started its hesitant way through a polite mixture of minor gossip, the weather, 'Please pass . . . ,' and some war news. There were smiles. There were downward stares and lulls, when only silverware spoke to china.

Robertson complimented the meal and went with his father to sit on the front porch. Katy excused Deuce from his normal table chores, and he joined the two men outside.

"Grandpa lets me use his whip."

"Oh?" Deuce's father said in a non-committal sort of way.

"Yes, sir."

"Use it for what?"

"Just messin' around."

"Umm." Deuce's father rocked slowly.

Grandpa and Robertson exchanged half looks. Grandpa winked and Robertson asked, "You any good?"

"Sir?"

"With a whip . . . are you any good?"

"Grandpa?" Deuce asked with one word that asked 'please, please. . .'

Grandpa gave in, unable to hide his enthusiasm any longer. The game of 'Let's keep Deuce on pins and needles' would end now. "Go get it. You know where it is."

Deuce leaped out of his chair. The metal chair thumped twice on the porch floor as Deuce bolted for the door with a yelp of joy. The sudden motion, the chair's rattle, the banging of the screen door sent two trees' worth of birds temporarily into the air, as if both trees had sneezed.

Bob Robertson smiled. As he turned to his father, the smile faded. "How's he doing?"

"He'll do," said Grandpa.

"Good," Robertson responded. "Thank you for all you've done. I'm sorry that I wasn't here."

"Think nothing of it. It's been great good times." Then returning to a more superficial subject, "Do you know what he practices on?" Grandpa chuckled. Bob nodded 'no.' "He practices on flies."

"Flies?"

"Yep. Swats flies with a whip. Gets 'em sitting. Gets 'em flying . . . well, sometimes he gets 'em when they're flying."

"That's clever, Pop."

"Yes it is. It's his idea, too. 'Course you see enough cow tails flicking at 'em, it doesn't take long before whippin' 'em seems like the very thing to do. Sort of ordained by Nature."

"He hasn't run out of targets yet," said Bob as he scooped a fly off the leg of his pants and clapped it between his hands.

"Well, as a matter of fact, he has . . . twice. We've had to have a whole new batch brought in. These here ones you see now are Logan County flies. Not the same quality as your native flies, but they'll do for target practice."

Bob raised a doubting eyebrow, "Logan County flies?"

"Yep. I'll show you. You see that one on the post there?" asked Grandpa as he slowly unfolded the stiletto awl blade of his pocket knife and held it briefly, mumbly-peg style. His hand hardly moved as the knife flicked the short distance to the post and impaled the selected fly.

"Missed," said Bob.

"Missed, hell! What do you call that?" said Grandpa, plucking the knife and its victim from the porch post and brandishing a very large, very dead horse fly.

Bob grinned. "I could tell when you let go of the knife, your throw was going to be low. Over-rotated your wrist. Just lucky there happened to be another fly there. Yep, just lucky."

"All right, wiseass, your turn," and Grandpa handed over the knife.

The knife flashed out of Bob's hand and stuck in the post once again.

"Not even close! Oh, flies are safe when you're throwing at 'em and that's for damn sure. Not even close," Grandpa laughed. "Not even in the same county with that fly!"

"What fly?"

"The one you were throwing at."

"I wasn't trying for a fly," said Bob, setting the hook, "I was aiming for the hole you just put in the post."

Grandpa laughed harder than before. He had thrown at the post many times, and holes were as plentiful as flies.

Deuce returned carrying his grandfather's whip. He crossed the porch and went into the yard beneath the trees. He had picked his spot purposefully. He uncoiled the whip and with the same action, set it in motion around and around over his head. A smile flickered across his face as he brought his arm arching down behind his back. The whip didn't crack, it roared - - a howitzer had been fired in the front yard.

Bob Robertson was impressed. The birds launched skyward screaming their alarms, and the sound began to echo, probably off the barn wall, but Deuce wasn't sure of that. He did know it happened here in this spot, and he loved it. He began arching the whip overhead again. Then he changed the pattern, and the whip flashed from front to rear, firing ahead and firing again behind. Deuce slowly increased the rhythm. Like a coxswain driving up the tempo of the oars of an eight-oared shell by rapping blocks, Deuce increased the explosions of the whip. Faster and faster in a hypnotic increase of rhythm and sound. And the crashes fired back their punctuation echoes. Like a train accelerating -- powerful, unstoppable -- the rhythm built, crash upon crash. Echo and crash.

Silence. A vacuum of silence. Deuce stood, trying to shroud his pounding heart in an air of casualness. He slowly turned his head to look his father in the eyes. The eyes smiled back. The screen door creaked, and Katy Robertson came onto the porch.

"Your son is very noisy," Bob said softly.

"See that fly on your shoe?" Deuce asked.

"Yep."

"Don't move." And Deuce delivered the whip's tip with a flick. The small popping seemed comical compared to the previous roaring of the whip, but the fly was gone and a small blood spot was left on the toe of the shoe.

"What do you think about that?" Deuce asked proudly.

"You're very good," Robertson said, and Deuce beamed. "Who's this coming down the lane?"

"That's Pete Miller. Neighbor," said Grandpa. "He's courtin' Katy."

Robertson looked at Katy. "Does he always bring flowers?" Robertson asked, but Katy did not answer. She shrugged and went off the porch to meet Pete as he got out of his car. Grandpa, Deuce, and Robertson waited by the porch, and Robertson watched as Katy and Pete Miller chatted in the driveway. Katy smelled the bouquet of daisies and smiled. She gave a little wave, and the two got into the car and drove off.

"He looked like a nice fellow," Robertson said flatly.

"He is," said Grandpa.

"They looked good together," said Robertson.

"Yep."

"He got bad breath or warts or eat crackers in bed or anything?" Robertson asked.

"I've never been in bed with him," Grandpa said.

Robertson's eyes flashed at Grandpa, flashed the question and held their stare, waiting for the answer.

Grandpa began slowly, choosing his words and speaking softly, "It has been lonely for Katy. She has had gentlemen callers over the years. Pete is about the most serious of the lot. He's a good man, a widower. Got a fine daughter named Rachel, his own farm, and a tractor. He comes by about once a week. Usually brings a little something, flowers or a candy bar. A little something he carved. He's pretty good at carving. Those figures over the sideboard in the dining room are his. Sometimes they sit on the porch here or in the parlor inside. Sometimes they go off together, and sometimes they come back late. But I don't know if he eats crackers in bed, and I never asked Katy if she knows."

"Well, shit." There was deep disappointment in Robertson's quiet oath. "This is not going the way I figured it would."

"You've been gone a long time, Bob." There was silence for a while and then Grandpa added, "Pete's a good man, solid man, stable man. That's his strength . . . and his weakness. He has a dull soul, and Katy needs a little fire, and she has been waiting for you. If you match her memories, then you've got a good chance."

"Well, I have come unprepared. I just assumed . . . you know. And that was really stupid. But damn. Pop, when I saw her this afternoon, just the back of her head, her hair down her back, the way she filled my mind . . . Pete Miller, huh?"

"Yep."

"Anybody else?"

"Nope."

Robertson slowly sat down on the top step of the porch. Deuce targeted a nearby fly. A small 'snap' of his whip and the fly was gone. The insignificant noise of a casual act. "You ever use a whip?" Deuce asked after awhile.

Robertson straightened his back and looked at Deuce. A smile crept upward at the corners of his mouth. "Go and get four beers and meet us in the barn."

The big barn doors were open in the front and rear of the barn, and a breeze wandered half-heartedly through the building. Robertson sat on a sack of feed and moved his fingers inside his knapsack as though he were typing. He was. He was entering retrieval codes on a touch screen.

"Oooo, Bobby, I love it when you touch me there."

"Molly, knock it off."

"Yes, Mister Jones, your worship, sir."

"What the hell is that?" Grandpa asked.

"It's a MollyPAC."

The knapsack made a dissatisfied noise.

"*She* is a MollyPAC," Robertson corrected himself.

"Portable processor?" asked Grandpa.

The machine answered, "Molecular Processing and Call Back, Unit 3166 of the Model 5 Series. I think of myself as a blond. And who are you?"

Grandpa was taken aback. "Who am I?"

Molly returned, "I do not know who you are. That is why I asked."

"Molly, be polite," Robertson said. "The Model 5 is the 'Companion Series.' Seemed like a good choice at the time. I didn't know I'd be getting a mother-in-law."

"Mister Jones, I'm hurt."

Robertson continued, "This is my father. Say hello."

"Good evening, sir," Molly responded politely.

"And he will be on access, Molly," Robertson directed.

Grandpa mused, "So, they've made the things portable. It figures, I guess. We had processors, but they were big and they didn't have personality chips."

Deuce entered the barn with the beers and saw his grandfather watching his father seated on a sack of feed looking at a knapsack.

"Very good, Mr. Jones," Molly continued. "I have his print."

"We're home now, Molly. It's back to Robertson."

"Ah, the Great One has returned."

"Molly, we are in a barn. Do you know what a barn is?"

"Yes, your lordship."

"Would you like to receive a program for about 200 kilos of cow shit?"

"No, sir." Molly was polite. "And the younger unit . . . will he have access too?"

Robertson saw Deuce in the doorway and motioned for him to join them. "Molly, have you been scanning without authorization again?"

"I have been scanning, sir, but your subset logic has an applicable directive on awareness, and I am but complying . . . poor humble servant that I am."

"He will have access too, Molly. He is my son."

"Oooo, Bobby, you never told me. I am crushed. Young man, please say something for voiceprint."

Deuce shrugged in confusion and Robertson smiled, "Just say hello or good evening or something."

"To a knapsack? You want me to talk to a knapsack?"

Robertson pressed the touch screen, and a beam shone from Molly and traced rapidly up, down and around Deuce's legs. As she worked, Molly said, "You are evil, Bobby, you know that, don't you." Another instant and the beam withdrew into the knapsack and with it went Deuce's pants, as if the beam had vacuumed them off of his body. Deuce's eyes were wide as he shouted his surprise.

"Deuce," Robertson said with a smile, "try to show a little respect for Molly here."

"My God, how did it . . . she . . . how did that happen?"

Grandpa was laughing very hard.

"What do I do?" Deuce asked, gesturing with open palms at his legs.

"Ask for your pants back."

"Give me my pants back."

Silence.

Inaction.

"Please."

The beam once again activated, and pants appeared on the barn floor, clean and pressed. Robertson chuckled.

Grandpa, laughing, said to Deuce, "It's a good thing you didn't really piss her off, or you could be asking for more than just your pants back."

"She only packs inanimate objects," Robertson explained with a twinkle in his eye, "so you might be on your guard, Dad."

"Oh, well a fat lot you know then," Grandpa returned.

"And certain dried food. Like jerked beef."

"Go to hell."

"How does it work?" Deuce asked.

"I haven't a clue," Robertson said, "but she's really handy for traveling. She'll hold more than you could carry. She'll scan and put the molecular structure into the program, then convert the mass and store it. She can also rearrange structures. Put in rags and ink, and she'll follow an example program and print up money. Very handy for travel. Molly, my whip please."

A magenta-colored beam traced rapidly back and forth, and in an instant there was the whip in Robertson's hand. He put two beers across the barn on the floor by the rear doors and looked out at the evening. Pigeons were returning to roost in the cupolas on the barn roof, and a swallow darted in the doorway and disappeared into the upper rafters. Grandpa had a hammer and two twenty-penny nails. He tapped each a little way into separate support posts in the barn.

The two men went over to Deuce and took the last two beers from him. They placed the bottlenecks near the edge of the hammer mill and came down with the flat of their hands on the top of the bottles. The caps popped off, and before they could hardly begin their fall to the floor, each man grabbed a cap in mid-air, squeezed it in half between his thumb and forefinger, threw the cap over his shoulder, and drained the beer from his bottle in a matter of seconds. Throwing the bottles into the air, they swept their whips into extension and lashed at the bottles as they fell. The bottles exploded from the whips' impact, and the men began an elaborate ritual rhythm.

They stood back-to-back and moved in and out and around in a circle, all the while their whips slashing out and roaring in the air. Deuce was mesmerized. Then he realized that as they turned and wove their bodies around the barn floor, the whips crashing out the rhythm, they were driving the twenty-penny nails into the posts. There never seemed to be a break in the movement. Always the whips were flashing -- never was there an opening in the blur of leather or a pause in the rhythm of the sound. Inside it was deafening. And the nails drove deeper. Crash and move. Drive. Explode and move. The shadows from the evening light and the barn's electric bulbs raced about the barn interior. The nail heads were only a fraction of an inch from driven. Less only an instant later. Imbedded now!

The two men whirled and the whips licked out in unison toward the beer bottles on the floor. The whips flicked at the bottles. The bottle caps flew off. The whips returned to their targets, the leather caressing each bottle. The sudden silent gentleness startled Deuce. Then the bottles were lifted and flown through the air to the waiting hands of each man. The whips arched backward, straightened hard and rod-like -- spear-like. They were thrown handle first at the nail posts. The handles struck. Impact blades extended and, unseen, drove into the wooden posts. The whip leather coiled around the handles, as if each whip had been casually hung on its own hook.

"Son of a bitch," breathed Deuce.

"Watch your language," said Grandpa.

"Here's to Pete Miller," Robertson toasted.

"To good old Pete," joined Grandpa, and as they rapped their beer bottles together, they said in unison, "Fuck him." And the two men, with sweat running down their faces, drank to the curse and confusion of Pete Miller.

"Yours empty?" Robertson asked, indicating his beer bottle.

"Empty," replied Grandpa.

Robertson raised his empty bottle in a toast,

"Faint of heart, oh faint of heart,
Rue ye the winds of change
That blow the dreams of men about
Exchanging might-have-beens."

And then, very solemnly, each placed his bottle on the floor.

"So they still toast the dead," Grandpa said.

"Yes," Robertson answered, "they do."

Deuce interrupted, "How do you guys do all that stuff with a whip?"

Robertson walked over to the post, took down his whip, and handed it to Deuce. It looked like an ordinary whip, the subtle woven leather was expertly braided just the way Grandpa's whip was. "Try it," Robertson said.

Deuce rolled his wrist backward, and the whip uncoiled behind him. He made a throwing motion, and the whip responded just the way Grandpa's always did. It felt like a living thing -- a giant snake. And it roared inside the barn and returned to lay behind Deuce.

"Feel the handle," Robertson said.

"You mean the little bumps?" Deuce asked.

"Yes."

"Grandpa's has them too. They help with the grip. So it doesn't slip in your hand."

Robertson took Deuce's hand and adjusted his grip on the whip handle. "What do you feel now?"

"I don't know."

"Press here," Robertson directed.

"Jesus Christ," Deuce said as the whip retracted into its handle. It was only about five inches long now -- just a leather-wrapped stick.

"Press again."

Deuce pressed as directed, and the whip extended clumsily onto the floor.

"Retract it again, Deuce."

The whip disappeared into the handle.

"This time when you release it, imagine that it is about ten feet long and that you are going to crack it just the way you have been doing."

Deuce pressed and moved his arm as he did when he cracked Grandpa's whip. The whip extended during the motion and wrapped around the flywheel of the hammer mill. Deuce tugged, but the whip would not let go.

"Press here," Robertson directed.

Deuce did so, and the whip released and returned to the handle.

"With a little practice, you can get these bumps to do some very interesting things," Robertson said, taking the whip back. "First of all, it is not really leather. It's morph-steel. It can sort of come and go as you want it to. Watch." And Robertson moved around inside the confines of the barn, dodging posts and equipment, all the while cracking the whip. The length varied and the whip never tangled. At one point, Robertson wrapped the whip around a pitchfork and hurled it across the room and into a hay bale. He set up a rhythm of metallic tones as he struck the hammer mill and an old hubcap that was lying about. He drove the hubcap farther and farther away with each crack of the whip, until the whip was at full extension of about twenty feet. And then, after a final deafening crack, the whip retracted into an innocent-looking five-inch handle. Robertson twirled the short handle in the palm of his hand, re-gripped it, squeezed, and a four-inch spike snapped out and flashed in the barn light.

"Show off," admonished Grandpa.

Deuce stood wide-eyed. Robertson retracted the spike and put the stubby handle in his pocket. "Pretty neat, huh?" he said to Deuce.

Deuce nodded. "How does it work?"

"The handle contains liquid morph-steel that is projected through this valve thing . . ."

"Valve thing?" Deuce sounded unconvinced.

"Yeah, a valve thing. Okay, it's an M.T.F.C., Molecular Transmorgraphic Focus Chamber. Does that sound better?"

"It's a valve thing," Deuce accepted.

"Right. Anyway, the liquid molecules are restructured and projected into a solid form that is flexible like leather and stronger than steel. And you can control the length and other stuff . . ." Robertson looked at Deuce to see if he had to define 'stuff.' He did not, and so he continued, ". . . by a combination of pressure and telepathic interactivity with the sensor controls in the handle."

"It seems unbelievably impossible," Deuce said softly.

Robertson chuckled. "Not at all," he said. "It's one of those nothing-new-under-the-sun things. Actually, it's just a technological imitation of what that spider over there is doing right now. That web starts out as spider juice and gets turned into solid silk that is stronger than piano wire and as flexible as rubber. And when he's through with his web, he'll eat it and turn it back into juices. Clever little critter. The same thing happens when the whip retracts. The solid reverts to liquid morph-steel in the handle."

Deuce looked overwhelmed.

"It works good and lasts a long time," Robertson said.

Deuce had so many questions now that he did not know where to start. "Why did the Molly call you 'Mister Jones'?"

"That's been our traveling name this time. Until I feel at home in a new time, I have found it useful to hang back for a while. Understand?"

"Not really. Why Jones?"

"Why not?"

The three men sat on feed sacks. The evening breeze eased through the open doors of the barn, and they talked about idle things, avoiding deeper subjects, until Deuce finally asked quietly, "Why were you away so long?"

"Deuce," Robertson began, "I know that I missed so very much, but this was the earliest that I could...I guess 'get away' is the simplest way to say it. 'Course, if I had known your grandfather was going to be corrupting you all these years . . ."

Grandpa smiled, "I did the best I could with the tools I got."

Deuce's eyes were wide, "What are you talking about? Where have you been, and why have you been gone so long? That's all I asked."

Robertson looked at his father, "Doesn't he know?"

Grandpa shrugged, "No."

"Pop. Damn it. Why not?"

"Well, it never came up. Hell, I told him all about sex. You gotta tell him some stuff yourself."

"But what did you tell him about me? Deuce, what do you think I've been doing?"

"Well, Grandpa told me a lot of stuff . . ."

"See," interjected Grandpa, "I told him stuff. There you are."

Deuce continued, "But I always thought it was like the other tales he tells. You know . . . about his bear, and El Cuchillo, the future . . .and, you know, . . . stuff. Stories."

"They were damn good stories too, Bob. You come out real heroic in all of them. How am I supposed to know what you've really been doing anyway?"

"Shit, Pop, it's the same kind of stuff you did. He probably doesn't know about any of that either."

"Well, I don't like to toot my own horn."

Deuce could not stand it, "What are you talking about?!"

Robertson looked at his father, then at his son. "Deuce, I guess the closest thing to an explanation is to say that probably all of your grandfather's stories are true."

Deuce looked at his father and grandfather, "Bull shit."

Grandpa spoke, level and straight, "No, Deuce, it's not bull shit. All the stories were true." Deuce only looked at him in silence. "Okay, some were . . . embellished a bit. Well, there were a couple that . . . shit, hold my hand."

Deuce was puzzled, "What?"

Grandpa's voice penetrated Deuce this time, "Hold my hand and don't let go."

Colors began to fill the barn, surrounding them and closing out the world. Deuce felt dizzy. Colors were passing through his body in waves. Deuce's eyes focused on something familiar, forming transparently in the color field. It was his father and grandfather with their whips. They were driving nails into the barn posts. Deuce saw himself watching. And then all began to fade. The colors left. The dizziness subsided. Deuce was standing next to his grandfather, holding his hand. His father remained calmly sitting on the same feed sack.

Deuce breathed in soft amazement, "Holy shit, what was that?"

Grandpa said, "Ghosting." Then he looked at Robertson and noted, "And it gave me a headache. No wonder I gave that stuff up."

Deuce slowly sat down onto his feed sack and muttered, "I traveled in time. We traveled in time."

"Actually, no. You can't go to where you've already been. You can't interact with your past. I showed you some of what was still fresh in time, but we did not go back there."

Deuce asked, "Why not?"

Robertson said, "Because you'd cancel. Ghosting is sort of like when you look at a bright light for a while, and then you continue to see it after it's gone. You can do the same thing with fresh time. Fades pretty quickly, though."

"What do you mean?"

"I'm not sure."

"What?"

"Well, I guess it's like death. Nobody ever comes back to explain it. Some of the snakes are . . . I'm sorry, the times, lines of time . . . it's like being in a pit of snakes, a rainbow of snakes all moving like waves. And if you try to go toward some of them, they disappear. I can't see them when I get close. I guess it is some way of keeping reality from breaking up. If we all went back and forth to any time, changing things, reality would become this vast variable. Am I making sense to you?"

"Only sort of."

"Well, I don't know how it works. I just know that I can do it."

"Do a lot of people travel in time?"

"No, not a lot. Very few, but some. And we can guide others who can't travel on their own."

"Could you take me with you to another time?"

"I don't think that would be a wise thing to do. And it is very tiring. Besides, I like it here."

Deuce looked disappointed, "So, you won't take me?"

"How do you know you can't go yourself?" his grandfather interjected.

"Are you serious?" Deuce asked excitedly.

"We'll see," Grandpa said.

Deuce thought about that late into the night, until he finally fell asleep to dream of the stories and to follow the colored snakes to other times.

Grandpa put a bucket over his alarm clock and went to bed thinking about what an interesting time he was living in now.

Robertson was on the couch in the front parlor thinking of Katy when he heard a car drive into the lane. He watched through the window as Pete Miller got out and went around to open the car door for Katy. She got out, and in the moonlight Robertson saw Pete brush Katy's hair, lightly touch her cheek, and let his hand move downward and trace the curve of her breast as he kissed her goodnight. Robertson could hear their voices through the open window, but he could not distinguish their words, only the soft tones of the conversation. He felt a sick tightness in his stomach as he clung to the thought that there had been only the one kiss, and Katy had not let Pete's hand continue its wandering for very long before she took it in hers and walked with him to the porch door.

'Tomorrow,' Robertson thought, 'tomorrow I will go and see this Pete Miller and see what I am up against.'

Katy went up the narrow back stairs and into her bedroom. She undressed and put on a light robe and took her thoughts out onto the balcony of her bedroom. Below her, was the kitchen where Robertson had surprised her that afternoon. She remembered. She thought of Pete. Good, sweet, Pete. And she thought of Robertson. Why had he been gone for so long? "The son of a bitch," she murmured into the night air, and tears of confusion filled her eyes. Pete and Rachel had prepared a dessert party for her. The two of them had spent the afternoon together, making all the little cakes with ever so much ration sugar. There had been daisies on the table. And candles. Rachel had worn her best dress. And it had been a wonderful evening. She thought of the knowing subtlety with which Rachel had excused herself to leave her alone with Pete. Katy stomped her foot, and through her tears came, "Goddammit!" as she realized that it was the thought of Robertson's touch on her arm that kept pressing into her mind.

"It's five in the morning, Robert." The voice was warm and whispered.

"Thank you, Molly," Robertson said. He liked Molly and had often wondered who she had been impressed from. Probably some ninety-year-old great grandmother who happened to have a special voice register. And an attitude, he reminded himself as Molly continued.

"Will we be wearing underwear this morning?"

"Work clothes, Molly, and yes, underwear."

"It is a chilly five degrees this morning, Robert, would you like a coat?"

"Yes, please," and he watched the magenta beam trace out the wardrobe. He had slept on the floor because the couch was too narrow for his habitual turnings during sleep, and now his back was stiff and his shoulder was sore from the unyielding floor.

Robertson was in the kitchen trying to find coffee when a variety of wake-up sounds began above him. There were bell noises and something that sounded like a bucket hitting the floor.

"What are you looking for?" asked Katy. She paused in the doorway and adjusted her robe.

"Good morning, Katherine. Coffee."

"I'll get it," and she began her breakfast routine.

"When did you get electricity?"

"Three years ago. The Millers have it too and pretty much all of the downtown now."

There was a long silence between them. Robertson fought the temptation to say something about the weather. Nothing else came to mind. Just the bubble rhythm of the coffee pot and the dinging and clicking of plates and pans and tableware as Katy assembled breakfast.

"Kind of chilly this morning." It had slipped out in spite of his efforts.

Katy paused and turned. There was a downward look, then a slight smile as her eyes rose and met his. Robertson shrugged apologetically, sheepishly, and scratched the back of his neck. "I'm more of a conversationalist later in the day. Usually, it's the weather from five to six-thirty, food and incidentals through the day, philosophy and rhetoric by dinner, and poetry around sunset. So . . . think it'll rain?"

Katy's smile released a breath of amusement -- not laughter -- only close to a chuckle, really just a warm sound. "How do you like your coffee?"

"Plain."

Grandpa came limping into the kitchen in search of bacon and coffee. "Well, I think I've got the son-of-a-bitch under control," he said with pride.

Robertson looked at Katy. She explained, "His alarm clock."

"Yep, absolutely encouraging. Pleasantly muffled, yet still authoritative enough to do the waking."

Robertson asked, "What was the crash I heard?"

"Ah, well," Grandpa continued, "the secret was putting the clock under a milk bucket, a towel under the whole pile of stuff. That was what made for the muffling combination. However, I forgot about the bucket, so when I reached for the clock, I sort of bashed into it and jammed my finger. The bucket knocked over the lamp. But that's all easy to control. All in all, a very satisfactory wake-up."

"Why are you limping then?"

"Stepped on the broken light bulb."

Deuce came into the kitchen. "Good morning. Grandpa, there is a dripping noise coming from your bedroom."

"It'll stop soon."

"Dripping noise?" Katy raised her eyebrows in Grandpa's direction.

"When I tripped over the bucket I broke the commode."

Katy's eyebrows raised further.

"I'll fix it. I'll fix it. It's a small price to pay for finally waking up in a good goddamn mood," and Grandpa headed out the door for the barn. He stopped and stood on the porch and greeted the morning chill, "Bring on fall!"

Deuce took an enamel cup of coffee and followed his grandfather out the door.

Robertson recovered from the onslaught and reviewed Grandpa's tale. He began to chuckle, then to laugh. "Stepped on the broken light bulb," and he laughed harder.

Katy was laughing now, "I can see him face down in the toilet bowl with a bucket on his foot."

"Stark naked," and Robertson howled.

Katy laughed so hard her sides hurt. "Bring on fall," she imitated, speaking in a low voice, puffing her cheeks, and holding her arms out like Grandpa had done on the porch.

The laughter subsided with occasional flare-ups, and gradually, bacon snapping in the frying pan became the dominant sound.

Robertson began, "Who lives in the house back behind the barn?"

"Nobody now. Merle Brady and his wife, Sue, used to live there. He was the hired hand. But he got called up to the war, and Sue went back home to her folks. I miss them. They were nice people."

"And who lives way up at the top of the lane?"

"Momma Chambeau. She's a Cajun, blind lady woman witch by damn," Katy said in her best Momma Chambeau voice. "I like her very much." And she put pancakes and bacon on the table. As she bent to set down the two plates, her robe parted slightly, and the hint of the curves beneath filled Robertson's mind. Katy stood and turned and wiped her hands on her robe. For her, it was just an unconscious habit, but the caress of her gesture again filled Robertson's mind.

"Katy, you look . . . nice."

"Poo." But she had spent extra time brushing her hair before coming downstairs this morning.

"No, you do."

"Nice?"

"Katy, I have been a soldier for a long time now. I have had to keep a lot locked away inside in order to survive with some sanity. I think it's all still there, but 'nice' is all that came out. But you do. . . you really do . . . look nice. I think, though, that I need to earn the privilege of seeing you this early. So, how about if I move into the house behind the barn and see how it goes for us."

"Okay."

Robertson nodded and finished his breakfast, while Katy self-consciously puttered about the kitchen. He carried his plate and cup to the sink where Katy was washing the frying pan. They stood very close to each other, and she took the plate and slowly lowered it into the soapy water.

"I have been gone for a long time. We have had lives we didn't get to share. Then, out of the blue, I just showed up on the doorstep like a postal package. I would like to start over, because you deserve more than some scruffy old soldier who shows up and says 'You look nice, let's screw.' I would like to come calling. In style. If you agree."

"Okay," she said simply. His crudeness jolted her. His manner was . . . unexpected. He was an unknown mixture of poetry and sunsets and 'let's screw.' And he was gone. "Well, shit," she said out loud when she realized she had been holding a soapy plate to her breast.

-----Miller farm-----

"Mr. Miller," Robertson said, extending his hand, "I'm Bob Robertson."

"I figured. You were the fellow sittin' on the porch the other night."

"I have heard some fine things about you from my father and from Katy, and I wanted to thank you for being such a good friend to my family."

"Where you been?"

"I've been away."

Pete Miller pitched hay into the feeder and leaned on his pitchfork. "What was it you said you did for a living?"

"I didn't say, but I understand your curiosity. I am retired now and looking forward to farming some."

"Ever been a farmer?"

"Briefly."

"Uh-huh." And Miller pitched more hay. "Some folks figure you were in prison, or dead, or you run off."

"No."

"What then?"

Robertson selected a stem of hay and peeled off a slender leaf. "I used to borrow cattle."

"Hell you say."

"Yeah. One morning just west of Amarillo . . . that's in Texas."

"I know where Amarillo is."

"Well, my associates and I were just west of there with about fifty head of borrowed cattle, when the rancher and his sons showed up. Now, their Winchesters were out and pointed, and ours were still in the saddle scabbards, so that was all she wrote about that."

"What happened?"

"Well, there isn't a tree in all of West Texas tall enough to hang anybody from, so they tied a rope around each of our necks, put the other end around their saddle horns and galloped off, dragging us by our necks through the sage and the mesquite. So, that's why I haven't been around. I've been dead for the last eighteen years."

"Bull shit."

"Yes, it is."

Pete spread hay through the feeding troughs for a while, and then said, "I've been courting Katy."

"I know."

"I didn't know she had a husband who was alive."

"I'm not her husband."

"The hell you say. What about Deuce?"

"Oh, he's my son. Katy and I just never had the time to make it official."

"Well, I'll be damned."

"So, I wanted to come by and meet you and introduce myself . . . as your competition. I'll be courting Katy, too. Again."

Pete leaned on the pitchfork. "I've already got a ring."

"Me too."

As Robertson turned to leave the barn, Pete asked again, "Where you been, really?"

"Pete, I could tell you, but it would just sound like the rustling story. And after I told you, I'd have to kill you." And Robertson smiled in a way that seemed to indicate a friendly joke, but Pete Miller would never ask again.

Rachel Miller came into the barn as Robertson was leaving. "Who was that, Daddy?"

"That is our new neighbor, Mr. Robertson."

"He seems nice."

"He is nice, I think. Damn it."

"Yes, quite nice," she said and then turned and left the barn, singing *Lady of Spain* at the top of her voice.

----- Robertson farm -----

The last cutting of hay came into the barn. Potatoes dug from the field were put into the cellar and closed away in the earthy darkness. The days were becoming progressively cooler, and Katy missed the glimpses of Robertson at the well pipe, stripping off his shirt to wash away the dust and sweat and the itches of grass and grain. She had so looked forward to taking the noon food out to the field where the three men worked. God, how alike they were. In the evenings she threw the peelings and scraps from dinner over the fence to the pigs, and she timed it to be there when Robertson walked past the barn and opened the pasture gate. From the hog lot fence she could see him go into the hired hand's house. And she felt guilty, as if she were being unfaithful to Pete. She had thought that she loved him. But still she worked to have her glimpses, and Robertson chose his routes carefully so she would have them.

And September passed.

In October the corn turned tan and brittle, and frost dusted the mornings. Ducks and geese passed overhead, and the wind lost its focus and blew warm or chill without a plan.

They took in the corn, and the farm's pace slowed to where one lazy Saturday, late in the month, Robertson came up the drive pushing a wheelbarrow full of pumpkins. He knocked on the door, opened it, and stuck his head into the room. "I was told by a small man with pointed ears that the world's greatest pumpkin carver lived within these walls, and I am come to challenge the champion."

Grandpa stood up from his overstuffed chair and said, "I am he of which you speak."

Deuce joined in, "Nay, not a whit. 'Tis I ye seek."

Robertson joined into the spontaneous mock Elizabethan, "Extempore rhyme then must I speak, to coax you gentles porchward ho, to carvings merry, carvings bold. Terror faces hewed from gourds, or humorous, whit-full bucktoothed orbs and candle-lit to be withal. But stay you sirrahs in your boasts, for truth be told, 'twas told to me, the greatest carver is a she! One so fair as stops men's hearts, and so good lady, come ye well to sit and carve and cast your spell on pumpkin, man, or what ye will."

Grandpa said in a hoarse stage whisper, "Well said, good sir, and well I see that she of speechless beauty now should speechless be. You got pumpkins, kid?"

"Yeah."

"Lemme at 'em. Come on Deuce."

Robertson held out his hand inviting Katy to rise and join them on the porch.

"You guys are crazy, you know that?"

Robertson returned, "Dulce est desipere in loco."

"What?"

"It is good to be foolish in the right place."

"I'll get some knives and be right there," Katherine said.

They sat in the afternoon sunlight, talked, joked and carved faces in pumpkins, not simple cut out triangle eyes and noses and saw tooth mouths, but faces carved in relief. Deuce was doing well in school and was very interested in a classmate, Margaret Porter. They watched as a flight of ducks came low over the treetops and landed in the pond. As they talked, a car drove down the lane and up the driveway. It was Pete Miller.

Pete got out and came up to the porch. "Nice pumpkins."

"Sirrah, sit and join the sculpt," Grandpa said.

"What?" Pete asked.

"'Twould give us joy," Robertson chimed in.

Katy explained, "Don't mind them. They're in a mood."

"Yeah, well . . . Katy, I'm sorry I didn't call," Pete began, "but I . . . could I talk to you in private?"

"Sure," she said and put down her knife and pumpkin and walked a little way off with him. "What is it, Pete?"

"Well, I need your help. Real bad. I . . . um . . . well, Rachel doesn't have a mother, and I . . . well, she is twelve now, and she . . . this afternoon, she . . . ah . . ." Pete wiped his hand nervously across his forehead and looked helplessly into Katy's eyes.

"I'll get some things and be right with you."

"What do you have to get?" he asked. Katy looked at him and raised an eyebrow. "Oh," he said, "right." She went back to the porch.

"I have to go over to Pete's for a while, but I should be back for dinner. If not, I'll call."

"Is everything all right?" Grandpa asked.

"Rachel started her period," she said quietly, "and if you tell anyone . . . ," and she pointed her finger menacingly at each of them and went into the house.

Pete and Katy drove down the lane, and Grandpa mused, "Seems Rachel isn't old enough. I mean she's just a little girl."

Deuce said, "Have you seen her recently, Grandpa?"

"No."

Robertson said, "I have. She's old enough."

"Time gets away, doesn't it?" Grandpa said. "Shit, that's the kind of stuff old people say," and Grandpa got a distant look in his eyes. "I think I'll go to town this evening. Maybe get a bite to eat at the Cafe."

"Or Miss Lilly's," Deuce said knowingly.

"Maybe," said Grandpa, and a self-satisfied smile broke onto his face. He got up and went inside and called Miss Lillian, a woman of great mature beauty and uncertain past who had come to town several years before the war and purchased a small house with cash money. She and Grandpa met at a Fourth of July picnic when he came upon her fishing. Acquaintance had become friendship, confirmed by Grandpa's frequent affirmation that he and Miss Lilly were 'very good friends.' Whenever he made such a comment in the company of others, eyebrows raised and smirks were exchanged by guests who knew or thought they knew better. And indeed, Grandpa had on occasion returned from town with a rumpled shirt.

Grandpa returned to the porch with a dissatisfied look. He sucked his teeth and then said, "Well, you two are invited to dinner. Lil says she is anxious to meet you and that Deuce is always welcome." He sniffed in a long breath and turned and went inside to get ready.

Deuce mentioned, "I think you and I should leave early."

"That was my impression," agreed Robertson.

They left a note for Katy clamped in a pumpkin top and headed for town and Miss Lilly's in the pickup truck. Momma Chambeau was on her porch, and as they passed, she waved to them and Grandpa blew the horn twice.

"I thought she was blind," Robertson said.

"She is," Grandpa returned, "but she knows all the different local vehicles by their sounds. Last time I stopped in to see her, she told me that this truck needed new plugs."

Robertson turned in the seat and watched the old lady rocking on her porch as they turned left and drove down Herbert Road.

Miss Lilly met them at the door. She was wearing a cotton print dress and glasses which she took off and placed in her apron pocket. She extended her hand. "Good evening, I'm Lilly. You must be Robert's son."

Robertson was taken aback briefly at the thought that someone would refer to his father as 'Robert.' "Yes, I am."

"And Deuce, get in here," she said in a friendly familiar way. And then simply, "Robert," and smiled.

"Lil. Thank you. I know this was short notice."

"Don't worry about it. I'm glad to have you," and then quietly with a hint of embarrassment, "Robert, there is not much meat . . ."

Grandpa asked, "Do you have beer?"

"Only on days that end in 'Y'," she said. "And vegetables and rolls and apple pie, but go easy on the meat. There isn't that much, and I don't want your son to think I don't know how to fix a proper meal."

"Lilly, don't worry about it. I raised him to be polite, and if he isn't, I'll see to it that something painful and medieval happens to him," said Grandpa.

The dinner was a delight for all of them. And Robertson was charmed by Miss Lilly's way of speaking. She repeated herself. A lot. But in a pleasant way, like a jazz musician toying with a melody.

"Young Robert, I am sorry for the meal. My mother always said a meal was not a meal without three meats, and this rationing of everything is just a big pain. I know I shouldn't complain. I'm not in a foxhole eating out of my helmet, but it is a pain anyway. If my mother were here, she would end this war single-handedly so that she could serve three meats, and that is the way of it. I am sorry."

"Miss Lilly, the meal was superb. Does Katy know how to do whatever it was you did with the potatoes?" Robertson asked.

"Oh, poo. Potatoes are just potatoes. But I'm glad you liked them."

"These came out of the ground as potatoes, but by the time they got to the table, they had received some sort of wizardry."

"Young Robert, flattery will get you anywhere. Butter, salt, fresh garlic, parsley, boil them in dragon's blood and leave some of the skin on. No wizardry to it. And yes, Katy knows how to cook my potatoes. Except for the dragon's blood. That's a secret."

"It's safe with me," Robertson smiled. "If your mother could end this war before Deuce gets involved in it, I would appreciate it."

"Mother is dead."

"I'm sorry. What was her name?"

"Silver."

"I beg your pardon."

"That was her name. Silver Louise. I am Lillian Louise. We don't really have a last name. Davis is just something that I sort of acquired."

Grandpa said, "Nice name, Silver. I didn't know."

"You never asked."

"Sorry."

"No, that is one of the things I love most about you. You seem to be interested in me, but you have never pushed. Do you know what I mean? You don't push. Too many people push."

Grandpa shrugged. Conversation lapsed, and then Lilly blurted, "Mother ran a sort of boarding house. And I grew up there. We always had three meats, you see. After she died, I carried on, as it were. With the boarding house. But it wasn't . . . I mean it was all I knew about at the time, but I never . . . well . . . ," and Lilly cleared her throat slightly, "and then I sold the boarding house and wound up here."

"I'm sure it was a fine, um . . ." Grandpa searched for a word.

"Yes, it was very high class. And I'm glad I told you finally. And I'm glad you never asked. Thank you, Robert. Well, that was a bit of a ramble wasn't it? Some more squash, Young Robert? Deuce? Please eat. This squash is not going back in the mason jar."

Grandpa interrupted, "Yes, have all of the squash and finish up those potatoes."

Lilly gave Grandpa a knowing look, "He wants the pie to himself."

"Pie?" inquired Deuce.

"Apple pie," said Miss Lilly.

"Eat your squash," Grandpa kidded.

Lilly had definite opinions about what a pie should be. The crust was a fragile patchwork that gave only tenuous support to the filling. The apples were thinly sliced, and surprise pockets of sugar and cinnamon lurked within their layers so that the flavors came attacking unexpectedly. There was also a bowl of thick cream, slightly sweetened and blushed with rum. This dessert was wonderful.

Robertson sipped coffee and said, "Miss Lilly, you are a delight. Thank you for everything."

"You are welcome. It is a pleasure having you here."

"You are also the first person I have met since I arrived who hasn't asked where I've been."

"I try not to push. I was new in this town once myself. It can be a trial."

Robertson chuckled. "Speaking of trials, do you know a thin lady, fiftyish, black dress with a high collar, grey hair pulled back . . ."

Lilly asked, "Was she doing needlework at Soal's Store?"

"Yes."

"Why do you ask?"

"Well, the other day as I entered Soal's, she got up and walked out, and she actually stuck her nose in the air as she passed me. I don't think I've ever seen someone actually physically turn up their nose."

"You were in the presence of Isadora Turner. She is something of a poot-root, but then she has her story, too."

Grandpa explained, "She was left standing at the altar apparently. And she takes gossip to a high art form. She was rather unkind to Lilly and me back when we started keeping company."

"Poot-root," interjected Miss Lilly.

"She was a horse's ass."

"Robert!"

"She was. And before us, it was Mary Pike when she turned up pregnant, and before her it was . . . I forget. And I don't care."

"It is a small town, Young Robert."

"Does it ever end?" Robertson asked.

Lilly nodded. "Oh sure. Eventually. You see, you are their new game. You and Katherine. Here, people farm. And visit. That's it. You farm and you visit. And you two are the hot topic. There is always some commonplace scandal. War brides with roving eyes. Girls with children and no wedding rings. Every high school class has the inevitable results of doing what comes naturally. They know how to gossip about those things. But you are driving them crazy. Between the telephone operator and the mailman and the folks at Soal's, there isn't anything that isn't known. Except about you. And it's driving them crazy. It's delicious for me, of course. Just delicious. But I think you have confounded their gossip resources, and they don't know what to do. It has been the most wonderful good time watching them try to figure you out. It was the same when I came here and Robert's hat began to hang in my parlor. Everyone wanted to push into my past. Push. Push. Then Bob Jenkins got his hand cut off at the mill, and . . ." Lilly shrugged. "There is one thing though. They gossip about morals . . . they gossip, and poo-poo, and raise their eyebrows. But they all read *The Scarlet Letter* in school and they liked it!"

"So, they're ostracizing us."

"No. They think they should, but they can't help rooting for you. It's driving them crazy. Great fun!"

"Where do they say I've been?"

"Oh, they're quite imaginative about that. Pete Miller says you rustled cattle. Imagine that. Then others say you were in prison. That's fairly common actually. You were on secret government business. You used to be dead, of course. That was sort of the tacitly agreed upon excuse for Katherine having Deuce and living with Robert. Miss Turner actually claims you have been off with the 'other woman'."

"Well, Miss Lilly, where do you think I've been?"

"Oh, I don't want to push, Young Robert."

"Have you read *The Scarlet Letter*?" Robertson asked with a smile.

"Yes, I have. I have also read *The Odyssey*."

"So?"

"Well, my rumor would be that you have been on a voyage, and that it has taken you all this time to fight your way back to the woman you love. And if that isn't true, it ought to be."

Robertson said nothing. Deuce looked at his father. Grandpa sniffed in a breath, cleared his throat and said, "Deuce would you like to show your father O'Malley's Bar or would the two of you like to stay here and do dishes?"

Deuce said, "I'll be glad to help with the dishes."

Grandpa glanced at Robertson. Robertson caught the request in his father's eyes and said, "Miss Lilly, thank you for a delightful dinner, and it is the least I could do to help with the dishes," and he looked back at Grandpa who glared. "But," he continued, and Grandpa softened, "Deuce has just recently received his draft card, and with your permission, Dad, I would like to have him show me this O'Malley's Bar."

"Fine with me. Be good for him," said Grandpa. Miss Lilly blushed slightly.

The table was cleared and the small talk continued, but nothing of substance was said until Deuce and Robertson were leaving. As they headed out onto the porch, Miss Lilly put her arm around Robertson's waist and said, "Welcome back."

"Thank you. And thank you very much for explaining things to me. I gather it's either make some friends or wait for someone to come up with a new scandal."

"That's about it."

Robertson looked at his watch, gave Lilly a friendly hug, and said quietly, "I think we'll be at O'Malley's until around . . . midnight?" Then he and Deuce walked toward Main Street.

Miss Lilly waved and said, "It was good to meet you. Please come again."

"What was that last thing he said to you?" Grandpa asked.

"He said we can wash dishes until midnight," she smiled, and the two of them watched Deuce and Robertson as they walked down the street toward O'Malley's. Then they went inside.

Deuce and Robertson walked in silence for quite a while. Finally, Deuce said, "It doesn't seem . . . I don't know."

"What?" asked Robertson.

"I mean Grandpa and Miss Lilly. You and Mom. It's as if, I don't know . . . I mean, I thought just young people . . . you know."

"We are young people," Robertson said quietly. "So what's special about O'Malley's?"

"I don't know. I've never been in there." And then, after another pause, "What did you do, really?"

"Just tried to keep the balance and make friends."

"I'm serious."

"So am I. Damn those guys are big. Who are they?" Two very big men had just entered O'Malley's.

"The Slakes. That's Barry with the hat and the other one is his brother, Ruben. Their father owns the mill and pretty much bosses the town. They played football in high school. They were something."

"How come they aren't off fighting the war?"

"Well, they're 4-F."

"What's that?"

"Physically unfit for duty. Ruben has a bad knee and Barry has a bad back. Everybody knows they're healthy as horses and it's just their father keeping them out of the war. He's on the local draft board, and so they came up 4-F. Sometimes you can hear them screaming at their old man even over the mill noise. They are really ticked about it. And then their best friend, Doug Drummond -- he played end -- he got drafted and got killed, and that's when they started going to O'Malley's pretty regular. And screaming at their old man and anybody else that looks at them funny. It's kinda too bad really. So what did you do for eighteen years?"

"I'll show you," Robertson said, and they walked into O'Malley's Bar.

The Slakes were sitting at a table drinking the first of their nightly beers when Robertson approached the bar and said to the bartender, "Sir, a beer for me and a beer for my son here who has got a brand new draft card in his pocket."

Low, under his breath, Deuce said to his father, "Don't bring this up."

"And a round for the house so we can all drink to the brave men who are fighting overseas."

"Oh, shit," Deuce whispered.

There were mutterings of appreciation, but the enthusiasm was minimal. The patrons knew who Robertson was, and they did not know whether they would drink with him or not, and they did not know what the Slake brothers would do. And so no one approached the bar to accept Robertson's offer. The bar got quiet. Very quiet. At the end of the bar, Slats Lyder was about to begin playing the piano. He slowly turned around on his stool and watched.

"Good evening," Robertson continued, as if everything were normal and friendly, "my name's Bob Robertson. Maybe you've heard of me. And this is my son, Deuce. The little . . . bastard . . . turned eighteen. Got himself a draft card. Liable to get called up to go serve any day now. So, we just came in to have a few beers to celebrate."

There was a hush. Then Ruben Slake said in a low growl, "Get the fuck out of here."

Robertson, with his back to the bar, said "Hey, friends, I'm new. What did I do? I offered everyone a drink in friendship. What did I do?"

Barry Slake answered, "You get your beer. You drink your beer. And then you get your new friendly ass out of this bar!"

There was a long silence while Robertson looked at Barry and Ruben. Then he turned to the bartender and said very meekly, "Two beers, please."

Barry adjusted his hat, Ruben wiped his nose on his sleeve, and the tension lifted from eye level to just above the heads of all the patrons. There it hovered. Waiting.

Deuce's stomach was in knots. He didn't know whether to feel relieved to be out of a dangerous confrontation or to feel humiliated. While he made up his mind, he chose anger.

"Dad, you could mop up the floor with these guys!"

"Why?"

"Why? Come on, Dad," Deuce said, already beginning to feel the beer. "All the things Grandpa told me about you . . . what were they? Some stories? Just stuff that he made up? I've wished those stories were true since I was just a kid. I've lived for them. I've wanted to meet my father for so long because my father was . . . somebody! I'm glad I never told anybody who my father was. They'd just be laughing now."

"So, you want a father who cleans out barrooms? That's a father?"

"That's being somebody!"

"Listen, I don't know what all your grandfather told you about. . ."

Deuce interrupted, "He told me, 'when in doubt, you'd kick ass!'"

"Your grandfather said I'd 'kick ass'?"

"Well, no, he said you would show them their fears, but it amounted to the same thing."

"So, you want to see Ruben's skull explode and blood spew from Barry's eyes. Is that it?"

"Well, no, not exactly."

"What then?"

"Show them who's boss. Kick their ass."

"That's too much trouble. I don't do that anymore."

"But, you said when we came in that you'd show me what you used to do."

"You want to spoil my retirement?"

"I want to leave here with some self-respect."

"By butting heads with the Slakes?"

"Yes."

"Deuce, if you think butting heads is the answer, you are very, very wrong. You butt heads every chance you get, and you are going to wind up with a headache you won't believe." There was a chilling undercurrent of horror in those last words, and then Robertson continued, "No matter where you wind up in this life, you remember that somewhere there is a father of yours saying 'I told you so!' You can't hear this now because you're so damn young. You've got hormonal immortality. You're immune to death and broken jaws. That's just how young people think, so I understand how you feel. I remember the feeling. God, I even remember this lecture. My father gave it to me. I didn't listen, either. And now I have got enough enemies and dead friends to last me a lifetime, and I don't want any more."

"But, Dad, these guys are just bullies. We could teach them a lesson."

"Now, that's a good idea. A lesson. I will now teach a lesson. You see those guys? You look at them very carefully. Look at those guys. They are very big. They have giant muscles. They can break things, like your pubescent ass. You want those giants for enemies? Not me. So, I am going to make friends with them. Did your grandfather teach you how to make yourself heavy?"

"Yes."

"Can you do it?"

"Yes."

"Then do it."

"When? Now?"

"You'll know when. Which one is supposed to have the bad back?"

"Barry."

"With the hat?"

"Right."

Robertson got up and went over to the Slakes and their friends. "Excuse me," said Robertson, and he tapped Barry on the shoulder.

"Get lost dipshit," said Barry. He and Ruben were arm wrestling for beers, and Barry was straining to keep from buying another round. His face was red and sweaty, and it was only a matter of time before he would lose again. Barry was getting mad. He couldn't hold out much longer. His forearm was at a 45-degree angle to the table. Ruben slammed Barry's knuckles into the tabletop.

"You buy," crowed Ruben.

"Bull shit!" screamed Barry. "I was distracted."

"Distracted, my ass."

"I was distracted, goddammit! How could I concentrate with this asshole asking me questions?"

Barry rose from the table and scooped the major portion of Robertson's shirt front in his huge right hand. "You are beginning to annoy me. How 'bout if I just throw you through the fucking wall?"

"Sir," Robertson began, referring to Barry, "I am sorry to have interrupted your contest." Deuce wished he were somewhere else. Deuce wished he were somebody else. This was humiliating. Robertson continued, "I tell you what . . . if you can throw me farther than I can throw you, I'll buy beer for all of you. If I throw you farther, you let me leave without beating the crap out of me. What do you say?"

"I say it's a trick, and I ain't lettin' you put a hand on me. You'll grab me by the nuts or something, sneak a knife into me when I ain't ready. No way. I ain't stupid. How 'bout this . . . you buy the beer, and then I beat the shit out of you anyway?" Barry said laughing.

"No, now wait a minute," Robertson continued, his voice wavering. "If you beat me up, what will happen to the kid?"

"Fuck the kid," Barry returned.

"Throw the kid," said Ruben.

"No! Absolutely not!" said Robertson.

"Yeah, the kid. He's the asshole with the big shot draft card."

"Not the kid," Robertson pleaded again.

"Listen asshole, you want to leave here alive, we throw the kid. I'm still gonna beat the shit out of you." Barry faked a punch. Robertson flinched, much to Barry's amusement. Deuce felt sick in his stomach. "But you'll be alive when you leave. Come here, kid!" Barry made a commanding gesture for Deuce to get over to the table. Deuce came hesitantly. This was not a situation that seemed to be in anybody's control, and he wondered what his father was doing. He certainly wasn't acting like the hero he had been told about.

"You first, dipshit," sneered Barry.

Robertson grabbed Deuce under his armpits and lifted. He didn't budge. Robertson whispered to Deuce, "Not now, idiot." Deuce smiled, relaxed, and Robertson lifted him and gave a heave. Deuce went through the air for about four feet and landed lightly, standing beside Ruben. Deuce noted that his head was level with Ruben's shoulder and that Ruben's arm was as big as Deuce's leg.

Barry roared with laughter. "I could throw the kid, you, and Ruben all at once, farther than that. This is gonna be easy beer."

"How far do you intend to throw him?" asked Robertson.

"I ain't decided yet," said Barry.

"Not over the table," Robertson said, setting the hook.

"Shit," returned Barry derisively, "I can throw him over the table, over the bar, and into the mirror. And you can pay for the damages. And the beer!"

"Don't do it. You'll hurt him. I'll just buy the beer now," said Robertson.

"Bull shit. A bet is a bet. This is gonna be fun." Barry spit on his hands one at a time and then clapped them together. Spittle sprayed from his palms into Robertson's face. Robertson wiped his face on his shirt sleeve and said again, "Look, I'll buy the beer. I'm calling the bet off. Please."

The bar patrons spoke in hushed tones and began picking spots to stand and watch -- close enough to see and hear, but not too far from an exit.

Barry laughed and moved to pick up Deuce. He grabbed a fist full of shirt and then bent to slip his arm through Deuce's crotch.

"What are you doing?" demanded Robertson. "You gotta use two hands under his arms like I did."

"I can do it any fucking way I want. The kid is gonna be an Olympic record here. So shut the fuck up!"

Robertson looked away to hide his smile. The hook was definitely set. Behind the bar, O'Malley braced himself to protect his mirror.

Deuce let his mind find his center and imagined it embedded below the floor of the barroom. For practical purposes, Deuce weighed about two thousand pounds. The bar was absolutely silent, everyone watching. Barry took a deep confident breath and gave a sudden violent heave. There was a popping noise like the popping of lake ice that sounds so much louder in the still tension of the first winter's crossing. A popping, and then Barry screamed and fell to the floor in agony.

Deuce caught his father's eyes and the subtle nod that said 'not bad.' He smiled back and then looked down at 275 pounds of bully lying helplessly in pain at his feet. His father moved close and whispered, "The bigger they are, the harder they fall. The trick is getting them to tip over." He winked and then joined Ruben and the others down on the floor beside Barry.

Barry was screaming about his back. His breath was coming in gasps. Rapid gasps. Barry was getting dizzy. He was only hyperventilating, but he thought he was going to die. Ruben was hollering for someone to get a doctor. Barry said he couldn't move, he was paralyzed. Onlookers pressed in and then flew out of the way as Ruben leaped up shouting, "Get a doctor, goddammit! Somebody get a fucking doctor!" His arms were waving around wildly in his frustrated concern for his brother. Tears were running down his cheeks. The bartender was already on the phone making the call, but Ruben wanted a doctor now! He was irrationally screaming for help when the low soothing words of Robertson eased their way into his mind. "Let's get him up and lean him over a chair. Just lean him over a chair. I can help him. I'll fix him, Ruben. Trust me. I'll help him. I can fix it, Ruben."

Ruben was too upset to reason about who was saying he would be of help -- he was grasping for straws. And so he and Robertson and Deuce lifted Barry from the floor and draped him belly-down over a chair. Robertson held Barry's vest and shirt briefly in his hands and then tore them in half to expose Barry's back. No one thought anything of it at the time, but later Ruben remembered the casual motion that had simultaneously ripped the two garments, and he wondered about it. Robertson rubbed his hands together hard and fast and then eased them onto the muscles of Barry's back -- smoothing motions along the spine and then circular rubbing on the knotted muscles of his lower back -- and finally slipped one arm under Barry's left armpit. He ran his right thumb and index finger over a portion of Barry's spine as he lifted the left shoulder. Barry gave a sigh of relief and relaxed. "Son of a bitch that hurt," he said with the soft exhalation of his first relaxed breath. Slowly, carefully, he sat up in the chair.

"You okay?" Ruben wanted to know.

"Yeah. I didn't know there for a while, but I'm okay now. Hey, O'Malley, your floor is filthy," Barry teased.

O'Malley returned, "Yeah, well look at the shit that lies on it!"

Barry made a friendly obscene gesture. Tension left the bar. Ruben looked at Robertson. "Thanks," he said. And then he became aware of his emotions, and pretending his tears were sweat, wiped them away on his shirt sleeve. "Sure is hot work trying to pick you up off the floor, you big shit." The two brothers smiled at one another.

"How far did I throw the little bastard?" Barry asked, and his big face swelled into a self-conscious smile.

There were laughs now and comments from around the room about the mirror being safe and the Olympic Committee's refusal to certify the record. There were comments that various individuals were glad they would not have to carry such a heavy sack of shit to the doctor's office. Barry interrupted, "All right you assholes, I just didn't want to break O'Malley's mirror, that's all." There were whistles and catcalls from the regulars who didn't often get a chance to joke with the Slake brothers. It was a good night at O'Malley's once again. "Yeah, yeah, well fuck you guys," called back Barry. It was the good-natured offensiveness that serves as banter between friends and death threats between enemies. They were all friends now, and obscenities flew for a while. There was a brief peanut fight in one corner, and then drinking and the conversations returned to normal.

Deuce and his father were seated with the Slakes by now, and somebody had bought a pitcher for them to drink. It was a pitcher of bourbon. Slats began to play the piano and sang *Clancy Lowered the Boom* which was O'Malley's favorite song. He and the whole barroom joined the chorus, 'Whenever he got his Irish up, Clancy lowered the boom, boom, boom . . .' *The One-Eyed Riley* and others followed. Deuce was amazed at the endless number of dirty songs his father was familiar with. Robertson continued to entertain the bar with limericks after all others had exhausted their store of verses.

Somewhere around 'There once was a pirate named Bates,' Deuce could no longer control the spinning room and careened to the toilet. Robertson noticed him leave and caught O'Malley's eye. Deuce threw up until his stomach muscles cramped. He didn't care. Neither did he notice the filth he was kneeling in as he stabilized his head against the cool porcelain of the toilet. The bowl was past cleaning, permanently stained and not that reliable when flushed. He didn't care. It was cool.

When Deuce returned to the barroom, he felt better. O'Malley handed him a mug of ice and club soda, delivering it casually as if serving a regular his usual boilermaker. Deuce liked O'Malley. Robertson was standing on a table in the center of the bar, singing something about 'A space-traveling man on Uranus' much to the delight of the patrons. Deuce drank soda water and watched his father juggle beer bottles, flipping them into the air and catching them by their long necks. Barry wanted to learn but broke too many bottles and was shouted out of trying by O'Malley. When Robertson and Deuce left the bar after midnight, they were the best of friends with the Slake brothers..

On the way back to Miss Lilly's, Deuce asked his father, "How did you drink all night and not have it affect you?"

"Drink one, pour three," was the answer.

"What do you mean?" asked Deuce.

"While you're sipping on one drink, pour three for the other guy. After a while, he loses count, and you're a he-man drinking buddy."

"I wish I'd known that earlier."

"I never saw a pitcher of bourbon before myself. Some of those guys' livers must have been made at General Motors. You did all right."

They passed a large home set back from the road. It was made of brick and had been built before the Civil War. Columns on the porch marked it as a place of distinction, and sitting on the porch in the early morning hour was a solitary figure.

"Who lives here?" Robertson asked Deuce.

"That is the Slake's house. That's probably Mr. Slake there on the porch waiting up for Ruben and Barry."

Robertson paused and greeted the figure, "Good morning there, sir. My son here tells me you are Mr. Slake. Is that right?" There was a slight slurring of the words as he spoke.

"I am."

"Well, sir, I'm Bob Robertson. This is my son, Deuce."

"I know young Mr. Robertson, and rumor has it that he now has a father in town."

Deuce whispered, "He can be a bit of an asshole."

"Umm," agreed Robertson. "You are up rather late, sir."

"What's it to you?"

"I figure you are probably waiting up for your boys to get home. Fine young boys they are, too. We met them just this evening. Fine boys."

"Are you usually this talkative in the middle of the night?"

"To tell the truth, I am not. But I did have more than a few little drinkies with your lads at O'Malley's tonight. Celebrating my son's draft card. Don't seem possible. I mean, one minute they're messing in their diapers, and the next minute they get a damn draft card. Too fast. Too fast, you know what I mean?"

"Yes."

"Yeah, ol' Deuce here got a draft card. Next thing, he'll probably be making me a grandfather, and I ain't hardly got used to him being out of kindergarten. Too fast. But what are you gonna do? Gotta turn 'em loose. Let 'em be men."

"My wife is trying to sleep, if you don't mind."

Robertson forced a whispered reply, "Sorry. Sorry," he said, holding his index finger in the vicinity of his lips. "Shhh. Don't piss off the missus. Well, nice to meet you, Mr. Slake." Then Robertson put his arm around Deuce and walked unsteadily off into the night. While they were still in hearing distance of the Slake home, Robertson said to Deuce, "Lucky man, that Mr. Slake. His kids ain't going to have to go to war. You know why?" he asked, not giving Deuce a chance to answer. "I'll tell you. Because they are too goddamn big, that's why. They couldn't pass the physical. Too big for a uniform. Can't fight naked."

It wasn't very far before Robertson began walking steadily, and his speech returned to normal. Deuce asked, "What the hell was all that about?"

"Just planting seeds."

"What?"

"Maybe something will grow. Maybe not. We'll see."

The fire of fall was ashes as Halloween rushed by, and Thanksgiving appeared out of nowhere. Robertson had been living in the Brady's house, taking an occasional meal with Katy, Grandpa, and Deuce, but mostly keeping to himself. He would walk the rolling hills of the farm and show up at the door with pheasant or quail and stay to see them become a meal. Katy looked forward to his visits and wondered if he knew enough to be playing hard to get so expertly.

One morning she went into the barn with a thermos of coffee and found Robertson forking hay to the cattle. Steam was rising from their backs, and the lower barn was filled with a sweet smell. She smiled and poured coffee into the thermos cup and offered it to him. The fog of breathing was everywhere. She wondered if birds' breath could be seen in the cold air, and she looked around the barn to see if a swallow or pigeon was there to give an answer.

"Thank you for the coffee," Robertson said.

"You are welcome."

"What are you looking for?"

"I was wondering if you could see birds' breath."

Robertson took a sip of coffee and deliberately let out his breath in a long, focused flow that met with Katy's. The two breaths swirled together. She breathed again. He intercepted hers once again and smiled at her in a boyish way. She took a deep breath and feigned its release. Robertson breathed into the anticipated space, but Katy held back, and Robertson breathed alone. She smiled playfully at him and puffed to intercept his. He looked at her, breathed in slowly, and then let out his breath in a long steady flow. She did the same, and the clouds joined and bobbed in the currents of the morning air. They did the same thing again, but they were closer together this time. And finally, they breathed together, Robertson's lips only a fraction of an inch from Katy's lips. Their lips touched and they continued to breathe together, looking into each other's eyes, looking deep and warm and long. And all the while the barest touch of lips together.

Katy turned slowly away and said, "Your coffee is getting cold."

Robertson looked into the cup and smiled.

Katy began, "For the past couple of years, Pete and Rachel have joined us for Thanksgiving dinner. I just wanted you to know . . . they are coming again this year. Rachel wants to help me in the kitchen. She is a marvelous help really. It's been fun seeing her get to be such . . ." Katy's voice trailed off. There was silence, except for the animals eating. In the outer barnyard a cow called a soft guttural moan.

Robertson was looking at Katy. He nodded. "I have a date, actually. We'll stop by later and say hello."

Katy's mind whirled. She had never thought he would not be coming for dinner. A date? Shit. Her stomach hurt. She could only say, "Please do," and then left.

Robertson followed her and leaned against the doorjamb of the barn. "Katherine," he said. Her pace slowed. "That kiss was the most . . . intense, bewitching thing anyone has ever done to me."

She looked back, and his eyes were on fire. She blushed and headed for the house, feeling a furious mixture of passions.

Grandpa stuck his head in the barnyard from outside. "Not coming for Thanksgiving?"

"I don't want to sit around making polite conversation with Pete Miller – 'What did you get for your corn, Pete? How do you like those Champion spark plugs, Pete? My, Rachel is looking all grown up, Pete. Why don't you and I help Katy with the dishes, Pete? Why don't you go piss up a rope, Pete?"

"So, who's your date?"

"There's nothing wrong with your hearing."

"So, who?"

"I'll think of somebody."

"Want a suggestion?"

"No."

"Very well."

"Yes."

Grandpa chuckled.

It began to snow, just a hint of snow at first, only noticeable because of the thrust of an occasional gust of wind. But by afternoon it looked like winter would come early. By evening the corn stubble was covered, and a tenuous slick of ice was on the pond, frosted over with snow and growing thicker.

Pete Miller was finishing the last of his second helping of pie. "That was truly magnificent, ladies," and he nodded to Katy and then to Rachel. "I don't think I will eat ever again."

"Just delicious," said Miss Lilly.

There was a brief silence, and Deuce thought he heard something outside. He cocked his head.

"What is it, Deuce?"

"Listen . . ."

"Well, I'll be damned," said Grandpa. "It's sleigh bells."

"Sleigh bells!" exclaimed Rachel, and she leaped up from the table. The others followed her to the window.

Coming across the field was indeed a sleigh -- a one-horse sleigh, just like in the song. And in the sleigh were two passengers. The driver halted the sleigh at the field gate, opened it, left it open, and drove on through. He was wearing a top hat, and his companion was covered in a furry robe. The horse, stomping and breathing fog, ready to continue, halted impatiently, and Robertson got down from the sleigh and touched the brim of his top hat.

"Happy Thanksgiving," he said and turned to help Momma Chambeau from the sleigh.

"Laissez les bon temps rouler!" she shouted at the top of her voice as she got down. "By damn, Big Robert, that was some fun. And now, to who-all am I talking?"

The Thanksgiving party had come outside, partially bundled against the cold, and greetings were exchanged.

"And I am happy for you to see me, too," Momma Chambeau said. "Now where is the fire, and where is the rum by damn?"

"This way, Momma," Grandpa said.

Robertson took off his hat and said to Rachel, "The horse is really just itching for some more work. Would you do me the honor of being my guest for a brief ride?"

"Ooo, Daddy, can I?"

Robertson looked at Pete, "Mr. Miller, I am sure you will agree that such a lady can make a choice of her own."

Pete waved his permission, and Rachel hopped into the sleigh and buried herself under the deep pile of the buffalo robe. Robertson twirled his top hat between his fingers so that it spun completely around, and then with a flourish he popped it onto his head, climbed into the sleigh, snapped the slack rein to the horse's rump, and off they went through the open gate.

"Katy, are you coming in?" Pete asked.

Katy smiled, took his arm, and the two went inside with the others.

The fire produced a bouquet of sparks when Grandpa put on another log. Momma Chambeau sipped her hot buttered rum and spoke in her quaint Cajun way of the dinner she and Robertson had shared. She spoke of the poetry of his soul and the charm of his manner. She wished she were young, for 'by damn' she would have him and that is a certain thing of truth.' She was Robertson's weapon, and her words drove sharply into Pete Miller's gut and softly into Katy's heart.

Miss Lilly got a ride next while Rachel bubbled and told of how she had driven the horse, and what fun she had had, and what a nice man Mr. Robertson was, that she should always call him Robert because they were friends now, and where the wonderful robe had come from. And she too was Robertson's weapon, and her words drove sharply into Pete Miller's gut and softly into Katy's heart.

Robertson returned and took Momma Chambeau home. Pete was leaving with Rachel, and as they said goodbye, Katy noticed the light still on at Momma Chambeau's house far away on the snowy hill at the top of the lane.

"Goodbye, Pete. Thank you for coming. Rachel, you were a great help." And so on -- the nothings of parting, when parting is only social. Pete held her hands and gave her a hard kiss on the mouth.

Rachel said in an embarrassed way, "Daddy!" But she really liked Katy, and she hoped her father would marry her so she could marry Mr. Robertson -- Robert.

Later, Katy was coming back from the dining room. She had put the silver away in the sideboard. She turned out the light and went to the kitchen table where her mug of hot buttered rum sat waiting for her. Robertson stood in the doorway to the living room. The firelight silhouetted his figure as he turned out the kitchen light. He stepped to one side and said, "You look lovely in the firelight." He had her coat draped over his arm.

"A bit presumptuous, aren't you?" Katy said, referring to the coat.

"Katherine, the others were only passing shadows this evening. The sleigh is for you . . . and the night . . . and the driver. All yours."

She took the coat from his arm and put it on, then took his top hat and put it on as well, and the two went out the door together into the chill of the night.

The door at the Chelsea Pub
----- O. C. 1944, London, England -----

Across the Atlantic Ocean in a stark temporary building outside of London, an army clerk answered the intercom on his desk, looked up and said, "Sarge, the lieutenant wants to see you."

And so George Washington Carver Johnson, sergeant of military police, checked his uniform to ensure that the edge of his blouse front and his belt buckle and trouser fly all formed a straight line, and then he knocked on Lt. Barkley's office door. He used his left hand; the knuckles on his right hand were still sore.

"Stand in the hole," and Johnson entered, closing the door behind him. He saluted and stood at attention.

"Sergeant Johnson. As ordered, sir."

Lt. Barkley returned the salute from his seat and opened a folder on the desk in front of him. He studied the sergeant, partly because he was trying to find the right way to begin but mostly because Johnson would expect it. There was nothing wrong. Everything that was supposed to line up did; everything that was supposed to shine, shone; everything that was supposed to be white and spotless was so. Johnson was not white. He was black. Not just a Negro -- Johnson was black, ebony, and very proud of it. Barkley leaned back in his chair and paused a moment longer.

"Johnson, when was the last time you saw Corporal Morris?"

"Last night, sir."

"What the hell happened?"

"Well sir, the corporal he ran into a door over at Chelsea Pub. There must have been somebody going out when the corporal was going in, sir."

"And he accidentally ran into a door."

"Yes, sir."

"And the door knocked out three of his teeth, broke his collar bone and two of his ribs."

Johnson's eyes narrowed ever so slightly. "Corporal Morris had an accident with a door, sir."

"Accident."

"Yes, sir."

"Johnson, I have been asked by Colonel Mayhew to investigate an incident that happened last night. Col. Mayhew for Christ's sake, Johnson. His Brits are really steamed, and do you know why? It's because they found two of their men tied to drain pipes this morning. They were very cold. They were very cold because they were very naked, except . . . ," and here Barkley had to look away to hide the smile that was going to ruin the chewing out. In fact, Barkley had to swivel his chair and continue while looking out the window, ". . . they were naked except for their dicks which were adhesive taped to opposite ends of an MP billy club. May I see your billy club, Sergeant."

Sergeant Johnson drew the club from its holder, rolled if deftly over his thumb and twirled it once between his fingers with a casual flourish, and then laid it on the lieutenant's desk.

"This is a new club, Sergeant."

"Yes, sir."

"Goddamn it, Johnson, they're allies!" The lieutenant paused and looked out the window again. It was raining. "Which door?"

"Sir?"

"The door Corporal Morris ran into . . . which one was it? The one on the side, or the one in front with the stairs leading up to it?"

"I think it might have been the one in front with the stairs, sir."

"Does this door have a sister?"

"No comment, sir."

"And does this sister work at Chelsea Pub where Morris spends more than a little of his time? And do you suppose that this door might get upset when his sister goes off for the weekend with a colored yank?"

"I suppose you'll need to talk to Corporal Morris about that, sir."

"Corporal Morris didn't tape the brother's dick to a billy club! They're sending the girl to Scotland to get out of the blitz, so that ought to be the end of it. But if Morris goes AWOL to Scotland, I'm going to send you to bring him back. You got that?"

"Yes, sir."

"Johnson, did you know that those two were hand-to-hand combat instructors for the British Commandos?"

"They must have got took by surprise, sir."

"I dare say they did."

Christmas on the farm
----- O. C. 1944, Robertson farm -----

The Thanksgiving snow lasted about a week before sinking into the landscape. Some remained here and there in shadowed areas and protected nooks, but except for these accents, winter turned again to tan and gray.

In early December, Robertson and Deuce went to town to the Liberty Mill to have feed mixed with molasses. Barry and Ruben helped unload the sacks of grain from the Robertson truck. They were enjoying their work and not above a little grab-ass in the process.

"Well, Mr. R., this is the last you'll be seeing of us for quite a while," Ruben stated.

"How so?" Robertson asked as he slid a sack of grain to the rear of the truck.

"Got orders," Ruben said.

"We're gonna be Marines starting next week," Barry said and picked up two sacks at once.

"Yep. Some kind of clerical error kept us down. Ain't that the government way, though," Ruben explained.

Deuce looked at his father as the two passed each other on the truck bed. Robertson winked.

Barry returned for another load of sacks. "We're kind of worried the damn war will be over before we can get in it."

Robertson asked, "You ever heard of Iwo Jima or Okinawa?"

"Nope."

Robertson said, "Don't worry. There's still some war left."

"You think so?"

"Oh, yeah," Robertson grunted as he pulled another sack to the rear of the truck. "Kickass Marines, huh?"

"Yes, sir! That's us! Funny, we were 4-F because they thought we were too big to fit any of the uniforms and stuff. Ain't so. That's all it ever was. Just a stupid size thing. Ain't that some shit now."

"Well, you boys remember, a hero is a guy in a motion picture with his own theme music. Don't you go Hollywood. Keep your heads down and kick ass from a foxhole. Then come back and tell war stories to your daddy's grandchildren."

"You bet, Mr. R."

"I'm serious now," Robertson said. "If something happened to you, O'Malley would go out of business. You keep your heads down, squeeze the trigger, and call for artillery, and I'll see you in a year or so."

"A year? You figure only a year?"

"Just a guess, Ruben."

Deuce caught a glimpse of Mr. Slake watching his sons work. He looked sad and proud at the same time.

Christmas came with all of the sounds and memories and family traditions, the feel of winter, and the bayberry, pine, and candy cane smells of the season. Katy could feel the sweet tension that children feel when Christmas is in the air. It comes from anticipation. Something wonderful might be coming. She hadn't felt this way in so long -- she thought it was a feeling only of childhood, a feeling gone for her forever. But it was back, and it filled her days.

She had managed to keep her gifts secret. Even the .22 rifle she and Grandpa were giving Deuce was still undiscovered. She knew the gloves and socks she had knitted had all been found in their traditional hiding places, but the rifle would be a surprise. And she hoped no one had told Robertson about the sweater she was making for him. She had gotten the size by measuring his shirt. She had insisted on replacing a button and had gotten all the data she needed. The fact that she had snipped the button off the shirt in the first place had never been noticed, and now she had the Irish fisherman pattern almost completed. She made a scarf for Pete Miller, and Rachel would get a cookbook. And she had gotten Grandpa a thing called a yo-yo and a book by Steinbeck, *The Moon is Down*.

But it was not the gift surprises that had her in the spirit - - it was suitors. She had become extremely fond of Pete, and she knew he would soon be asking her to marry him. If he had asked last year, if he had asked in July or in early August, she would be Mrs. Miller now. But he hadn't asked, and an entirely new and deeper emotion had swept over her when she saw Robertson again. He had been lying on the kitchen floor in dirty pot water, but now all she remembered was a thrill that darted from her throat to her spine to her stomach to the top of her head. And now it was Christmastime, and she felt like a girl again.

Pete and Rachel stopped by on Christmas Eve. Rachel had made an apron for her and embroidered it with flowers. Pete had been working for more than a year on the manger scene he had carved. He had wrapped the delicately carved figures in a box of sawdust. The stable building itself had been built just the way a real one would be built, with joined posts and rafters and individual siding boards all made of cedar. He had even handmade the shingles for the roof. The Holy family and all the beasts, two kneeling shepherds, the wise men and their camels, and three angels were all carved in basswood. It was magnificent. As Katy found each piece in the sawdust, she marveled at the artistry, and her heart sank thinking about the crude scarf she was giving him. She had spent hours of work and romantic fantasy making a sweater for Robertson. She had made Pete's scarf in two days. When she saw the angels and the intricate way Pete had used the folds of their robes and the position of their wings to disguise the supporting connections so that they seemed to float over the stable, tears came to her eyes.

"Oh, Pete, it's the most wonderful thing I've ever seen. How did you do it?"

"I had someone to do it for," he said. "Don't look too closely at the shepherds. I did them first, so they aren't quite as good as some of the other ones. I like the pig family. And Mary. I tried to get her to look like you."

Rachel said, "I told him to have pigeons on the roof because there are always pigeons on the roof."

"I love the pigeons. They are so small, how did you do it? And the angels, my God, Pete how . . . ?"

"You just cut away everything that doesn't look like an angel."

Katy sat and looked at the manger scene without speaking. Deuce and Grandpa studied the figures and complimented Pete. It would be a family treasure.

Pete said how much he loved his scarf, and he wore it inside the house until he left. And Rachel was pleased with the cookbook which had a special section on French pastry.

As they parted, Katy kissed Pete and said, "You have given me so much. Thank you."

Pete looked into her eyes, "No more than you give me, Katy."

"Next year, I'll have to knit you an entire suit."

Pete smiled at her and said, "Next year . . . that sounds real good."

Rachel pulled on her father's sleeve and moved her head from side to side. Pete said to Katy, "Rachel has been all ga-ga since that sleigh ride. So now we have to . . ."

"Daddy!" Rachel interrupted.

"What? You baked some cookies. Is that a big secret?"

"You just wouldn't understand," and she got into the car and slammed the door.

"Sometimes . . . ," Pete said and made a gesture of confusion common to fathers of teenage daughters. Then he glanced toward the house where Robertson lived. "Are you and him . . . I mean, he's living on your place. Have you two . . . you know?"

"No, Pete, I don't know."

"Yes, you do. I mean, he's Deuce's father. I just wanted to know."

"Pete, don't spoil it."

"What?"

"Christmas. Don't spoil Christmas." Her voice had a coldness in it.

Pete raised his hands and shook his head. "I don't know. I'm sorry, I guess. I can't talk about cookies. I can't ask you a simple question. I just don't know."

Rachel blew the horn and Pete called out, "All right, Rachel Ann, I'm coming. Katy, I didn't mean to get off base, but I've got a lot involved here. I've got plans . . ." Rachel blew the horn again, and Pete waved at her to be quiet. "I love the scarf. Thanks again. Merry Christmas." And he called to Grandpa and Deuce, "Merry Christmas."

As he got in the car, he muttered to himself, "Shit," and then reluctantly headed down the lane so his daughter could deliver cookies to the man he wished had never come back.

"Now don't spend all night giving him those cookies. Just give 'em and come on back to the car. Okay?"

"Okay, Daddy."

Robertson opened the door and smiled at Rachel. He looked past her and waved at the car, even though he could not make out Pete sitting behind the wheel. "Come in, Rachel," he said and held the door open for her. She blushed and held out a shoebox she had decorated and filled with oatmeal cookies.

"I can't stay, Robert," she said.

"Well, some other time, then," he said.

He probably could have said anything and she would have written it in her diary inside a big heart, but the simple sincerity in his words churned in her. Her Christmas had just become magical.

"They're just cookies. Merry Christmas," and she went down the porch steps. At the bottom, she turned and said, "And a note."

"Merry Christmas, Rachel. Thank you." He watched as Rachel and her father drove off into the night. He did not know why he stayed out to watch, but Rachel spent the whole drive up the lane looking back at the man on the porch and thinking and of 'some other time,' and of the intimate entry she would make in her diary, Pete Miller did not realize how close to a woman his daughter had become.

Christmas dinner was a late afternoon affair, and Robertson had been invited. The awkwardness of Thanksgiving was easily bypassed because Christmas was a family day in the local community and very little visiting ever went on. About four o'clock, Robertson arrived and was welcomed into the living room. Katy came from the kitchen with some hot spiced wine in a pottery mug. Robertson put down the burlap sack he had brought and took the wine.

"Thank you, Merry Christmas."

"Merry Christmas, Bob," Katy returned.

Robertson took a sip and nodded his approval, put the mug on the coffee table, took off his coat and gave it to Deuce. When he took up his mug again, an ornament on the tree caught his eye. He sat on the couch beside the tree and touched a small brass angel hanging from a lower branch. He looked up at Katy and smiled. She smiled back. He had given her that ornament almost twenty years ago.

"Wow," he said softly.

"I didn't know if you'd remember."

Robertson reached in his bag and took out a small box. He handed it to her, "I didn't know you'd still have it." In the box was a small brass angel.

After dinner, other presents were exchanged, and the family listened to a Decca record album of *The Christmas Carol* narrated by Ronald Coleman that Robertson had given as a present. They enjoyed it so much that they took the Victrola with them when they went to see Momma Chambeau. Before departing, Grandpa piled the hot ashes and coals of the fire over four potatoes to roast while they were gone.

Momma Chambeau loved the recording, especially the visitations of the ghosts. "Dat could really be. I bet de Scrooge, him live from de bayou by damn. I know him, dat Scrooge."

Before they all left, Momma Chambeau held each one by the hands. She made little noises as she held them. She would hold for a long while, then let go and turn her palms up as if releasing something. Then she would beckon with her fingers for another to come and let her hold hands. Deuce got in line twice. The second time Momma touched his hands, she quickly let go and slapped the backs of his hands with a friendly reproach and a laugh. "I am one hard-to-fool ol' lady woman. You watch out or I turn you into a toad."

When she had finished, she said, "Big Robert, Deuce, Old Robert, all the same. You are all the same. This, I think, being last final Christmas together this journey, but we will meet at Christmas again. Maybe next journey, maybe journey after next, but we meet again, by damn. And next time, I get to see you," and she smiled a big broad smile. "Now go home. Your potatoes are done."

They took turns carrying the Victrola as they walked back home. Deuce asked, "Did we say anything about cooking potatoes?"

"No."

"I don't think so."

Deuce said, "She is really spooky sometimes."

When they got home, Grandpa took the potatoes out of the ashes and got the fire going again. As they ate, Robertson said, "It seems my bag isn't quite empty yet," and he reached into the burlap sack and pulled out a bottle and handed it to Grandpa.

"A little Black Label Nebula that Molly brought back for you."

"My God," Grandpa exclaimed softly as he recognized the contents. "There are a lot of memories that go with this stuff."

Katy asked, "Who is Molly?"

"It's a slang term. An old drinking buddy term. It's hard to explain really. And Deuce, here is something absolutely useless, but I thought you might like it," and he handed Deuce a tomahawk. "The handle is new. I made it from some of that old cherry wood in the orchard, but the blade is authentic. I found it on the prairie."

"Wow, thanks."

"With all those feathers and leather wrap, it doesn't throw that well, but it might look good on your wall. Oh, by the way, I found it sticking in this." He tossed Deuce a piece of a human skull with a hole in it.

"Wow," Deuce exclaimed again. "Where did you find it?"

"On a hill in Montana. And this," he said, tossing a tarnished crossed-saber insignia of the 7th Cavalry.

The touch of the bone and the old brass insignia filled Deuce with a melancholy he had not known before. He saw things, bits and pieces of battle and fear. He felt a swirl of energy and a deep sense of loss that comes with living inside of great moments that will never come again. He grew very quiet and then said, "It really did happen, didn't it." His father nodded.

Katy was not enthusiastic at all. "What kind of gift is that?" she whispered. "A skull? At Christmas?"

Robertson could not answer her. There was no way to explain his intention for the gift. But he felt that Deuce knew -- that Deuce had felt the ghosts, that the ghosts had touched him, and that he realized how precious and fleeting life was. But all he could say to Katy was, "Kids like that sort of thing. Boys anyway."

Katy's Christmas was more confused than she had expected. Pete had hinted that she was sleeping with Robertson -- hinted in a very possessive way that made her uneasy. And now this grotesque gift for Deuce. It just was not the pine and bayberry and candy cane Christmas she had planned.

Late in the evening after Deuce and Grandpa had gone to bed, she and Robertson sat together in front of the fire, leaning back against sofa pillows they had put on the floor. The old house made occasional popping noises. The fire would hiss and blow a miniature spark comet.

In this quiet peace, Robertson found the words to say, "Katy, there is a line from *Cyrano DeBergerac* that says, 'There comes one moment once, and God help those who pass that moment by.' I want Deuce to treasure life . . . his life . . . all life. Each moment. That is why I gave him a little piece of death."

"I never read *Cyrano*," Katy said softly.

"Ah," Robertson mused and reached into his bag one last time. The rather small volume of *Cyrano* was bound in dark green leather with fleur-de-lis embossed in gold on the front. Inside was an inscription that made Christmas whole for Katy as she read, 'Christmas, 1925, for Katy, all my love.' It was signed 'Bobby,' and below the faded ink of 1925 was a second inscription in the same hand. 'Christmas 1944, for Katherine, the love of all my journeys, all my times. Know that whatever life we are in, I will come in the hope that you will choose me. Love, Robert.'

"I didn't get to give you this last time. I had to leave . . ."

Katy held the book and delicately turned the pages. There was a thin woven strap that came from the binding and rested between the pages to mark where she read in the fire's glow, 'There comes one moment once . . .' She closed the book and placed it beside her on the floor.

"Thank you." Her words were soft and their tone made Robertson's heart jump. She unbuttoned her sweater and the blouse beneath and took his hand, kissed it, ran her tongue between his fingers with a teasing briefness, and slowly eased it inside the lace of her bra to close on her breast. "Don't leave again."

Robertson looked in the barn door. The commotion that had attracted his attention as he walked by outside turned out to be Deuce swearing as he pawed through the haymow.

"What's the problem, Deuce?" Robertson's words startled Deuce, and he whirled to face the sound.

Deuce threw his hands haphazardly in a gesture of frustration. "I can't find my knife."

"In the hay?" Robertson asked with a chuckle.

"Well, I missed the post, and the damn knife disappeared into the hay. And I can't find it." Deuce was on the verge of tears now. "It's the knife Grandpa gave me for my twelfth birthday. I can't lose it. I can't."

Robertson took a pitchfork and began distributing hay that Deuce had been searching through. Deuce joined him, and in silence the two men spread hay all over the barn floor. It wasn't long before one of the pitchforks made a clinking sound as it hit the knife.

Deuce clutched his prized knife and said, "I won't do that again."

"Do what?"

"Throw my knife in the barn."

"That's wrong," said Robertson.

"What do you mean?" Deuce asked.

"The problem is not throwing the knife in the barn. The problem is that you missed the target."

"So?"

"So, learn not to miss the target. What were you aiming at?"

"That post."

"Where on the post."

"Just anywhere. Just so it stuck in the post."

Robertson lowered his head and looked at Deuce out of the top of his eyes. If he had been wearing glasses, he would have looked over the rims. It was that look. Deuce had seen Grandpa use it often. Without speaking, Robertson walked to the post and took out his penknife. Into the post he scraped a square as tall as the post was wide. The color difference between the old exterior wood and the newly exposed wood became a target.

Robertson took the knife from Deuce and flipped it in his hand and from hand to hand several times. "Nice knife," he said as he turned suddenly toward the post and threw the knife. It embedded in the target with a solid 'thunk.' "Throws good too," and he went to the post and retrieved the knife. Then he went outside, picked up several rocks, and handed them to Deuce. "Throw these and hit the target. Now you aren't pitching for the Yankees, so just leisurely throw and hit the target."

Deuce did fairly well, and small dents from incoming rocks peppered around the target.

"Now," Robertson began, "imagine the knife turning in the air one and a half times and hitting the post in the center of the target. Imagine it. See it. Feel the weight of the knife in your hand and watch it travel with your mind. I'll be back in a little while." And he took the knife and went out of the door.

An hour later Robertson returned. Deuce was sitting on a block of salt. "How did it go?"

Deuce shrugged.

Robertson handed him the knife and said, "You have one try. Hit the target."

Deuce threw the knife and hit the post about six inches above the target.

"Better," Robertson said. "Now, you come in here to practice an hour a day. And for that hour, imagine each throw. You see and feel the knife with your mind. At the end of the hour, throw the knife." And he left.

A week later Robertson stopped in on Deuce's practice. He watched unnoticed from the shadows of the barn until Deuce threw the knife. It hit the target in the upper corner. Deuce pulled the knife from the post. He had a broad smile on his face. But when he began his practice the next day, he noticed a white circle in the center of his old target, and so he practiced with this reduced target. The knife hit the circle three times and was never far from the mark.

Robertson told him, "See the target, closer, magnified. See the grain of the wood through the paint. Make it as big as a pie plate and then make it bigger and put the knife right in the center."

The next Monday the white circle was smaller -- no bigger than a silver dollar. As Deuce began his practice, he noticed that white circles were on other posts, and one was on the vertical support of the mow ladder, and one was on the narrow molding that surrounded the small window by the door. He practiced, and the knife hit the circles, even the one on the window molding.

Robertson returned one afternoon and told Deuce to close his eyes and see the target. Then he placed the knife in Deuce's hand and told him to open his eyes one more time, then close them and hit the target. Deuce did as he was told, and to his astonishment he heard a solid 'thunk.' He opened his eyes, looked, and saw the knife sticking in the center of the target.

Robertson nodded approvingly, said "Good throw," and brought up his hand in front of his body. He was holding the knife. Deuce, confused, wide-eyed, looked from the knife in his father's hand back to the target. There was no longer a knife there. No knife, but there was a gouge in the center of the target -- an imprint. Something had been there. He did not understand, and as he wondered, his father took the knife by the handle, bent slightly at the waist, and flicked his hand back away from the target. His wrist and fingers and elbow combined to throw the knife around and over his right shoulder. It blurred past his right ear, turned one and a half times, and stuck into the same target gouge Deuce had just noticed. 'Thunk.'

Deuce's jaw dropped, and he looked at his father. Robertson brought up his hand in front of his body, and there again was the knife and again the empty gouge mark in the target. Robertson handed the knife to his son and said quietly, "Kind of makes you wonder what's real, doesn't it?" and walked out of the barn.

Deuce followed rapidly after his father. He had questions to ask, but all he could think to say was "Dad . . ."

Robertson stopped abruptly and turned toward his son, "Dad?"

Deuce looked embarrassed. "Yeah. I guess it just slipped out. But, well, yeah . . . Dad."

"I like that."

"So, what the hell were we doing in there?"

"Your mind is an amazing thing. Be careful from now on how you use it."

"You mean I, we, just . . ." and Deuce made a throwing gesture from his forehead toward a fence post.

"Yes," and Robertson duplicated the gesture.

"Holy shit," Deuce murmured, barely believing he had formed an image of a knife and thrown it from his mind into reality.

They walked for a while toward Robertson's house, and then Deuce asked nonchalantly, "So, what happened to your hand?"

Robertson held up his left hand and wiggled the fingers, "Nothing."

"Your right hand. With the stumpy fingers."

"Frostbite."

"And Grandpa, too? Same hand, same fingers?"

"What did your Grandpa say?"

"Frostbite."

"Umm," was Robertson's only response.

And so Deuce lowered his head and looked at his father out of the top of his eyes. "Frostbite?"

Robertson scratched his neck in an idle way and drew in a breath, "See that stump?" A tree had been hit by lightning years ago, and its jagged stump remained as part of the fence row that separated the old orchard from the path that went to the pasture gate and on into the meadow. The fence wire had grown into the tree before it had been hit, and vines grew all around it. Deuce looked at the old hulk and nodded.

Robertson bent the middle fingers of his right hand into his palm and clamped them there with his thumb. His index and small fingers were extended skyward. Deuce looked at his father's hand and then blinked. He thought he had seen a spark or a flash of light connect the fingers. He looked at his father. Robertson leveled his hand at the stump. A flash from his fingers. Wire to the left of the tree severed and curled back. A flash. Wire to the right flew back. Quick flashes. Vines flew. All the wire ruptured. Some of it glowed red, and drips of old steel fell and hissed. Flash. An old stubble of a branch disintegrated. Flash. 'Thunk.' A knife stuck in the trunk. Flash. 'Thunk.' An arrow hit the knife handle and split it! Flash. 'Thunk.' Another arrow split the first. And then one more flash, and the stump was blasted out of the ground and flew into the air. Another final flash, and the stump exploded in mid-air. Splinters and bark and termites splattered into the trunks and leaves of the old orchard. There a rabbit could stand to hide no longer and ran and jumped his jagged hop and dart way out of the fence row, leaped sharply to his left, and was gone.

Deuce stared in fright at his father's hand. He swallowed and said, "Forget I asked."

Robertson rubbed his fingers on his shirt. "Wears the fingertips down. Makes them itch, too." Then he flexed his fingers and rubbed his temples. "And it gives me a headache."

Reassigned
----- O. C. 1944, London, England -----

The firing range where the Military Police practiced was Sergeant Johnson's favorite place in all of England. It was a wonderfully picturesque spot, even on a raw March day. The Brits had a fanaticism about proper appearance, and so white paint accented the wooden structures at the range. Even the firing tables were made of wood, joined with dovetails and mortises, and the surfaces had a furniture finish. At several spots the local garden club had planted flowers. The target backstop had ivy growing on it. The whole thing was a denial of war, as if by pretending the range was a garden, nothing violent would really happen there.

In keeping with this, Sergeant Johnson had taken to the idea that his target practice was an artistic skill that somehow complemented the order of the range. The dark black circles of his targets were his canvasses, and the .45 caliber holes that he grouped so closely in their centers were his art. He was contentedly at work on an especially small group of shots when his lieutenant came up to speak with him.

"Sergeant . . ."

"Just a minute, sir,' and Johnson squeezed off his fifth shot. He reeled in the target and examined it. The center of the target was missing. A scalloped hole the size of a 25-cent piece was there where the ten ring had been. Johnson smiled.

"I think you just shoot one shot in the middle and then shoot the rest high and pretend that they went through the same hole."

"It is hard to tell, isn't it Lieutenant?"

"Sergeant, we have a problem."

"We, sir?"

"The Brits have found out about what you did to their combat instructors, and I have it directly from their CO that you are *persona non grata* as of now."

"Sir?" asked Johnson.

"Latin for 'not wanted'."

"Sir, I am from Georgia. I am used to being 'Latin for not wanted'."

"Well, I'm shipping you stateside anyway. Frankly, you are just too embarrassing to have around."

"Stateside, sir?"

"Yes, Sergeant. You are going to disappear before the Brits kill you and Mayhew kills me. You leave tonight for Box 1662 in Santa Fe, New Mexico. Report to 109 East Palace Street. See the lady there."

"What's there, sir?"

"Who knows. But it has Presidential priority, and it does not exist. And whatever is there -- that does not exist -- needs guarding. Have a good trip."

NEWS!
----- O. C. April 12, 1945 -----

The April Thursday had been lovely, and the evening air still held some of the day's charm.

Rachel Miller was in the kitchen listening to the Captain Midnight Show on the radio and opening a mason jar of green beans.

In town at the Avalon Theater, Deuce and Margaret were just beginning to share their popcorn as the early show newsreel was on the screen.

Slats Lyder was playing *Night and Day* on the piano at O'Malley's.

Grandpa was leaning on the pasture gate as Robertson and Katy came up from the meadow creek where they had been walking together.

Rachel was still holding the jar of beans when she entered the barn where her father was milking. "Daddy . . ."

At the Avalon Theater, the newsreel flickered to a halt. Just the blaring light of the projector lamp was on the screen. The mutterings of the audience and the ritual rhythmic clapping of their dissatisfaction died out sporadically as a man came onto the narrow stage and stood in front of the screen, shielding his eyes from the projector's light. "Ladies and gentlemen, . . ."

O'Malley put two fingers in his mouth and whistled loudly. Slats looked over his shoulder. "Hey, listen to this," and O'Malley turned up the volume on the radio.

In New Mexico, Sergeant George Washington Carver Johnson reported to 109 East Palace Street, handed in his orders, and was met with silent stares. "Ain't y'all ever seen a black man before?"

"I'm sorry, Sergeant. It's not that," the lady said, turning down the volume on the radio. "Welcome to the Manhattan Project."

In the dusty dimness of the Liberty Mill, Mr. Slake reached past his foreman and pressed the rounded red button on the main control panel. The roar of grain and grinding machinery wound down to silence. "Come into the office . . ."

Grandpa watched a ladybug crawl along the top board of the gate and thought 'what a strange thing to notice.' "Bob, Katy . . ."

All over the town, all over the farmland, all over the country, the word spread, things stopped, and people grew quiet.

President Roosevelt was dead.

In O'Malley's, someone breathed a twisted epitaph, "Oh shit, Truman's President."

"Who the hell is he?"

The lovers' shroud
----- O. C. 1945, Robertson farm -----

The next to the last day of April began as a drizzly Saturday. By noon, the light rain had stopped but the clouds remained, their gummy grayness holding 1200 feet above the ground. Grandpa, Deuce, and Robertson were using the inclement day to cut the weeds along the fence row of the lane – 'brambling' Grandpa called it. About 2:00 in the afternoon a truck came down the lane. The driver blew the horn, and a mechanical moan came out from under the hood.

"Herman's here," Grandpa said.

"Yep," agreed Deuce.

Robertson asked, "What the hell is that noise?"

Grandpa explained, "It's Herman's cattle-caller. He's really proud of it. This is his best one, don't you think?"

Deuce agreed, "Definitely."

Robertson leaned on his scythe and asked again, "So?"

"Oh, you see, Herman has been perfecting his cattle-caller for some time now. He is forever beating and strangling that truck horn, sticking things in the bell and such. Claims he's going to patent it when he gets done. He's here with the spring gasoline ration."

Herman pulled to a stop beside the three Robertsons and offered, "Hop on the running board, and I'll ride you home."

Deuce climbed onto the truck bed, and Grandpa and Robertson put their scythes in the back, climbed onto the running board, and held onto the frame of the open door window.

"How do you like her?" Herman asked.

Grandpa said, "Best ever. Closest thing to a sick crow I ever heard."

162

"Heard about you," Herman said, looking at Robertson. "Glad to meet you. I'm Herman."

"Bob Robertson," nodding a 'hello.'

"How do you like my horn?"

"It's great. I never heard anything like it." Herman's face lost its smile, and Robertson quickly added, "Except for a cow, of course. It sounds just like a cow."

Herman was triumphant, "There! You see," he said to Grandpa.

"How do you get it to make that noise?" Robertson asked.

"Secret," Herman said.

Grandpa chimed in, "Secret, hell. He's got a crow under the hood with a stick up its ass, that's all. That ain't no great secret."

"Go to hell," Herman said good-naturedly. "You wouldn't know a proper sound if Mozart came up and bit you in the ass."

Grandpa countered, "That would be for the famous *Concerto for Crow and Windbag in C Sharp.*"

"Fat lot you know. It's in D," and Herman blew the horn the rest of the way down the lane.

Between the garage and the house was a slab of concrete where 55-gallon barrels of gasoline were kept to supply the farm equipment with fuel. Herman backed up to the slab and parked. He got out, climbed into the truck bed, and he and Deuce unchained the barrels and moved them onto the hydraulic lift gate at the end of the truck bed. While they worked, Herman gave glowing forecasts for his cattle-caller and the fortune it was going to make him. Grandpa would interject 'bullshit' whenever he thought it appropriate.

Herman hopped off the truck and operated the tailgate controls. As the barrels slowly descended he continued his forecast. "Patent attorney over to Hillsdale says it's a sure thing,"

"Bullshit."

"Sears and Roebuck are gonna be beatin' down my door."

"Bullshit."

And so on.

Herman and the Robertsons re-stocked the fuel slab and returned the empties to the truck and chained them in place.

"Yep, you old fart, when Sears buys my caller, I'll just see to it that you get to pay double price for yours."

"Pay? You mean you think people are going to pay for that god-awful noise maker? You ain't got the sense God gave a goose. So shut up about your damn horn and tell us the news."

Between the telephone operator, the mailman, and Herman, all local events were cataloged. Herman began, "Well, Roosevelt died."

"No shit."

Herman chuckled. "Did you hear Truman's speech the other night. Ol' Harry's different, ain't he? Okay, now here it is. You know about the bank robberies?"

"No."

"Well, it's gettin' to be a real Bonnie and Clyde affair," Herman said. "Only these are some nasty-ass guys. They killed I don't know how many folks by now. Raped that twelve-year-old girl over to Middletown. Now, I'll admit she's a good bit older lookin' than your average twelve-year-old, if you know what I mean. But even so, these are some real nasty-asses. Word is they are deserters from the army, and they got machine guns and everything. Then I heard they were escaped convicts. And they're fast, too. They've gotten to where they can be several places at the same time. You know how that goes. Any crime gets done, why it's just got to be those deserter-convict guys, which is bullshit, of course. But there are some for-sure, bad, nasty-asses roaming around over three states, so watch yourselves. The sheriff says he got a bulletin that there were four for sure and maybe six of 'em. And that's from the sheriff himself.

And Mrs. Wicks had another girl. The Dunn boy died of polio. He was a nice kid, too. That's about it. Here's your receipt. And sign this for me so the war department fellows know I ain't sellin' on the black market. And sign this for the local allocation board. That's three copies, so press hard. More damn paper. Oh well, what are you gonna do?" Herman got in his truck and leaned out the window. "So what do you really think?" he asked Grandpa.

"You're real close. It's got a bit too much high-frequency vibration. But it's real close."

"Damn straight. See you next time. Say 'hi' to Katy for me. Want me to pass anything along about the courtship or just let folks stew?"

Robertson smiled at Herman, "Tell them she has decided to marry an inventor."

Herman laughed. "Yes sir! You and Pete watch out. I'm already good lookin', and I'm gonna be stinkin' rich," and he laughed again as he licked his fingers, took off his greasy cap, and slicked his hair. "Smell good too."

Grandpa said, "You smell like gasoline."

"I rest my case." And Herman drove off singing, "Oh, she jumped into bed and she covered up her head and she said I couldn't find her . . ."

Robertson said, "Didn't I see a horn like that advertised in the *Journal*?"

"Yes, you probably did," Grandpa said.

"Does Herman know you can already buy such a thing?"

"Oh, he knows," Grandpa said with a shrug. "Clearing up a bit. Gonna be a fine evening."

And a fine evening it became. In its humid sweetness, Katy walked with Pete Miller.

"Katy, I like Bob. I can understand how you could fall for him. But where has he been? Gone, that's where. I've been here. I'm going to be here for you forever. You've already been a mother for Rachel. I don't know what I would have done if you, well, you know. Thank you. She's still young. She needs you. I need you. And all that with Bob . . . that was years ago. Deuce is a fine boy, so I guess it was for the best, and I can forgive you for it. I can overlook it. It doesn't matter, and I really mean that. It's past. This is now. And I . . . I want to marry you. I want you to be Mrs. Miller. Share my life. Please, Katy, will you marry me?"

"Do you love me, Pete?"

"Well, that goes without saying, doesn't it?"

"Does it?"

"Come on, Katy. I'm a farmer. I'm not some . . . I don't know, some poetic movie guy. This is hard for me."

Katy reached out and touched Pete's cheek tenderly. "I know it is, Pete. I love you for it."

"Then you will?"

"I'll let you know."

"Let me know? Tell me now. I want to hear it now. Good God, Katy, it's been two and a half years. And we've had some close times. And I said I didn't mind about . . . about you and him and all, and . . . what can I say?"

Katy kissed him slowly and waited for the magic. It was a warm kiss, a nice kiss. But 'nice' is the shroud that lovers' hopes are buried in. It makes a hollow sound in the heart like the whistle of a train disappearing into the distance. Katy put her head on Pete's shoulder so that she would not have to look into his eyes. He held her and shifted his arms in tentative caresses. Pete imagined her sitting in a lawn chair next to him, sipping coffee and talking about the day. He thought how beautiful she was and how much he wanted her for his wife. Katy was thinking about Robertson, about his words, about the magic.

"Give me some time, Pete."

"How much time?"

"Some. I'll let you know."

"Well, I'm not gonna wait forever."

"I know."

Robertson and Deuce were sitting on the steps of the old Brady farmhouse where Robertson spent his nights. They could see Katy and Pete walking together in the lane.

"Are you and Mom going to get back together for good?"

"That's my plan," Robertson said.

Deuce nodded. Two women discussing such a topic would have filled hours with questions and answers, details and thoughts.

"How are you and M'Gee doing?"

"Margaret, Dad."

"Right."

"We're doing good. Real good actually."

Robertson nodded.

Then after a silent while, Deuce said, "I've been thinking about that stump you blew all apart and the knife throwing. It's all the same isn't it? It's all been about how to use my mind."

Robertson was silent.

"You and Grandpa, you've been training me, haven't you? To be able to do all that stuff you and he did in the stories. But I don't want to do those things. I like it here . . . the farm, everything . . . Margaret. I don't want to leave and go off into some great blood-and-guts adventure like you did."

"I didn't want to go, either."

"Then why did you?"

"It was the thing to do at the time."

"What do you mean?"

"I hope you never find out. Maybe you won't get called up. God knows I hope you don't."

"I'm not talking about the draft, Dad."

"Neither am I."

"What then?"

"It's a nice evening isn't it? The balance is good tonight." The two sat silent once more, then Robertson began again, "Your mother and I were so much in love back then that nothing could possibly upset our world. Then there was this . . . situation. And there seemed at the time to be two choices. One really bad one, and one that was worse. And I chose. And it turned out to be a lot of years filled with things that can't be shared or explained, and I wish I had never had to live them like I did. I hated it . . . goddamn I hated it. But I was good at it. Anyway, it worked out. Many a night I dreamed about getting back, though. Getting away from where everything was right on the edge all the time. I am never going back. I promised myself that. I am done. Retired with a capital 'R.' I have always thought it would be nice to own a tavern, a nice but informal place with good food. The sort of place people would go and meet a friend or two. I don't have the bad dreams so much anymore or the headaches. I've got evenings like this. You,

Pop, Katy. Family. Family and friends, Deuce. I even like Pete Miller."

Robertson was looking at the couple in the lane. He was quiet now as he saw their embrace. "Of course, if he doesn't start leaving your mother alone, I'll have to come up with something painful and medieval." He saw the couple kiss. "Thumbscrews maybe. So, to answer what you were asking . . . yeah, you've been in training. For your own protection really, and we hope you will never need it. But . . ."

"Do you miss it, the 'being on the edge' as you call it?"

"Do I miss it? After all that wonderful great speech about retiring and running a tavern that I just gave you, you ask if I miss it?"

Deuce looked at his father in the over-the-glasses way of the Robertsons. "Do you?"

Very softly, Robertson said, "Sometimes."

The tentative shoots of early May flourished in profusion by the end of the month. And now, in mid-June, all of the meadow's variety was in bloom. The work of the day was completed to a point where Robertson could excuse himself from the remaining chores. Katy had prepared a simple dinner for Deuce and Grandpa. And now, she and Robertson walked together through the meadow toward the creek.

Robertson had requested the date a week earlier with a written note. The note was now in a small cedar-lined chest in Katy's bedroom. It was there with others, wrapped in yellow ribbon and resting on top of a leather-bound edition of *Cyrano de Bergerac*. The thought of a stroll and dinner had filled her mind for days. Which dress? How to do her hair? And, oh God, what to talk about? She knew the talk would come easily. It had always come easily for them. She did her hair up, but with only a few pins. She chose the white cotton dress with the scoop neck. The sleeves were short and loose, the waist was held by a sash and bow, and it had few buttons. She considered it flattering to her figure, and it was easy to take off. She knew this because she had practiced. If the sash bow was not tied too tightly, a gentle tug freed the waist. Three buttons, slowly released, allowed the scoop neck to flare and ease off of her shoulders and flow over the curves of her body to land at her feet.

As the couple passed the barn, Grandpa noticed what Robertson had already noticed. What the backlight of the setting sun revealed was that Katy was wearing a cotton dress -- and nothing else.

Beets and blood
----- O. C. June, 1945 -----

The next day Katy had a special glow. She had returned to the main farmhouse in time to fix breakfast, still wearing the white cotton dress from the night before. By afternoon she was humming to herself while she worked, scrubbing and preparing beets for canning.

Deuce came into the kitchen and asked, "So, Mom, how's it going?"

"Wonderful," was the dreamy reply.

"I meant the beets," Deuce said with a twinkle in his eye.

Katy cocked her head and returned the banter, "So did I."

"It's been sort of steamy around here. Must be the new pressure cooker."

"The new pressure cooker is really something, but to answer your question, Mister McSnide, I am in love with your father," and she spun around like a schoolgirl. "And you and Margaret, are you two cooking beets, too?"

"Mom . . ."

"Ah-ha. Love's amazing, isn't it?"

"I suppose."

"Well, you two certainly have seen a lot of each other lately. She is a wonderful girl. Hand me a potholder."

"Sure. Wow, you've done all these this afternoon?" Deuce exclaimed as he saw rows of mason jars. They formed a rather impressive parade on the countertop -- a deep maroon regiment cooling by the window.

Deuce was in the middle of a question to his mother when it began. "Mom, I was wondering . . ." One of the jars of beets exploded, sending fragments of glass and the contents of the jar into the air. Deuce's mother dropped the pressure cooker. Its lid flew off in spite of the clamp handles, and hot beets erupted from the giant pot and splattered on the wall and stove. Another jar on the counter exploded. Another. Glass and beets flew about the kitchen. A fourth jar exploded. Deuce's mother shouted for him to go into the next room. She followed immediately, both of them ducking, then crawling as quickly as they could. Deuce shut the door. The two sat and listened. The jars continued to explode.

"Sounds like a war in there," Deuce joked. Katy sat with her back up against the closed door and said nothing.

The noises from the kitchen stopped, and Deuce reached for the door handle.

"Wait!" insisted his mother. "Just a little longer. To make sure."

After a time, Deuce opened the door. Beets, beet juice and glass were everywhere. The walls. The floor. Even the ceiling and the light fixture that hung from it. A few jars remained on the counter, miraculously untouched by the mayhem.

"You know what Grandpa would say, don't you?" Deuce said with a chuckle, and then as if on cue, both he and his mother echoed one of Grandpa's time-worn expressions: "Looks like a bear's been in here." And the two began to laugh.

"It looks like the beets lost. They put up a hell of a fight, though," Deuce joked. It really did look like a battle had been fought in the kitchen.

"Why don't we just leave it and see if anyone notices. 'What did you do today?' 'Oh, canned a few beets, redecorated the kitchen.' 'Looks nice. Kinda sticky, though'." And Deuce and his mother began to laugh all over again as they imagined the reaction of Deuce's father.

A jar exploded. Its sealed top with the jagged glass remains of the jar flew just past Deuce's head and hit the wall behind him.

"Here we go again!" he shouted, and once more the two retreated to the living room and closed the door.

"I'm not sure the beets lost," his mother said, and both lay on the rug of the living room and laughed.

In the kitchen another jar exploded, and then silence returned. The silence remained. It seemed deeper after the tension of the random explosions.

After a time, Katy said, "You know, I always liked the country. It really is peaceful. Even when it's not." She smiled and looked at Deuce and reached over to him to stroke his hair. Her hand was just about to brush back his hair from his forehead when a violent explosion shook the house. This was not beet jars.

The incoming anti-personnel sphere had homed in on the kitchen's activity and exploded, sending shards in an outward spherical pattern. The entire kitchen was covered with steel needles like the inside of a pincushion. There was a needle-shard embedded in every inch. Everything was bristling. If Deuce and his mother had been there, they would have been shredded.

Deuce opened the door to the kitchen, "Jesus Christ, Mom, look at this!"

"My God! And don't say Jesus Christ like that all the time, Deuce." She had barely finished speaking when a metal canister flew through the room and slapped onto the far wall. It fell into the sink, and gas began hissing out, filling the kitchen with fumes. Katy grabbed her son and whirled, and the two crashed once again into the living room and shut the door.

Muffled shouts could be heard now. The splintering wood noise of the outside door being kicked in was followed abruptly by what sounded like automatic weapons fire. Deafening staccato blasting and breaking noises. Deuce and his mother flattened themselves on the floor, afraid to move, not knowing what was happening.

"What's going on?" Deuce asked.

"I don't know," his mother shouted over the noise of the attack.

The wall between the kitchen and the living room turned to shreds just above Deuce and his mother. Closer shouting. The door flew open. Light came in briefly from the smoke-filled kitchen, and then the light vanished, blotted out by the figure in the doorway. Full body armor. Contained-air helmet. A machine rifle on a floating hip mount. The muzzle began to spit fire, and a roar filled the room as the mercenary fired waist-high. Below the floor a grenade went off. As the figure leveled the machine rifle at Deuce and his mother, the floor beneath them vanished, and they fell into the basement as the pulse shells blew apart the piano and the sofa. The sounds of the piano strings breaking made a brief eerie sound, like the cry of a loon.

Deuce and his mother found themselves in a smoke-filled basement without any idea of what was happening or why. They stood in the rubble, confused, when an armored figure began descending at half-gravity through the jagged hole above them, firing as he came down into the semi-darkness. Canned goods on their storage shelves blew apart in the barrage. Deuce grabbed a pickaxe and swung it at the figure's back. The ax glanced off the body armor, and the shock stung Deuce's hands. The figure swung his hip-mount toward Deuce and began to fire. Deuce dove for the floor, and the burst missed. His mother swung an ax at the figure's firing hand. The ax blow hit his armor glove, spoiled his aim, and then glanced upward and wedged in the gasket where his C.A. helmet joined the upper body armor. Blood from his neck sprayed out in a red mist as the helmet's air supply escaped through the gash.

A second figure descended. A third. The first one now slumped onto the floor. The second and third landed back-to-back and began firing their hip mounts. Deuce threw a jar of canned tomatoes at the helmet of the nearest one. The jar shattered and the tomatoes obscured his vision plate. He stopped firing to wipe it clean. Deuce threw a second jar. The jar broke on the mercenary's armor glove, and the tomatoes splattered onto the vision plate further obscuring the screen with their red lumpy goo. The two mercenaries abandoned their back-to-back formation and turned to direct their fire at Deuce. Deuce's mother grabbed a paint can from the corner and frantically tried to open the lid.

The firing began again. The basement turned into splinters and flying pieces. The burst of one mercenary cut through a center post which dangled briefly and then vanished as the ceiling beam it supported crashed down, pinning the trooper helplessly under it. The remaining mercenary whirled his hip mount toward Deuce's mother, firing as he turned. She was still struggling with the paint can. She had a chisel in her hand and was trying to get the paint lid off so she could throw the paint just as Deuce had thrown the tomatoes. The line of exploding basement rapidly approached her as the mercenary blasted. The machine rifle barrel slammed into the other center post and stopped. Its fire ate a hole through the stone wall just three feet from Katy's head. The lid came free, and she hurled the paint at the figure's helmet. Nothing came out of the can. The paint was too old and thick.

"Shit!" she screamed and rammed the paint can onto the muzzle of the machine rifle. The old paint was like glue, and the can stuck on the barrel. The merc's attention focused on the ridiculous can stuck to the end of his devastating weapon, and in that instant, Deuce's mother drove the chisel through his helmet gasket. Milky fluid seeped from the hole, and he slumped to his knees. Katy ripped the machine rifle from his hip mount just as another pair of mercenaries came through the ceiling. She fired and shouted, "Spit blood and die you snake fuckers." The first round coming out of the barrel blew the half-dried goo of white paint into mist. Then came death. Blood and pieces of body armor slapped onto the far wall.

Deuce ran for the door to the potato cellar. He reached the door, but a ceiling beam angled across it. His mother backed toward him, the rifle pointed at the hole in the ceiling. There was a lull in the attack. "If we can get this beam out of the way, maybe we can get out up the stairs from the potato cellar," Deuce shouted as he heaved against the weight of the beam. The beam was not moving as Deuce struggled.

"Deuce," his mother said frantically, "your grandfather has been teaching you to focus your energies for years. Now would be a very good time to do some of that."

It hadn't occurred to Deuce before, but his mother's urging was all it took. He stood erect. Took a deep breath. Let it out. Another. In. Out. He wrapped his arms around the beam, and slowly, seemingly effortlessly, he lifted it out of the way as if it had been only a two-by-four. He smiled at his mother and tossed the beam to the side. As he did so, a jagged splinter of wood from the beam stuck in his right index finger. He instinctively shook his hand, and as he did so, his middle two fingers bent inward and were momentarily clamped down by his thumb. The frustration of the battle-without-reason, and now the sudden pain, shot into his mind. His index finger and small finger felt unusually warm. His mother was just realizing how easily he had tossed the huge beam, when Deuce's fingertips flashed, and as he shook his hand upward, arrows formed and flew from his hand and imbedded in a vertical line in the door just to the right of his mother. The two exchanged shocked glances.

"What was that?" Deuce gasped.

"You did it and you don't know?"

"Not really. It just sort of happened."

A silver sphere descended into the basement and hovered. Deuce's mother fired at it, and the shots glanced off the bottom of the sphere and propelled it back up through the hole in the ceiling. It had just gone out of sight when it exploded. A cone of anti-personnel shards fired downward into the basement and stuck in the debris on the floor. The rest sprayed into the room above. Two mercenaries fell through the hole, their armor riddled and seeping blood from the shards that had fired from the grenade above the floor.

"Let's get out of here, Deuce."

"After you, Miss Oakley," Deuce said and threw open the door.

Deuce and his mother stood in disbelief as they starred at what should have been the hallway to the potato cellar. It was filled with rock and dirt and the remainder of what had been the hallway roof beams.

"It's been nice knowing you, Mom. We were pretty tough rats there for a while."

"And what happens to the tough rat when he thinks he can whip any cat that comes along?"

"He meets up with a bear."

"Deuce . . ."

The firing began again and two more mercenaries eased into the basement, their machine rifles blasting up glass, wood, stone, and blowing apart the bodies of their comrades that remained in the line of fire.

"Who are these guys?" Deuce screamed.

Deuce's mother aimed from her hip at the two attackers. She pulled the trigger. Two rounds were all that remained. The machine rifle spit twice and quit. She threw it at the two attackers.

"Deuce!" she screamed and looked hard into his young eyes. There was no fear in them, only determination and anger.

"What!" he shouted.

"Deuce, be the bear!"

The mercenaries spotted the two humans standing in the doorway that now led nowhere. They leveled their machine rifles and pulled the triggers.

Robertson stepped from the post office with a package in his hand. It was neatly wrapped but had no return address. He looked toward the mill, thought of the Slakes, and smiled. He realized he had been smiling at things all morning. The sky was a special blue, greens were greener, all colors brighter, all of life was warmer. Down the wooden steps and toward the truck, he hummed a tune. Even the reluctance of the truck to start seemed to fit the lilt of the melody. He drove to the east edge of town and turned onto a dusty patch of ground dotted with farm equipment.

Robertson parked the truck and went inside Gladstone's. The faded green and gold sign painted above the door always seemed odd to him. 'Gladstone Farm Implement Company.' The price of a new tractor, if you could get a new tractor, seemed to make 'implement' an understatement of giant proportions.

"May as well say 'farm utensils'," Robertson thought to himself as he passed the shelves of tools and racks of handles for scythes or hoes or whatever needed a handle. He liked the curves of the scythe handles, the snake-like grace that made a thing so simple into just the right shape for efficiency.

In the rear of the store, Margaret was drinking a carton of chocolate milk. "Hello, Mr. Robertson," she said with a friendly smile. She wore a white shirt, overalls, and a baseball cap with an International Harvester emblem on the front and a black feather on the side, its quill threaded through the eyelet vents in the cap.

"Nice feather, M'Gee."

"Thank you. Found it this morning out back. Crow feather, I think."

"Looks like. I got a note that my mower sections came in."

"Yes, sir, they did. Silly war. We have to special order mower sections during haying season. Come fall, that's probably all we'll be able to get. 'Course, by then, anything having to do with a corn picker will be on the restricted list." And she disappeared down a row of parts shelves to get the mower sections.

Robertson leaned on the countertop and idly looked at the huge parts books that bulged in their special bindings.

Margaret emerged from the parts darkness but stopped just short of the counter, looking toward the front door. "Well, if that isn't something," she said quietly. "Look at that silly crow now, will you."

Robertson turned slowly and looked. A crow was inside the store and sat perched on the top of a scythe handle. Its black feathers shone with the light coming in the door and windows. It did not move but seemed to stare at the two humans -- a piercing, unsettling stare.

As Robertson looked, three more crows outside the store lighted on the old pickup truck. "Oh, shit," he said softly and headed toward the door.

"What did you say?" Margaret came around the counter and followed him out the door. "You forgot the mower . . ." She never finished the sentence. Crows were perched on the buildings and equipment that surrounded Gladstone's. Black punctuation marks everywhere. And not a sound. The crows were all quiet. The insect noises that should have been in the subconscious background were not there, and their absence intensified the quiet. Margaret closed the screen door slowly, as if she might have been in church, and whispered, "What is it?"

"Look," Robertson said.

In the distance, toward the Robertson farm, smoke rose like some indistinct scrimshaw in the sky. The siren of the volunteer fire truck could be heard, haunting in its faint and distant sound.

"You coming?" Robertson said as he opened the truck door and got behind the wheel. Margaret hurriedly joined him in the cab without thinking, without pausing. She was drawn into the situation and now she hung onto the door frame as Robertson gunned the pickup in reverse, spun the wheel, shifted gears, and tore off toward his farm and family. The dust churned up in the Gladstone parking area hung in the air. By one's and two's the crows solemnly left and flew toward the horizon and the smoke.

Dust lines converged toward the Robertson farm as the various volunteer firefighters left their normal activities and sped to the fire. Robertson had the accelerator on the floorboard, and the pickup rattled and lurched down the road through town. A horn blared behind him, and a red convertible roared past the old pickup. The driver waved his right arm from side to side as he passed, and the red car disappeared over the slight rise ahead.

"Who was that?" asked Robertson.

"That was Branson Thomas. He's a fireman," Margaret said.

"Damn, he's got a hot car."

"Yeah. I tuned it for him."

"You what?"

"I tuned it for him. I tune the fire truck, too. I'm really good with motors and mechanical stuff."

"M'Gee, you amaze me."

Margaret smiled and continued to hang on to the door of the truck. After a few more bumps, the road smoothed out and she asked, "What do you suppose all those crows were doing all over the place?" Robertson was intent on the smoke on the horizon and didn't answer.

"The crows. You ever see anything like that?" Margaret repeated.

Robertson glanced at her. "There are those in other cultures who believe that when any really significant confrontation is about to take place, the souls of dead warriors gather to warn the living."

"Are you talking about the crows?"

"Yeah."

"You mean the crows were dead people?"

"Probably not."

"No, I guess not! They're just crows . . . right?"

"Probably. They also hang around with wolves, play tag, keep-away with sticks. They scout for the wolf pack and get to share a kill."

"Do you believe that the crows were souls come to warn somebody?"

"No," he said.

"Good," was her unsure response.

"They probably just came to watch the fight."

"What are you talking about?"

"If you don't think it's true, why get so excited?"

"I am not excited!" Margaret blurted. Robertson smiled and looked at her briefly out of the corner of his eye. The lines around his smile and his eyes projected warmth that indicated knowledge beyond the words spoken.

"I am not excited about a bunch of crows," Margaret said quietly as the truck bumped along.

"Good."

"It was just kind of spooky, that's all."

"Yes, it is."

"And you're being awfully glib."

"Glib?"

"Glib, yes, glib. Your family could be trapped in a fire. Deuce could be . . . and your wife or whatever she is, Katy anyway . . . they could be in danger, and you're joking about birds."

Flashes of the past flickered in Robertson's mind. He did not like what fire did to the flesh of comrades, turning friends into charred hulks, smoking and oozing on the battlefield -- mouths burned shut, no eyes to look into, no face at all. His thoughts automatically reeled away from the image of Katy and Deuce looking like that. Crows. He forced the blackened images to be the feathers of a crow and watched it fly off into a clear sky. A great deal of past horror had been sent into his mind's sky over the years or had been boxed and placed on the baggage car of a train that would carry it into the prairie horizon.

"Sorry," he said returning to the conversation. "Damn, this truck is slow."

"Needs new plugs."

Robertson looked at Margaret, then back to the road. "Probably needs new plugs," he said with a controlled satirical emphasis.

"Men," she said feebly. Her comment made Robertson smile in spite of his concern for his home and family.

"I could tune it for you."

Robertson's mind had returned to the unknown dangers possibly awaiting him at the farm, and he did not answer.

"It's going to be all right," Margaret said, trying to believe it, hoping he might believe it, but he did not answer, and the truck roared on as the two sat in silence.

Robertson drove along the ridge on Herbert Road and looked toward the farm buildings on his right. The smoke was noticeably less.

"The boys got it out," Margaret said with relief.

Robertson rounded the turn into the lane to the house and slowed the truck. He had expected activity, volunteers unrolling hoses, spraying water, running lines to the pond that was only a few hundred yards from the house. But there was no activity. There were only spectators. Cars parked in random patterns and men standing looking toward the dying smoke. The fire truck was backing slowly away from the fire as Robertson pulled to a stop and got out of the pickup.

He went over to Marv Peters, school principal and volunteer fire chief. Marv was just stepping down from the running board of the fire truck. He walked around to the front of the truck and shook his head. The paint was blistered, the chrome bumper was various shades of purple like a black eye, and the license plate had melted and hung in a pathetic distortion from the steel bolts that held its remains to the truck's bumper.

"Son of a bitch," Marv breathed softly. He winced as he took off his fire helmet and became aware of the burning sensation on his face, especially his nose. "Bob, we did everything we could . . . it just . . . ," and Marv's voice trailed off. "Figure it was the 55-gallon gasoline drums somehow got set off. I guess. Anyway, we couldn't even get close enough to hose it down. Best we could do was keep it from getting the barn. That west wall was burned some, even so. Couldn't save the hog house. Pigs got out, though. They're around somewhere. The house behind the barn got to burning pretty good. We put it out, but it's a mess inside. Son of a bitch. That was some fire."

The rest of the firefighters stood in silence and watched the smoke disappear on a light breeze that began to blow from the southwest. They began taking off their gear and putting it into the trunks of their cars. A few near to Robertson muttered condolences and regrets that they could not have done more.

"Hell of a fire, Bob." "Sorry, Bob." "If there's anything we can do, Bob."

Marv offered, "You need anything, you just call. You got a place to stay tonight?"

"Yeah. Thanks. Sorry about the truck, Marv."

"Oh, it'll paint. It will give Jimmy something to do. He's really good with bodywork. There was no sign of your family, Bob. They, ah, . . . ," Marv sighed, "I'll talk to the coroner. He'll come back and poke around, I guess. Hey, Katy and Deuce might just be visiting somewhere, you know. Maybe. Oh, we found some of these sticking in what's left of your trees. Tore my coat on one of them." Marv held a sooty metal spike for Robertson to examine. "Any idea what it is?"

Robertson took the spike and slowly, knowingly, shined away the soot with his thumb. He remained silent.

Marv suggested, "Probably what's left of something that blew up in the fire. Piece of water heater, maybe. I don't know. Hell of a mess. Damn, I'm sorry, Bob."

"Thanks, Marv."

Margaret's heart sank, and she walked alone toward the barn. Marv Peters had said Deuce might be visiting. His words had said that -- not his eyes. Ben Wilkes approached her. "Maggie, we hardly got the hoses out, I mean...Damn. What can I say? I can think of a lot of four-letter words, but they have no comfort. Well...if you need anything, if I can do anything..." His words faded softly into the charred air.

"Thanks, Ben."

One by one the cars departed. Margaret watched Ben get on his motorcycle and roar up the lane, so devil-may-care, so alive. The fire truck was the last to leave. Marv gave two farewell rings on the bell and drove up the lane, turned left on Herbert Road, and disappeared over the rise.

Margaret walked slowly along the barn wall, tapping at paint blisters with a stick and letting tears flow in torrents down her cheeks. She and Deuce had had such a beautiful, strong love and such an open future -- so much promise, so much hope. She let the stick fall from her hand and started to scream, but she held the agony noiselessly inside where it built and roared and then burst out with her renewed tears. She beat the side of the barn slowly with her fist. Over and over, through her clenched teeth, over and over to the beat of her fist on the barn wall, over and over, "Shit. Shit. Shit." The awful sudden unfairness of the loss was inexpressible. "Shit." Incomprehensible. "Shit."

After a time the tension eased, and she turned to lean her back against the wall. Robertson appeared in front of her. His presence startled her. Her eyes flashed open, and then she pushed forward into his arms and sobbed again.

He was saying something to her. She did not hear it. He was speaking in a warm tone, but the words were not coming through. His hand held her head close to his chest. Finally, he sensed she was listening, and he put both hands on her shoulders and moved her away from him. He looked directly into her eyes. "They are not dead, M'Gee. And I don't mean they are with God in Heaven or any of that stuff. I mean they are not dead."

Margaret was surprised by his tone of voice. He sounded excited, almost jubilant. She sniffed and wiped her nose on the back of her hand. Robertson gave her his handkerchief. She blew her nose. The sound made her laugh. It seemed so basic. So un-solemn. It was a life-goes-on sound. She smiled faintly.

"Walk with me, M'Gee."

"What do you mean they're not dead? Where are they? They're just visiting, you think?" But even she could sense the false hope tone in her voice.

"It's 'when are they'?"

"What are you talking about?"

The two walked toward the foundation of the farmhouse. Robertson paused and looked into the charred hole that had been the farmhouse basement. Residual heat made the area uncomfortably warm even now.

"Look M'Gee, what do you see?"

"I don't see anything."

"Exactly. You don't see anything. Just a big black hole. Where are the partially burned books? The unburned couch cushions? Where is the cast iron tub? The water pipes? Where is the fireplace?! Where are the firebricks?! This was no 55-gallon gasoline fire. They magged the place."

"They who?"

"I don't know."

"What did you say happened?"

"They magged the house. Used magnesium grenades . . . well, *a* magnesium grenade. One would have been more than enough. And they wouldn't have done that if they had been successful. If they had done their job, then they would have left the bodies. It would have been a regular fire, and Marv and the others would have put it out, and there would be those partially burned books and cushions and the bathtub. But they must have wound up with bodies they couldn't explain and probably body armor and weapons. So to cover all that up, they magged the whole lot. Mags can cover up a lot of tracks."

"What are you talking about?! Who are you talking about?"

"I don't know. I already said that. But they weren't the National Guard. Oh, they came here all cocky and ready for sport, I bet, and then all of a sudden found themselves hunting bear with a stick, and they got their asses kicked, and they didn't leave any bodies to be found because the only ones they had to leave were their own, and that would have raised some really big questions."

"Will you do me a favor and talk sense. I don't understand any of this."

Robertson ran his fingers through his hair as he searched for a way to explain. "Well," he began, "my family has developed some, I guess you'd say, some unusual capabilities over the years. Kind of a father-to-son, grandfather-to-grandson thing."

Margaret looked at him. She suspected that the shock of the fire and the loss of Katy and his son were more than he was willing to admit. "Is this going to be like the crows again?"

Robertson chuckled. "Yes, I suppose it is."

"Oh, brother." Margaret turned and stared into the ashes.

Robertson looked at her for a long time, saying nothing. Deciding. Then he said, "Hold my hand because this can get a little confusing. You're going to have trouble because there isn't going to be any up or down . . . but don't worry. Just keep holding on."

"What?!" But it had already started to happen. Colors like the shimmer of oil floating on water began to surround them and close off the world. Familiarity faded and she had a feeling of sound without really hearing anything. The colors flowed through her body, and she became dizzy. There was no longer any reference for reality. No up. No down. She felt the pressure of Robertson's hand, but nothing else was familiar. Only swirling colors. Then in the area above her head, a vision formed and moved from right to left and toward her feet. It continued to move and at one point passed through her as the colors had done. She screamed, but the scream only echoed in her head.

Robertson squeezed her hand and pointed at the vision. The two of them swirled with it, and she could make out Deuce. She called out to him, but he did not hear her. Then it looked as if Deuce and his mother were standing in front of a door -- the door in the basement of the farmhouse that led past the potato cellar and then up to ground level. Smoke was all around. Bodies in strange armor lay on the floor. Everything was in ruins. Two evil-looking figures with weapons were turning toward Deuce and his mother. Why don't they do something? They should run. Margaret screamed for them to run, but they could not hear her.

As if in slow motion, Margaret saw the action as the two figures closed in on Deuce and his mother. She could see the pulse sounds start from the muzzles of the weapons. "Run Deuce." But she could only watch in horror as the deadly projectiles got closer and closer to Deuce and his mother. The roar of the weapons filled Margaret's head, and then above even that deafening sound, there came another. Louder. It penetrated everything in the vision. She couldn't see Deuce's lips move. But she heard him. She felt the vibration of his mind as it reached way down to his center of being and screamed, 'NO!' And as she felt his mind, she saw him roll forward toward his attackers. He rolled under the fire from their weapons and came to a halt on one knee. She saw his hand form in a strange way, index and small finger extended, the center two fingers clamped down by his thumb. And then from his hand came a flash that pointed at the attackers, and from the flash flew a barrage of arrows.

She did not understand. She had never seen anything like this before. Arrows for God's sake! Forming and flying from Deuce's hand. The arrows were faster than the pulse rounds. They sliced through the body armor like it was made of paper, and after they hit they exploded, and the two attackers' torsos vanished. Their heads fell unsupported to the floor. Behind Deuce, the rubble-filled doorway molded into the shape of an arrowhead, and within the outline of the arrowhead a starfield formed, as if the doorway opened into a starry night. Colored threads undulated among the stars. Margaret saw Deuce and his mother turn and disappear into the starfield. The starfield vanished. There was only the doorway filled with rubble.

The vision faded. The colors melded into farmland. In the distance she could hear cows. A lone crow's raspy call sounded almost like Taps. She felt sick to her stomach and fell to her knees in the scorched grass as familiar reality returned to focus.

"Jesus God," she whispered and fought to keep from throwing up. "What was that?"

"Did you see Deuce?" Robertson was excited, glowing with pride.

"Yes. Or at least I think so. But what was that?"

"We just saw some of what happened here about an hour ago."

Margaret's eyes were wide, and her mouth was slightly open.

"Deuce will be back. If he's skillful, and I know he's skillful. And if he's lucky. He'll be back. He'll find you."

"How?"

"When you're in love, you do things. And he is in love with you."

Tears welled up in Margaret's eyes and silently spilled over and ran down her cheeks. "I know," she said. "I don't understand any of this, Mr. R. I don't understand." And she pressed her face into his chest and cried there. "Sorry," she said after a while. She cleared her throat and in a sure voice repeated, "Sorry."

"Come on. I'll give you a ride back to the store."

They walked away from the pit that had so recently been a home full of family and laughter and memories. Robertson opened the truck door for Margaret and she got in. As he closed the door, he looked back up the little hill where the farmhouse had been, surrounded by trees, now reduced to ashes and charred stumps.

Margaret asked softly, "Are you okay, Mr. Robertson?"

"Oh, yeah. I was just thinking how hard it's been to keep up with those two. I'm gonna miss them. Again."

"I'm sorry."

"Me, too. You know, M'Gee, somebody is going to a whole lot of trouble and expense to spoil my retirement, and it's about to piss me off."

"I can't imagine you angry. You've always been so . . . I don't know . . . so nice."

"Big teddy bear."

"Something like that. What's it like when you get angry?"

"It's very tiring. And there's usually some breakage."

"I'd like to see that."

"No, you wouldn't." And he walked around and got in the driver's seat, shut the door, and cranked the engine. After several seconds the truck reluctantly started.

"Needs plugs," said Margaret.

"Yeah." And they drove up the lane together and turned left on Herbert Road.

Visitors
----- O. C. June, 1945-----

Robertson dropped Margaret off at Gladstone's and continued on to Miss Lilly's to pick up Grandpa. He parked the pickup and tapped the horn twice, waited for what he thought would be a discreet amount of time, and then got out and headed up to the door. He knocked and Miss Lilly opened the door and invited him in. As he passed into the room she buttoned the last button of her dress and hoped he had not noticed. He had.

Grandpa came out of the bedroom. "You oughta have more respect for . . ."

Before he could finish his complaint, Robertson interrupted, "Dad, didn't you hear the sirens?"

"No, I did not."

Miss Lilly ran her hand past a strand of hair and tucked it behind her ear and turned away saying, "Would you like some tea, Robert?"

"No, thank you, Miss Lilly."

"What about the sirens?"

"The farmhouse is burned to the ground, Dad. And Katy and Deuce are gone."

"My God," breathed Miss Lilly. "They're dead?"

Robertson glanced at Miss Lilly for a moment, "Gone." Then he turned to Grandpa and looked into his eyes and said steadily, "Gone."

Grandpa raised an eyebrow and gave a slight nod. "Lilly, I've got to go. It was wonderful to see you again. I'll let you know . . ."

"I'll be outside, Dad," said Robertson. "Don't be too long. We've got some things to do."

"Right."

Robertson went back to the truck and sat behind the wheel. While he waited for Grandpa to say his goodbyes, Robertson took the package he had gotten at the post office earlier and opened it. Inside were a letter and two objects. He opened the letter and found it was from Quigley Bates. Under his breath Robertson sighed, "Well, shit," as he realized that if Quigley could send him a package in the mail, anybody could find him. And his family.

"Dear Robertson, you were right, I did find the book again with your whereabouts in it. All my best to you and Katherine. I hope that this package reaches you in time. Beware. I have had a visit."

The first man of the small group took off his hat and nodded at the lady peeling potatoes on the porch. "Evening, Ma'am," he said smiling.

Momma Chambeau stopped rocking. "And hello be to you your-ownself," she said. "Dere seem like a plenty many of you. What you want?"

The first man was staring at Momma Chambeau. He had not seen many women who smoked a pipe. He waved his hand back and forth, but her eyes did not follow it. He raised his middle finger and motioned rudely toward her.

Another whispered, "She's blind."

A third muttered with a twist of his lips that raised his nostrils, "Perfect."

"Shut up," said the first man over his shoulder. "Why, Ma'am," he continued with mock sincerity, "we just were looking for a place to rest for a bit and maybe a drink of water."

"Water be where you are standing. And a cup. Make the water yours. Leave the cup."

The six men gathered by the well pipe and drank from cupped hands and from the tin cup. While they drank they argued.

"Let's hide out here for the night."

"Hell no, it's too close to the road."

"So what."

"So people drive by on the road, that's the fuck what!"

"Shut up."

"Jesus, he's got his fly opened up again."

"Shit, that's disgusting."

"Well, the pants are too damn small, is all."

"You mean you don't really love me after all?"

"Go to hell."

"Quit splashing, goddammit!"

"So, if you had killed a guy your own size, your damn pants would fit."

"Yeah, well you're about my size."

"Knock it off!"

The first man had finished drinking and walked over to the porch and stood with one foot on the first step. "So, you all by yourself?"

"Maybe," said Momma Chambeau.

"You got a husband, Ma'am?" he continued.

"Had one once. He got lost somewhere."

"That's too bad," and he motioned the others to come over to the porch as he climbed to the top step.

"If you don't mind my asking, Ma'am, what is that burned smell that's all in the air?"

"Oh, dere was a one big-by-shit-damn fire dat burned all de Robertson's house to ashes in a hole. Thought maybe you were leftover wit de firemen. But din you would not be asking dis stuff. Who are you?"

The first man began, "Well, ma'am, we're just out of the army. We got us medical discharges from being shot and all. So now we're looking to find some work maybe . . . kinda make a few dollars to get the rest of the way home."

One of the others at the bottom of the steps remarked, "She ain't bad looking, you know." He said it low and under his breath to those standing beside him, but Momma Chambeau could hear the passing of a shadow, and she did not like the tone of these men. And she did not like the way they smelled. She tightened her fingers on the paring knife and took her pipe from her mouth, nonchalantly changing the grip so that the pipe stem extended between her fingers like the spike on brass knuckles.

"Ma'am, let me help you with those potatoes, what do you say?"

"Thank you a nice lot, but I am happy wit no help for the potatoes."

Momma Chambeau rose slowly and began to head toward the door. "Drink all you want and be havin' a good journey home now."

The first man was at the door with his hand resting on the handle, blocking her way.

From below, one said, "I'm first this time."

"Go to hell. We'll cut cards for her like always."

"We could take her two at a time."

"A blind pussy. My friends, we have gone to Heaven."

The man at the door looked down at Momma Chambeau's wiry body and wondered if her breasts were still firm. "Looks like we'll be staying awhile," he said, "just to help you get over being lonely. I know you'd like that. Wouldn't you?"

Momma had listened to his words and knew his height. She had heard the screen door tell her where his hand was. The porch boards described the position of his legs when he shifted his weight to his right. She knew how he stood as surely as any sighted person.

"Wouldn't you like that little lady?"

"Spit blood and die snake fucker!" and Momma Chambeau drove the paring knife into his stomach.

The letter was direct. The prose was simple. And Robertson had been captivated by the words. "Old Quigley can write a hell of a letter," he thought as the images danced in his mind. Two men had appeared. They talked with Quigley. One played fetch with Mose, throwing a stick, and idly asking about any visitors that might have come by recently. Quigley on the porch, offering beer and being polite – "No, no visitors. Not many come this way anytime but especially not in the heat of the summer. Kinda lonely . . . ," and so on, in that pseudo-countrified way Quigley used for his own amusement. "Come on up and set a spell. Dadburn hot today. . . ," and that was how Robertson remembered Quigley at his hick best. He smiled at the memory. Playing fetch and talking.

But damn! For in an instant, the one man had taken the stick from Mose, slipped it through his collar, and twisted. Robertson could live it through Quigley's simple words. Twist and lift. Mose held in the air, his back legs just touching the ground. His tongue hanging out. The gurgling sounds and the lunging against the pressure. Trying to escape. Trying to breathe. "Tell me about the visitor."

"Leave the dog be!" And the hand of the second man wrenching Quigley"s arm behind his back. Where was the hurt? In his arm? No, it was in his soul as he watched Mose die. Die just to ensure that his answer was satisfactory. Robertson could feel the hate burning from the pages as Quigley wrote. Long after the two had left, Quigley still sat in the dust, cradling Mose in his lap. Stroking the dog's head. Trying to wish it all away. "But I never told them. I remain respectfully yours, Quigley Bates."

"Shit. Shit," Robertson repeated. Where had he heard that same oath recently? "Shit," he said and rummaged in the newspaper inside the box and touched the objects Quigley had included, an old gray tennis ball and a tin pie plate. "Shit!"

"Sorry I took so long." The words startled Robertson. "What have you got here?" Grandpa asked as he sat down in the truck and closed the door.

Robertson started the truck. "Dad, somebody hit the farm. They were light-armed travelers, or at least they had a traveler guide to get them here. They . . ."

"Deuce and Katy?" Grandpa interrupted.

"They kicked some ass, Dad. They really did! But the house is gone. It looks like whoever attacked magged it. Probably to cover up the body count. I locked in on the fight for a bit of it. Deuce and Katy are off and gone. So, we're going home to a big black hole in the ground and some cows that don't know anything except it's milking time."

"Why did they do it?"

"I have no idea," Robertson said and handed Grandpa Quigley's letter. Grandpa read it as the truck headed back to the Robertson farm.

"Nice dog, was it?"

"Yes."

"Who are these two guys? Why are they looking for you?"

"I don't know. They might be looking for you, you know."

"Not after all these years."

"There are some very long memories out there, Dad."

Robertson turned off the main road onto the lane that lead past Pete Miller's and on to the Robertson farm.

Robertson shrugged, "What should we do about the cows?"

"Take them over and give them to Pete Miller. Pigs too. The steers will feed themselves for the summer. Hell, just lease Pete the whole farm." Robertson nodded his approval, and Grandpa turned to look out the window at the passing farmland.

The sun was lowering, and it appeared that amber would be the color of the evening sky. Grandpa stood at the edge of the burned ruins of the house, holding Beatrice by a tether rope and looking into the ashes.

From a short distance away, Robertson called, "You coming or not?"

Grandpa did not answer.

Robertson came closer, bringing Matty with him. The cow sniffed the charred ground and raised her head again. "It was just a house. We'll build another one."

"Just a house," Grandpa said softly. "But you weren't here when Deuce was two or something and dug up all Katy's flowers. Or the time when . . . ," and his voice trailed off. "There were photos. That wooden stool, notches on the door frame that marked how tall Deuce was on his birthdays. Letters. Stuff. Memories. It wasn't 'just a house.' It was someplace you could come back to and there would be all the old times waiting in the woodwork and the closets and the porch chairs. A lot of stuff . . . lots of memories."

"You never lose the memories, Pop."

"Yeah, I know," Grandpa said, "but I used to have a place to keep them. Well . . ."

"Well what?"

"I don't know." Grandpa's eyes were full. "Well... shit! Come on, cow." And Grandpa led Beatrice off toward the Miller farm.

The last blush of evening was fading as the two Robertsons walked the gravel lane back from Pete Miller's. Grandpa was talking, "I am surely going to miss those cows. When I get up at four in the morning tomorrow, I'm not going to have anything to do. Might just have to go back to sleep. What a waste. And our evenings and our weekends and our holidays. Why without those cows, we're going to have to become sociable. Might even have to spend some more time at Miss Lilly's. I am going to miss the shit, though."

"Right."

"No, I honestly mean it. Not that ammonia stench when it's fresh and you gotta clean it out of the barn. But there is a certain sweetness to the smell of the stuff when it floats at you on a little breeze."

"Dad, you are weird."

"And the cats. I'm going to miss those cats draped all around waiting for a squirt of milk."

The two walked on in silence for a while, each listening to the crunch of the gravel beneath their feet. Robertson stopped, put his hands on his hips, and looked at his father.

Grandpa noticed and turned back, "What?"

Robertson bent forward slightly, "A certain sweetness to the smell when it floats on a breeze?"

Grandpa chuckled. "Well, maybe not," he said. "What did you say to old Pete back there? I mean he positively brightened up, especially for a guy that just lost the girl of his dreams."

Robertson answered, "Oh, I told him that Katy had said that she loved him and not me."

"Is that true?" Grandpa asked sadly.

"No."

"Ah. So Pete Miller will have a warm memory at the cost of a little white lie."

"Something like that."

"Unless he ever reads *Cyrano de Bergerac.*"

They came to the top of the hill and turned left. Slowly, and almost at the same time, each man stopped walking. Robertson was slightly farther ahead. Both looking down the lane. Both realizing the discrepancy. They spread apart automatically and resumed their walk on either side of the road. In the grass. There was no crunch of gravel now. The pace quickened. They became two shadows moving silently toward Momma Chambeau's house. Toward a blind woman's house. Where there was a light on in the window.

The front yard of Momma Chambeau's was empty. Inside the house there was a murmur of voices. The light flowed through the porch railing and past the posts and spilled out into the yard. Among the stripes of light and shadow Robertson silently studied footprints around the water pipe. Both men paused and watched and listened. Then they met at the porch steps. Grandpa's finger extended downward, pointing to the foot of the steps. Robertson picked up the object. It was a partially peeled potato. There was a dark stain on one side, and Robertson smelled it. He held it for Grandpa, and he smelled it. It was the smell of blood.

The two men went up the porch steps, keeping their weight over the nail heads that indicated substructure support. At the door, they paused and studied briefly the blood spatters on the screen and the floor. Grandpa held up six fingers and then moved the single finger across his abdomen in a slicing motion. Robertson nodded. A glint on the porch floor caught his eye, and he bent to discover a bloody tooth. He stood and noticed Grandpa had extended his whip from its handle. Robertson did the same and then gestured toward the door as if to say, 'After you.' Grandpa inhaled slowly and quietly released the air. He eased the screen door open. It creaked. He released it. It swung closed with a soft thud.

Inside, the voices stopped. Then, "Check it out." The light went out. The main door opened inward. There was a pause, and then one of the men cautiously pushed open the screen door with the barrel of a shotgun. Robertson slammed the screen door on the protruding barrel, denting it. The man pulled the trigger. Double O buckshot with a blocked exit blew the gun apart in the man's hands. He screamed and fell back inside, clutching his arm where it had been shredded by the exploding gun.

"What the fuck!?"

A burst of machinegun fire ripped through the porch wall. The window disintegrated. Belt-high lead and splintered wood flew into the night. Twenty rounds -- a full clip burst. Ragged holes every three inches. A pause. The metallic clink of the next magazine. Men took positions on either side of the window, their faces and weapons barely visible. Silence. A face peered through the lacerated screen of the shattered door. The porch was empty. There were no signs of anyone or anything. Only wood splinters and broken glass.

"Well?"

"Nothin'. Fuckin' nothin'."

"Well, you killed the shit out of that fuckin' nothin'."

"Piss off."

"It's a joke, dumb ass."

"Go to hell."

"You just woke up the whole fucking countryside."

"So, what's your point?"

"My point is we gotta get out of here now."

From the bedroom, one of the men called, "What?"

"We gotta go now that ol' dead eye here unloaded on a mouse or something."

"But, I ain't finished my second turn yet."

"Forget it, the old bitch has been dead for three hours anyway."

"I ain't neither gonna forget . . . ," and the words in the bedroom ended with an odd sound. Something rolled across the floor.

"What's that?" The man with the machine gun whirled around.

"Don't shoot! We're in the room remember!"

"What's that smell?"

"You smell that?"

"Who farted?"

"Smells more like rotten meat."

"It's coming from the kitchen. Gimmee a flashlight. Old bitty probably wasn't a very good housekeeper." The speaker took the flashlight and stepped into the kitchen doorway. There was a vibration. The floorboards quivered. A sound. Very low, very deep, very big. As if a cave had growled. "Jesus . . ." The man spun around, facing into the room. Five deep parallel claw gashes had opened his entire chest. The parallel sections of rib cage fell haphazardly away and blood and the shreds of internal organs flowed past shattered ribs and onto the floor. His knees buckled. The flashlight slipped from his bloody hand hit the floor and illuminated the eyes of the man who had just called from the bedroom. On his forehead there was an 'X' drawn in blood, and the head was all there was of him.

And then began the sound of rapid-fire explosions as the whips filled the darkness with motion.

The 10:00 a.m. sun was warming to the task of pushing the temperature into the 90's by afternoon. It bothered the police patrol officer, made his collar seem too tight, but regulations were regulations, and he did not loosen his tie. The shade of the building was growing smaller, and he had to inch closer to the doorway to remain in the dwindling shadow. The closer he got to the doorway, the more uncomfortable he became. He had been inside that building already. It was he who had first opened the door this morning. He had gone inside two hours ago, had been the first one. Now the sergeant was in there. Inside with the victims, with the flies.

The sergeant appeared suddenly out of the dark inside, braced himself briefly at the door jam, and then reeled outside, turned to his right, and threw up, violently trying to separate himself from what he had just been looking at. He was still gagging when the sheriff's car drove up. He wiped his hand across his mouth. Flies were starting to gather in the vomit. He could not shake the acid taste from his throat or from his mind. All of his years, both in the army and on the force, had not come close to preparing him for what was inside Momma Chambeau's house.

Sheriff Conklin approached slowly, uncomfortably, the smell and the flies almost physically hitting him. His breath shortened, and he stopped and beckoned the patrol officer to him. "What's with Stewart?" he asked, nodding toward the sergeant.

"He just got out from in there," was the response. The words came in the hollow level tones of a man in shock.

"Sergeant, what have we got here?"

The sergeant came over, taking a cigar out of his pocket. He tried to light it, but the match would not strike. He stood before the sheriff like an automaton, mechanically rubbing the match against its cover, trying by the repetition of a basically meaningless act to get control of his mind again. At least the cigar in his mouth helped to keep away the taste of vomit and the smell of death that flowed from the building. He dropped the match on the ground and spoke.

"Goddamned flies. Goddamn the goddamned flies."

"Sergeant," the sheriff repeated in a level voice, "what have we got here?"

The sergeant spit a speck of tobacco from his tongue. "We have got six...the remains of ...remnants of six...oh Christ." The sergeant suddenly became silent, wiped his mouth and continued, "I think it's those guys they wanted down-state for shooting up the bank, and that twelve-year-old little Middletown girl thing. I think we've got them in there. Sort of."

"That's wonderful, Sergeant. Just wonderful. Great work."

The sergeant looked at the sheriff. The sheriff didn't know what he was talking about. He hadn't seen; he didn't know. "You better take a look in there, sir."

"Damn straight," said the sheriff, and he walked toward the building, stepped inside the door, and disappeared into the darkness. The smell was overpowering in the small room, and the flies swarmed and darted from spot to spot. As the sheriff's eyes grew accustomed to the light, he saw what his men had seen before him. It froze his body and branded his mind. All three would have nightmares of this morning for the rest of their lives. The sheriff stepped unsteadily into the sunlight.

"Jesus Christ," he murmured, "what the hell did that to those guys?"

"Maybe Momma Chambeau put a curse on them. You know, voodoo or something."

"Wild animal, maybe," suggested the officer. "Maybe a cougar. Bear maybe. Bear could have done it."

"Stewart, that was no cougar, no bear. They were not mauled or eaten or clawed. They were shredded. They're spread all over the fucking room. And you damn well know there ain't no damn wild animal so damn tidy that it kills six damn men and then lines their damn heads up in a row on the goddamn mantel!"

"I'm telling you, she voodooed them."

"Oh, bullshit!"

"So what did it?"

"I don't know. But I damn sure don't ever want to meet up with it."

"Or him," said the sergeant quietly. "What for the report, sir?"

"Well, we sure can't put down 'voodoo.' Make it read 'wild animal attack.' Make it a bear. Shit, make it two bears. And go on down to the Robertson's and ask if maybe they saw or heard anything unusual last night."

"It's kind of a rough time for them right now, sir, what with Katy and the boy and all."

"Well, it's been kind of a rough time for Momma Chambeau, too. Never mind, I'll go ask them. I want to do it myself, anyway."

Grandpa was standing outside the door to the lower barn, drinking water from a coffee can when he spotted the sheriff's car coming down the lane. "Bob, come on out. Buck Conklin's coming."

Robertson came out of the lower barn. He was wearing shoes, trousers, and a T-shirt. From inside, the Molly called, "Bobby, your shirt is ready."

Robertson went back inside. "Thank you, Molly." He came back outside crumpling his clean shirt.

"What the hell are you doing?" Grandpa asked.

"Putting a little straw in your hair. You look entirely too neat."

Buck Conklin approached, "Good morning, gentlemen."

"Morning, Sheriff. What can we do for you?" Robertson asked.

"Well, Pete Miller called early this morning and suggested that we might want to come out here and investigate some gunshot-sort-of sounds he heard last night. And sure enough, Momma Chambeau's place is all shot to shit."

"Is Sienna all right?" Grandpa asked.

"She is dead. Murdered," answered the sheriff.

Robertson allowed his shoulders to sag. "Damn," he said softly. "Damn."

"You boys hear anything last night, say a little after sunset?" the sheriff continued.

"No. Do you have any idea who killed her?"

"No," the sheriff said as he looked at the Robertsons' clothing. "You sleep in the barn?"

"Yes."

"But you didn't hear anything?"

"Hear anything, like what?"

"Well, it looks like Momma Chambeau was gang-raped and murdered by a group of very undesirable folk that various departments across the state have been looking for. And they shot up the place. Then some . . . I don't know . . . creature, bear or whatever, tore them apart. There are blood and body parts all over the place. I have never seen anything like it. It is most untidy. And you didn't hear anything unusual?"

"No."

"Just up the lane, at the top of that hill," the sheriff gestured toward Momma Chambeau's, "spitting distance from where we are now standing, there was the local equivalent of the Battle of Gettysburg, and you did not hear anything?"

"Yesterday was not a good day for us, and your news is not helping. Katy and Deuce . . ," Robertson stopped in mid-sentence, took a couple of subdued breaths, and haltingly continued, "They always enjoyed . . . they . . . we all loved Momma Chambeau. But we did not hear anything we haven't heard before. There was a full bottle in the barn. It's not full anymore, and I have a hell of a headache."

The sheriff nodded. "I've been there. Well, sorry to bother you so soon after . . . damn shame, that fire and all. But I've got the damndest mess of dead people up there, and I was hoping you could give me something to explain what happened. You got any of that bottle left?"

"No. Wish we did."

"Yeah. Well, thank you," and the sheriff walked back to his car. "I hope I never meet up with whatever tore into that place. I mean . . . Jesus . . ." He started the car and drove away.

Grandpa noted, "The sheriff looked a little pale."

"Yes, he did," Robertson agreed.

The two returned to the shadows of the lower barn where Robertson removed a canvas cloth that covered six rectangular objects. They had been part of the personal gear of each of the men at Momma Chambeau's. Six men. Six standard issue MollyPACS. This had not been an encounter with deserters and convicts -- at least not deserters and convicts from 1945.

"These things are getting smaller and smaller," Grandpa observed.

Robertson nodded and retrieved his knapsack from behind a pile of hay. "Molly, take a scan of your little friends here and take an inventory."

"Yes, your worship," and Molly began the computer-to-computer translation of data. There would be no way to retrieve any of the items without the security codes individually entered by the owners. This was a standard precaution to prevent looting or use by an enemy, but with enough perseverance, another MollyPAC could gather data and estimate the inventory of any other PAC.

"How's it going, Molly?"

Molly reported, "These are standard issue inventories with occasional personal additions, mostly pornography. There is one that has a code-only sanctuary, indexed as '71545ABQ.' It has a standard auto erase for false code entry."

"Can you gain access, Molly?"

"No, sir."

"Do you have any data relative to 71545ABQ?"

"Not at this time, sir."

"Thank you, Molly."

"Well, there it is," and Grandpa finished his water. "What do you want to do about breakfast?"

"We could get a squirrel and roast it," Robertson said with a subtle smirk.

"Squirrel, hell! We could go to Miss Lilly's and have food!"

"Eggs," Robertson suggested.

"Sausage."

"Pancakes."

"Steak."

"Kippers," Robertson teased.

"What the hell are kippers?"

"I have no idea. You want some?"

"No, I do not want any kippers for breakfast. I do not want squirrel en brochette, I do not want pigs feet boiled in panther sweat. I do not want . . . ," and Grandpa continued to spout out a long list of barely edible possibilities, none of which he wanted for breakfast. The list continued, on and off, until the pickup truck pulled up in front of Miss Lilly's home. Robertson turned off the engine and sat still.

"Albuquerque."

"What about it?" Grandpa asked.

"ABQ. That's the destination code for Albuquerque. I saw it on the train ticket coming out here. Do you want to go?"

"Go where?"

"Albuquerque."

"Are you going?" Grandpa asked.

"I thought I would. Do you want to come along or not?"

Grandpa scratched his neck and looked toward Miss Lilly's house. "I don't know, Bob. I'm getting a little long in the tooth for that sort of thing."

"There are six guys strewn about Momma Chambeau's who might disagree with you. And you keep saying how you miss being on the edge."

"Yeah, but if you had paid attention, you'd have noticed that I only talk that way after a few beers. Nothing like a little alcohol to turn back the clock and start a battle song running through your mind. It is fun to remember back to when I was this awesome, immortal force. But that is only old warrior fireside bullshit. It goes away by morning."

"Did you feel old last night?"

"No. But the bear did. She's got arthritis you know."

"Hogwash."

"No, I mean it. It tires me out something fierce to call up that old bear. It takes a toll after all these years. You'll find out."

"Dad, when Miss Lilly thinks we're not listening, she calls you 'Bear.' Now why would that be, I wonder? I mean, I get this image of . . ."

"Never mind," Grandpa interrupted in a playfully gruff tone. Robertson smiled and rolled his eyes. "Go to hell," Grandpa continued. "It's nice here. I like it a lot."

"I could use your help."

"Well," and then Grandpa changed the subject, "do you miss being on the edge?"

"Not until somebody turned my life into a smoking hole. Now there is a definite itch. But I hated it. Still do. Always will, I suppose. There were times I would cough in this low key way to cover up the fact that I was a hairbreadth from throwing up. I remember the fear. I would wrap it in gauze bandages and put it on a train and watch the train roll out of sight with my fear closed up inside. There was never a time I did not hate and fear what I was doing. But shit and God help me I was good at it, and in this twisted way I miss it. Isn't that the stupidest thing? I do miss it."

"I would hold my fear by the throat way up over my head, and an eagle would come down, grab it, and fly off. Smaller and smaller. Just a dot in the sky. Then gone."

"I didn't know."

"Yeah, well . . . ," then Grandpa turned toward Robertson, tucking his chin down so as to look out of the top of his eyes at his son, "Albuquerque, huh?"

"It's in New Mexico."

"I know where Albuquerque is."

"Climate they say is really good for arthritic bears."

"You are an insolent son-of-a-bitch, you know that don't you?"

"I love you too, Dad."

"I wonder why men don't say that much?" Grandpa got a faraway look in his eyes as he remembered the hills that rolled around the farmhouse in overlapping waves, the greens and tans of the crops rotating from field to field as years of seasons passed. Bits and snips of days and words, flashes of family and newborn calves, cats, dogs, distant crows, cold winter mornings, the oppressive heat of the haymow, the taste of the spring water, so much gone by so fast. "I'm going to miss green," he said. "I don't think Albuquerque is very green." After a pause, Grandpa turned to look at his son.

Robertson noticed his father's gaze. "What?"

"I love you, too," Grandpa said as he opened the truck's door and climbed out. "You might visit more often."

A third party would surely have wondered why the two men walking up to Miss Lilly's porch were laughing so hard. At the foot of the porch steps, Robertson stopped. "71545."

"What are you talking about?"

"7.15.45. It's a date. July 15, 1945. It's next week. Next week in Albuquerque. It could be a rendezvous point for their recall."

"Don't go. It's probably a trap."

"Probably. A trap exposed is but a challenge. At least I was told that by someone once."

"By me. When you were young and would still listen."

"You coming with me?"

"Sure."

"Did you enjoy last night . . . the fight, I mean?"

"Yes, I did."

"So did I. Is that dangerous?" Robertson asked.

"I don't know. Let's eat."

Robertson had noticed his father's actions change during the morning. Back at the barn when the sheriff had driven up, there had been something wrong. Something odd. He realized it now as he watched his father eat the breakfast Miss Lilly had prepared. He was using his left hand to eat, to hold his coffee cup. Robertson thought about the slight miss-step his father had joked about when he tripped after he had gotten out of the truck. It was adding up.

Grandpa spoke softly, "I'm sorry, I . . . I have a bit of a headache. Maybe the air on the porch will help. Fresh air . . . ," and he rubbed his temple. With his left hand. Grandpa walked haltingly to the porch and sat in one of the rocking chairs. His right arm hung limply in his lap. He turned his head slowly to Robertson and began, "I want to go." His speech was very slow and had a forced deliberateness. "I want to go . . ."

"I know," Robertson said, and he sat beside his father. Hard memories came. He knew what was happening to his father. He had seen it happen to other bowmen. It had happened to him. He didn't know all of the physiology involved, but he knew that it felt like his mind had exploded. Not just his brain, his mind had exploded. And he was this small inner thing screaming helplessly for the pieces to come back together. He had been able to hold the scream after awhile and go into the darkness and find the bits and pieces and coax them to return. But while he searched, there had been a terror deeper than anything he had ever known, like a fire infused with a soul from a predator, loosed and free, roaring and consuming.

When it was over for him, the terror had become a warmth that surrounded his mind. He had taken the life support invasions from his body, folded his bed linens, coiled the tubes and hoses, and walked out of the Guardian Hall in search of other times.

"I want to go . . ." Grandpa's speech was slurred now.

"Listen, Dad. Listen . . ."

Miss Lilly didn't hear all of the things that Robertson said to his father there on the porch. Some of the things about rebuilding and how to control the terror she didn't understand at all, but the final words -- those words sank deep into her heart.

"Dad, thank you for all you did for Katy and Deuce. You taught him the balance, and he knows where the center of the world is because of you. And he has the memories of when everything was warm and sure, and those will keep him sane. And me, even though you were gone for a long time, I always knew that you wanted to be there, and that made all the difference. I love you, Dad. I'll be back."

And then he rose and saw Miss Lilly. "My father is going to go through a rough time now. He's going to need a dark place to rest, chicken soup and mother things. And be sure to talk to him. He won't answer, but he will hear. And after a while, he'll come back to you. You are important to us. I will try to get back. Tell him that when he . . . tell him that I'm always trying to get back." Then he smiled and said, "Goodbye," and got into the truck and drove away.

Miss Lilly followed the truck with her eyes as it drove away. It led her gaze to the porch rocker where her Robert sat. She saw him move his left arm and take his limp right hand and place it palm up on the rocker's arm. Still using his left hand, he slowly closed the middle fingers into his palm and brought his right thumb down over them. His shortened index and small finger straightened briefly, and then the effort became too great and his hand relaxed. He raised his head, and tears ran down his cheeks.

The journey begins
----- O. C. July, 1945 -----

Robertson drove to Gladstone's. As he approached the door, two of Margaret's friends were leaving, and Robertson held the door for them and waited.

Their conversation was ending, " . . . It's denial. I did it when Jack was killed. It's part of the grieving process, Father Michael says."

"Good morning, ladies."

"Mr. Robertson, we are so sorry about Katy and Deuce and all."

The second young woman -- Robertson thought her name was Sally or Silvia -- had lost her husband in the early going against the Germans in North Africa. She put her hand on Robertson's arm and said, "I know. If you need anything . . . ," and she lowered her eyes. When she raised them, the look was very different, " . . . anything at all, call me."

"Thank you very much." She was good looking and twenty years old. Robertson felt much younger.

"M'Gee, may I talk with you?"

They went outside into the equipment yard and walked slowly among the used and the new, the rust and the grease, and stopped beside a new Farmall tractor that had been ordered for three years and had just come in.

"This is some catch with the war on," Robertson said noticing all of the metal and rubber which were generally as available as hen's teeth.

"It'll pull a four-bottom plow."

"How did you manage to get it?"

"I have no idea. You want to buy it?"

"Me? No. I came by to tell you I am leaving for a while and that I would be leaving you under the protection of my father, but there is a bit of a problem now with that idea."

"What protection?"

"How many people know you and Deuce are courting?"

"Courting?"

"Dating . . . going together . . . I don't know what the term is now. How many people know you two are in love?"

"Everybody knows."

"And how many of them know you are pregnant?"

Margaret's eyes widened, and then she lowered her head and studied the ground where a discarded gear seemed suddenly in need of attention. "Not that many. I wasn't sure until just recently. A couple. No more. How did you know?"

"Well, I'm guessing, but I noticed you have started to wear a wedding ring, and I thought that might be because of...," Robertson said, pointing gently toward her stomach. "And you've told a couple of people. Two people?"

"Yes. Sally and Rosie. They just left. We were talking about Deuce and everything, and I just mentioned it."

"Whoever attacked the farm yesterday . . ."

"Attacked," Margaret was reminded of the news and interrupted, "my God, did you hear about Momma Chambeau?"

"Yes."

"Isn't that just awful?"

"Yes."

"Do you think it's related to the other . . . to Deuce and Mrs. R.?"

"That is a possibility," Robertson lied. "And you just told Sylvia and Rosie that you were carrying Deuce's baby?"

"Sally, not Sylvia. They promised not to tell."

"M'Gee, this is a small town. Maybe they won't tell anyone, but that's a big maybe. And in six months they won't have to keep it a secret, anyway."

"What are you getting at? I love Deuce. And yes, we actually did get married. Sally and Rosie know that too. I am proud to have his baby."

"Well, the key phrase here is 'Deuce's baby'."

A sudden thought burned in Margaret's mind. The horrifying images of strangely armored men, tanks with arms and legs, images of Deuce and his mother, of the fire and violence. "Oh, shit. Oh, God. They'll come for the baby."

Softly, Robertson said, "I think so. Yes."

The blackest fear of a mother filled her eyes. She wanted to say something brave: 'Let 'em try. Just let 'em try.' But she had seen the power of the attackers, and there was no reality for her.

"M'Gee, as I see it, you sort of have two choices. If you stay here with your folks and your friends, it'll be like serving in the Navy. You'll have a warm bed and a hot meal every day until the first torpedo hits. Waiting for that torpedo can get to be nerve-wracking, and the end result is not all that acceptable. Staying here would have been all right with Dad around, but he's had a kind of stroke . . ."

"A stroke. No. Is he doing okay?"

"He'll be all right, but it will take him some time, and he can't help now. Second choice is to come with me."

"My dad can take care of me. He wouldn't let anything happen, believe me."

"Do you want your house to look like my house?"

Margaret thought of the gaping charred hole that Robertson was talking about and did not like the thought. "What makes you think you can do anything?"

"Hand me that gear, and I'll show you."

Margaret bent to pick up the gear she had looked at earlier. "No, the other one," Robertson said referring to another larger sprocket that was barely visible under the tractor tire. As he spoke, Robertson calmly grasped the tractor hitch and lifted the machine until the rear axle was high enough for the tires to be off the ground. Too stunned to think, Margaret retrieved the sprocket, and Robertson returned the tractor to the ground. He held out his hand, and Margaret gave him the heavy metal gear. "You see that fence post over there that's a bit taller than the others?"

Margaret nodded.

"Watch," he said and threw the gear like a discus. The post splintered. The severed end flew into the air. Margaret saw Robertson's hand move. Quickly. Was there a flash? Not sure. The air -- a sudden heat. The post end disintegrated. Powdered. The gear continued and embedded in the concrete wall of the shed behind. The metallic impact echoed. Silence.

Robertson looked at Margaret, "I can do some other stuff, too."

"Who are you guys?"

"Come with me and find out."

----- Santa Fe Chief -----

There's a rhythm and a roll to the riding of trains. They have their own music, played in steel by rail joints and wheels. Subliminal, hypnotic, like a drummer ticking his sticks on the drum rim waiting for the horn section to pick up the beat and come in. Trains have a special feel about them and a garden of fragrances that forever haunt the minds of all those who travel on them.

Margaret noticed that Robertson seemed to be somewhere else most of the time, his gaze focused in some distant realm, and he was silent for long periods of time. She enjoyed the trip. It was new, and she had never been far from home before. The view changed with a leisurely pace. It did not really change so much as it flowed, one moment easing into the next. She loved it.

Margaret asked the steward, "Where are we now?"

"Kansas, ma'am."

"I thought Kansas was flat."

"Oh, no. It rolls pretty good in spots."

"Mr. Robertson, isn't this lovely?"

He did not answer.

"Mr. Robertson, are you all right?"

He did not answer. He did not hear. His mind was filled with Katherine and their last night together. There was a deep ache that filled him. She was gone again. She was not there to touch -- to touch him. Her smile, her eyes -- the smiles they held -- the slight toss of her head when she let her hair down, the way the candlelight licked over her body, all were memories now.

He was facing the window of a train, but he was seeing her dress slide off her shoulders and crumple to the floor. He felt again her softness, her firmness, the curves and recesses of her body. He saw again the room in the farmhouse where they stood holding each other. He felt her close against him as she raised on her toes to accept him, and he re-lived the motion of her legs against his as they danced, hardly moving, joined as lovers, slowly edging in a circle, slowly building their sensation together. He had been looking into her eyes, his lips resting gently on hers, breathing her breath. That sweet slow agony. The sensation that fills true lovers when they use their bodies to join their souls. The stuff that creates galaxies should not be lowered into words.

"Mr. Robertson, isn't the view beautiful?"

He did not answer.

He did not hear.

And the rolling grass of Kansas passed the window by.

The mountains of Colorado and New Mexico stretched tightly across the horizon, and like a long arrow, the train headed through the rolling plains toward them. Margaret and Robertson were in the dining car finishing their dinner. The day was slowly fading, and the train began to pick up speed for the night. The water in the glasses quivered, and the waiters adjusted to the sway and roll as they carried trays to the tables.

"Mr. R, could I ask you something?"

"Of course."

"How did you know that I was pregnant?"

"What?"

"Back at Gladstone's, you knew when you came to get me. You said then that I was pregnant, and I didn't know much before that myself. All you said was something about a ghost which I didn't understand. So how did you know?"

"You had two voices. They were loudest at the farm after the fire when you thought Deuce was dead. So I knew."

"What do you mean two voices?"

"Men, women, creatures of intelligence . . . I've known some very smart dogs, by the way. Pigs. Wolves . . . my God they're something. You know. And whales. Bears. All of them. Anyway, intelligence feels and thinks meaning. A mother feels for her young -- wolf, bear, Chinese lady, you. That feeling tries to express itself in language, but whether it's a growl or Chinese, or you crying on my shoulder, it is the same. The meaning is there. That's how I have been able to speak with so many different beings. I can sense what they are feeling. You can do it, too."

"How?"

"You ask me if I want dessert, and I'll make up a word for an answer, and then you tell me what I meant. Go ahead, ask if I want dessert."

Margaret giggled, "Okay. Do you want dessert?"

"Kangee."

Margaret looked at him, smiled and nodded, "You want dessert."

Robertson nodded.

"But do you want the pie or the ice cream?"

"Ah, that is more difficult to tell, but when the waiter asks, you order for me, okay?"

"You're on."

The waiter came soon thereafter and filled the water glasses as much as the rhythm of the train would allow for. "Ma'am, would you care for some dessert?"

"Yes, please. The ice cream. Thank you."

"And for you, sir?"

"What are the choices again?" Robertson asked.

"We have ice cream and some very fine apple pie."

At the mention of fine apple pie, Robertson pictured a slice in all of its flaky, fruit-filled glory, but he said nothing. Margaret said with a smile, "He'll have the pie," and Robertson nodded his agreement to the waiter.

"Very good, sir," said the waiter as he departed to fill the order.

Robertson said, "See, that was not so hard, was it? And now, the next time you meet up with a whale or a wolf or a Chinese lady, you will be able to tell exactly what dessert they want."

Margaret smiled at this, but her mind was really wrapped up in the charm of the thought of her two voices. That glow women get was in her eyes, and so Robertson ate his pie in silence, in deference to life's magic.

Sancho's prediction
----- O. C. July 1945, White Sands, New Mexico -----

Five days later, Margaret Porter sat on a rock in the New Mexico desert, a very long way from home. "You'll be cooler if you can get off of the desert floor," Robertson had said as he handed her an umbrella. "Instant shade," he quipped, "and drink this before you get thirsty. If you get thirsty, drink all of it. Forget about all that crap from the movies about just one sip now and all that rationing hooey. If you're thirsty, drink," and then he had walked off across the dunes and disappeared into the scrub vegetation of the desert. He had taken his backpack with him to go 'investigating' and said he would be back 'whenever.'

And so Margaret sat. 'That backpack,' she thought, 'what a thing that is.' She had been introduced to Molly on the train ride, and it had been like meeting a friend. Their needs came from the backpack by way of Molly's direction: clothes, strange bits of equipment, money. Now there was a good trick. Molly produced money. And the sassy way Molly talked to Mr. R. They must go way back, Margaret concluded.

She thought about the silver and turquoise in the market in Santa Fe and wondered what it was that so fascinated Mr. R. about 109 East Palace Street. He had heard about it in a bar, he said, and knew it was important because when he asked about it, he was told it didn't exist. That really excited him, and he was gone for the better part of a day after he heard about it.

The next day they had gotten on a bus and gone to Albuquerque. The mountains and hills of Santa Fe changed to red rocky thrusts and rough-cut river banks as the bus wound south. She remembered the tuberculosis hospitals that had made Albuquerque a large city, growing in the clean dry air. She remembered the expression on the car dealer's face when

Robertson had purchased the old Ford with cash. She thought about how much she had hated Mexican food and how quickly she had grown to love it. She was fascinated by the cruelty of the land here. 'Everything either has thorns or it bites,' she thought. But in the austerity, there was beauty. There was balance. Deuce had talked about 'the balance.' God she missed him. She missed home and the everything-is-right feeling she had left behind there.

She still was not sure why they had come here to New Mexico to the White Sands. But Robertson had seemed to know what he was doing. She went back to the car to sit, but the black Ford was like an oven inside, so she soon returned to her rock. Without the shade of her umbrella, the rock had become uncomfortably hot. She poured some water on it. The water hissed and vanished immediately, but the rock was cool enough to sit on. Then she finished the rest of the water and wished she had not poured any on the rock. When Robertson returned, she knew she would be grumpy. Tired. Hot. Grumpy.

"It's very hot here, your Worship."

"I know that, Molly. Tell me something I don't know."

"The scan is quite difficult to conduct at this range and provide anything resembling detail. The thermal interference from the sand . . . did I mention it is very hot here? . . . makes it hard to pick up and maintain contact with the life units, but one does what one can."

"So?"

"A tower. Steel. A radioactive device is being raised by the life units. Do you need an accurate height on the tower?"

"No."

"One hundred feet plus or minus ten feet. Close as I can get in the heat. In the sand. With no shade. There are motorized transports and radio transmissions. That's about all I can give you without an active scan. Or maybe being positioned closer to the target. If your Worship would see fit to . . . ," Molly stopped in mid-sentence.

Robertson glanced at Molly's function screen. It was all normal. He was about to question her when she spoke again.

"I know something you don't know."

"Molly, knock off the bullshit. It's hot out here."

"Ah-hah," Molly paused and wished she had a face so she could create a smirk of triumph. She knew the significance of her discovery, and in the level tones she used when things were serious, she continued, "There was a lifescan pulse sweep from the target area. Interrogation of temperature, carbon content, oxygen utilization, motion. Maybe more, but the pulse was very brief, and that's all I got."

"Thank you, Molly."

"You're welcome. Are we done being hot now?"

"Yes," Robertson said, and he dragged Molly back down the dune, closed her in the pack, and walked back to Margaret. She had drunk all of the water and was holding the umbrella and sitting on the large rock, just where he had left her.

"It's very hot here," Margaret greeted him.

There was a vibration in his backpack and Robertson returned, "So I've been told."

"Did you find out what you wanted to find out?"

"Yes."

"Which was?"

"Which was, I'm going to have to go to work tonight."

"Are you being enigmatic on purpose? Some sort of man thing?"

"Enigmatic? Enigmatic?"

"I read books. I have a dictionary."

"You also like Hopalong Cassidy movies," Robertson countered as they climbed into the old Ford.

"And *Casablanca*. What's your point?"

"Are we fighting?" Robertson asked as he started the engine.

"No, this is fighting," and she reached over and turned off the ignition key and threw it out the window.

"Shit." He got out of the car and searched for the key. When he returned, he was ready to give Margaret a lecture about behavior, but her voice was soft and she did this thing with her eyes that completely disarmed him.

"Mr. R., what's going on?"

He leaned on the door's window opening. The hot metal burned his forearm, and he dropped the key. "Shit," he said, but as he bent to pick it up, he could not resist the balance of the new mood between them, and he pretended to hit his head on the door, simultaneously hitting the car's side with his fist. He stood up rubbing his forehead and wincing.

"My God, are you all right?"

Robertson rolled his eyes back and sank from view. Margaret hurriedly opened her door and ran around the car to find Robertson sitting on the running board, smiling. Margaret put her hands on her hips and tried to glare at him, but a smile formed in her heart, nudged at the corners of her mouth, and then took over her whole face. "You goof. Deuce used to catch me with that stupid trick all the time." Her smile slowly retreated back into her heart with her memories of Deuce and love. Then with a sigh, she released the sadness and took up determination. She looked at Robertson and with a silent gesture, her palms asked, "So?"

Robertson spoke, looking out across the rolling sand dunes, "Do you remember what I showed you about Deuce not being dead?"

"Yes."

"Remember the attackers. The ones you said looked like men sticking out of machines."

"Yes, tankmen."

"They're back."

"Over at the tower?"

"Yes."

"But there can't be tank men over there. We saw all the soldiers running around over there, and they were just regular soldier guys. Jeeps. Guns. Regular stuff. And you can't get close. You said so yourself. So, if there are any tank men, then our guys must know about it."

"Nobody knows, M'Gee."

"How can that be?"

"Well, if I were doing it, I'd have my guys go underground with rations and environment suits. I'd set up a perimeter defense with lifescan monitors and random active search pulses. Communication would be by shielded laser or conduit radiovision. And then I'd just wait."

"For what?"

"For me."

"That's why we came all this way?"

"Yes. For some reason, they want me to show up. I think they want to mess with my retirement some more. Anyway, I showed up."

"So they know you're here?"

"No, probably not."

"Well then, just sneak up on them and mess with *their* retirement."

"I like the way you think. Good plan. It's the sneaking up that's the hard part. By now, they've got a computer log of every life form in the area. Every U.S. Army man and vehicle. Every scientist. They know if somebody sneaked a girl into the barracks last night. They know when the last eagle flew over and how many rabbits he had to pick from."

"All from holes in the ground?"

"Yep."

"You know, I only understand about half of this?"

"I know."

"So you can't sneak up on them."

"Nope."

"What are you going to do?"

"I'm going to sneak up on them."

"Great, now the half I do understand, I don't understand."

"I learned long ago, when you are forced into a game of 'Last Man Standing,' the best way to win is to cheat. I am going to cheat. Are you thirsty?"

"Yes."

"Then let's go back to civilization, running water, and beer on tap," and Robertson stood up and stretched. He seemed to stiffen more easily lately, and with that thought came another - - he wondered how his father was doing. He thought a lot about his father as he drove the old Ford to Socorro. They had found a restaurant there that they liked. Good food, real people, and a very entertaining proprietor, Ruiz Alvarez.

Ruiz had been a reader in the cigar factories of Cuba. There in the pungent air, he had entertained the workers with stories as they cut and rolled the tobacco. To be successful in this, Ruiz had developed the projection techniques of an opera singer, so that his voice could be heard throughout the factory above the constant staccato chopping of the workers. He had loved his work and had become one of the most sought-after of the readers. His most requested story was *Don Quixote*.

In the late 1930s, Ruiz developed an asthmatic reaction to the fragrance of tobacco and emigrated to Mexico City and then northward to Monterrey, Ciudad Juarez, then across the border to Las Cruces and Socorro. Here he met the dark eyes, winning smile, and fine cooking of a Navajo woman. She was known locally as Denny from a corruption of *Dineh,* the name the Navajo call themselves. They married and opened a small restaurant that served the simple corn, bean, and lamb staples of the Navajo, combined with the spicy hints of Cuba, to create a very popular local establishment, The Dineh Bekeyah. Denny cooked and Ruiz waited tables and recited stories to the customers.

Here Robertson and Margaret rested and ate and listened to Ruiz's voice fill the room with passages from *Don Quixote*: " '*And I have heard say that she whom commonly they call Fortune is a drunken whimsical jade, and what is more, blind and therefore neither sees what she does nor knows whom she casts down or whom she sets up.*' Soon, Sancho was weeping for his dying master: '*Don't die, master, but take my advice and live many years; for the foolishest thing a man can do in this life is to let himself die without rhyme or reason.*' "

Denny brought out a peach dessert as Ruiz continued, "'*You must have seen in your books of chivalry that it is a common thing for knights to upset one another, and for him who is conquered today to be conqueror tomorrow.*'" There was applause from the several customers as Ruiz finished.

After dinner, Robertson and Margaret drove back into the desert. "You know," Margaret said, "I had never heard of Don Quixote before now. What a fun story. I'm sorry we got in the middle of it." She remembered the simple plea of Sancho and chuckled, "'*Don't die, master, but take my advice and live many years.*' You might pay attention to that, you know."

"Good advice," Robertson said.

"Beautiful evening," she said as the dunes passed by and the sun went down in a cloudless sky.

"Looks like rain," Robertson mused.

A scraggly, improvisational fence of barbed wire and various vertical objects and posts followed the road that Robertson drove down. The sun was poised on the horizon, about to dive into the desert night, when he stopped by a break in the fence. Two ruts headed off from the road and skipped over the scrubland of White Sands.

"M'Gee, that is the road we were on this afternoon. You drive down it for ten and a half miles, and you will be at that big rock you spent the day sitting on. Wait there and I will meet you by dawn."

"Where are you going?"

"I am going to do some things. My plan is to get them done, meet you, and then we go home."

"Back to Albuquerque?"

"No. Home. Gladstone's, cows, my dad, your folks. Home to wait for Deuce. Hopefully, Katy too. That home."

Margaret nodded and tried to feel good about what he said, but Robertson's mood had been different since the afternoon, and she knew that it was going to be a long night.

"So, you drive on down there, and I'll meet you by that rock, okay?"

"Okay."

Robertson got out of the car and closed the door. Margaret slid into the driver's seat and said, "Good luck." It seemed a small thing to say, but it was all she could think of.

Robertson studied her face. His intensity embarrassed her, and she lowered her eyes. He began softly, "Either way, I think when the night is over, it will be safe enough for you at home. So. Drive slowly. Keep the headlights off. Do not go any further than that rock. And wait for me."

"No problem," she said weakly.

"Margaret, when the dawn comes, if you see the sun over the mountains and I am not back, you drive to Albuquerque, get on a train, and go home." Her eyes pleaded 'No,' so his tone turned hard, "Do it."

"Yes, sir," she said, thinking that she had never seen him like this. His easy manner was vapor, and what she saw in his eyes scared her.

"What?"

"I just never have seen you so . . ."

"Most of those who have are dead," and he stood back from the car. Talk was over.

Margaret started the car and turned to follow the two ruts into the scrub and dunes. She was just about to top the first rise when it struck her. "My God," she said to herself aloud, "he called me Margaret," and she stopped and turned to look back toward the road.

Robertson was visible but indistinct, surrounded by ribbons of color that undulated around him. A bluish glow slowly swelled and shrank like something breathing. The blue became dominant, and like a fog, began to obscure the colors and the man until all faded and disappeared. Clouds began to form in the west. Clouds erupting where there had been only clear sky. A sinister, rolling, vertical wall of clouds. The red glow of the sun's last light had just enough power to coat the edges. Clouds edged now in blood. Darkness took the sky, and a low, long rumble rolled over the desert. A chill wind coaxed a rattling noise from the scrub foliage, and the desert whispered like the death threat of the snake's tail.

Of dead cows and boogiemen
----- O. C. July 16, 1945, White Sands, New Mexico -----

Just after midnight the phone at S-10,000 rang, and Sergeant Johnson picked it up. "Sugar 10. Sergeant Johnson."

"This is General Groves. Get a patrol together and get on down to the tower and check around. Check for . . ."

Johnson interrupted, "Who is this?"

"This is General Groves! General goddamn Groves, and I want you to get your insubordinate ass in gear!"

Johnson was not impressed. "My ass is always in gear, sir. Do you know the password for the day?"

"Tangier," came the curt reply.

"I am sorry, sir, who did you say you were?"

"Goddamn it, whoever you are . . ."

"Sergeant Johnson."

"Johnson, what the hell do you think you are doing?"

"That's Sergeant Johnson. Now, whoever you are, I don't know how you got this number, or who you really are, but you have ordered me to leave my post, and you don't know the password of the day." And Johnson hung up the phone.

"Who was that, Sarge?" a soldier asked.

"That was General Groves," Johnson replied calmly.

"You hung up on General Groves?"

"He'll call back."

The soldier gave a soft whistle of amazement.

Groves went into orbit, and his aide asked him what the problem was. Groves glowered. "The code for the day is 'Tangier,' right? Because I just got some insolent son-of-a-bitch sergeant who doesn't know that, and I want his ass on a pike."

The aide pursed his lips. "I'll check, sir," and he opened his dispatch case.

"What?" demanded the general.

"Well, technically, 'Tangier' expired three minutes ago, sir. If you want to be absolutely accurate. As of 0001, 'Grover Cleveland' should have been in use, sir."

"Shit," the general said in exasperation.

"Sir?" questioned the aide.

"Well, I just talked to either an insubordinate asshole or the sharpest security guard in the outfit, and I don't know which."

"What is his name, General?"

"Johnson."

"He's both, General."

Groves smiled. At least this was army. He had always understood army. The longhairs, as he called the scientists, were always driving him crazy with their informality and lax security. Groves chuckled. "Hot damn," he muttered and picked up the field phone one more time.

"Sugar 10. Sergeant Johnson here."

General Groves spoke calmly, "Sergeant, this is Grover Cleveland. Do you recognize my voice?"

"That would be General Cleveland, would it not, sir?"

The general laughed. "I am told you are the best we've got, and now I believe it, Sergeant. Well done. Now there really is great concern about the possibility that either the Japanese or the Russians or both might be trying to sink us, and I want you to take a detail down to the tower and check around. Babysit Kistiakowsky and the arming crew. Make sure everything is as it should be. No Japs. No Ruskies. No stray cows chewing on important wires. You got that?"

"We are on our way, General."

"Good. And Sergeant, I have heard that in addition to being good at security, you are also sometimes disrespectful, but

I am sure that is not the case. Now move it." Groves hung up the phone and went to bed.

"Who was that?" the soldier asked Johnson.

"That was General Groves. Come on, Stupen. And Simpsky, you too, and Valentino. Get your stuff. We're going on patrol."

It started to rain as the four soldiers climbed into a jeep and headed the six miles from S-10,000 to the tower where the 'gadget' hung in silence. Dr. George Kistiakowsky and two assistants waited atop the structure to throw the arming switches. The rain began to splatter on the tin roof and made conversation difficult, so the three men sat in silence, each with his own thoughts and questions about what they were all about to try.

Rain was coming down hard at the test sight when Johnson and his men arrived at the base of the tower. The tent at the bottom was vacant, and the sergeant tried to call up to the scientists, but the noises of the weather prevented him from being heard.

"You guys take the jeep and make a wide sweep of the area. I'll see if the longhairs are okay."

"What are we looking for, Sarge?"

"Boogiemen. And watch out for dead cows. You do not want to drive into one of those and break the front end, cause if they arm that thing up there tonight we are really going to want that jeep. Got that?"

"Hell yes."

"Make your sweep and come back here."

The three men drove off complaining about getting wet while the sergeant would be all cozy in the tent or up at the top drinking hot coffee with the longhairs. They headed toward the barracks compound that had been built to house construction workers, and later guards, while the tower was being built. It was empty now, and the soldiers figured to use its shelter for a while and then return to pick up their sergeant. Their patrol was another ridiculous piece of army make-work.

Valentino grumbled as they drove, "This is a crock of owl shit. The only reason we gotta do this is because some brass hat is jumpy. If you were a saboteur, do you think you would be out in this shit? Hell no. Let's just get our asses in the barracks and kiss it off."

"Yeah," agreed Simpsky, "you can't see shit anyway."

Valentino griped, "Nobody in his right mind would be out here."

"We're out here."

"Go to hell."

Johnson started up the ladder to speak to the scientists. He was halfway up when a bolt of lightning imbedded itself in the desert. The violent illumination froze Johnson in his climb. "Jesus, I am climbing a steel tower in a lightning storm. This is really dumb," he said to himself and started down. Lightning fired again. Close. The thunder was quick to follow and deafening. Johnson thought briefly about jumping the rest of the way off of the giant lightning rod he was on.

In the tin room at the top of the tower, the large sphere that was the first atomic bomb swung ponderously on its chain. Someone wondered aloud, "Is this thing grounded?"

"Good question." And they all wondered if the lightning might set off 'the gadget.'

The storm became more violent, and Johnson huddled in the tent at the base of the tower. The canvas offered only partial protection from the gusty wind and the torrents it blew. Johnson checked his watch. It had been far too long since he had sent Valentino and the others to check the perimeter.

The first doorway the three soldiers had tried was locked. They considered shooting open the lock but did not. Simpsky said, "Screw this," and headed over to the second building. He tried to jump a puddle and slipped on his landing, falling unceremoniously on his butt. The other two laughed. The lightning that had startled Johnson on his climb lit up the area, and Simpsky looked between his sprawled legs. An antenna came up out of the mud. On the end of the antenna was a small rectangular device about four inches long.

"What the shit. . . . hey guys, look at this."

"Hey, Valentino, Ski finally found something between his legs."

Simpsky looked over his shoulder and fired back, "In your hat, asshole. Get over here and look at this!" And he got on his knees in the puddle and stared at the strange antenna. The rectangle on top of the antenna turned slowly, scanning parallel to the ground. Simpsky jumped up and aimed his rifle down at the object that was just in front of him.

His companions were still laughing, "Ski, you gotta be some kinda proud of your dick to want us over for a look."

"Yeah, besides, you seen one you seen 'em all."

Simpsky shouted through the rain and wind, "It's an antenna or something." And the rectangle continued its slow scan.

Valentino roared, "Ski's dick has got an antenna." The two were leaning on their rifles under the roof overhang of the barracks. They had fallen into contagious laughter when everything was funny. Ski was funny. Their own drenched appearance was hilarious. And bits of joke punch lines and single word cues brought laugh and laugh again.

The rectangle stopped. It was pointing at Simpsky's right leg. It paused. The rectangle rose vertically to become a lumpy end on the antenna, and then the whole thing disappeared down into the mud.

"Hey, fellas . . ."

The mud quivered.

"Hey, Ski . . ."

Water, where Simpsky was standing, flew into the air. The ground beneath his feet gave way. He screamed and disappeared. There was a flash of lightning, and the others stared at a brightly lit emptiness.

"What the fuck . . ."

Valentino had a tommy gun, Stuben had an M-1. They both had .45's. They looked at each other and became soldiers. In overlapping runs they approached the puddle where Simpsky had vanished. Stuben got there first. He looked down into the dark water. Valentino looked behind him to see if any threat was coming from that direction. He turned back to see something come up out of the ground. This was no antenna. It looked like a helmet of some sort. Not exactly like the ones the Krauts had, but similar. "Holy shit," he said under his breath and sighted his tommy gun in the direction of the emerging shape.

Stuben had already begun to empty his clip into the rising figure. Muzzle flashes and .30-06 rounds at point-blank range. And still the figure rose. The whine of deflected rounds mingled with the wind. And still the figure rose. It had arms. Legs. The right arm grabbed Stuben by the throat and raised him gagging into the air. The figure was silhouetted by lightning. A hulking man-shape. Armored in a strange way. Helmeted. Black. Matching the night.

Valentino flipped to full automatic and mashed his trigger. The clip emptied at the shape, and the bolt locked back.

Valentino rolled to his left and put in a new clip as he rolled. When he righted himself, he saw Stuben's limp body being thrown into the hole from which hell had risen. The ground where Valentino had been firing erupted as something blasted from the armored shadow. Valentino fired. Rolled. Fired. The figure was always facing him. It wouldn't die. It didn't move. It just turned as if driving Valentino to his left. A new clip. His last.

As he rolled, he glimpsed other shapes rising from the ground. Dark armored shapes. He fired a three-round burst to distract his foe. To buy time. Why wouldn't the damn thing die. He could see his hits. Shoot for the belly. Always the belly. Shit. No good, no effect. Go for the head. Another three-round burst. The rounds impacted the center of the helmeted head. Nothing. Valentino rolled again. Lightning flared. Valentino, on his back in mid-roll, stared up in horror and emptied his last nine rounds into the belly of the looming black armor that stood above him.

The thing had been waiting for him to roll to him all the time. They were playing games with him. It moved its hand. Something in the hand pointed. A finger? Not sure. Valentino screamed defiance, "Fuck you, machine!" and he kicked where a groin should have been. There was only armor. Valentino scrambled to his feet and ran. The ground to his right exploded. He dogged left. The ground there exploded. They were having target practice. The fuckers were playing with him again.

He stopped and turned to face the shapes. There were five of them. Two spaced to his front, one 90 degrees to his right, and he saw two more maneuvering in the night. The rain lessened. Valentino wiped the wetness from his face. "All right, you fucks," he shouted, and he deliberately drew his .45 and aimed. He fired one round at each figure, hitting each squarely in what should have been a face. He had three rounds left. He fired them in a two-inch group into the chest of the first of the shapes, the one that had taken out Simpsky and Stuben. The thing appeared to look at its chest, studying the spot where Valentino had hit it. The thing looked up slowly and stared at Valentino. Valentino tossed his empty gun almost casually into the mud and drew his knife. The figure raised his arm and saluted.

"I'll be a son-of-a-bitch," Valentino said softly.

The dark figure lowered his salute and fired.

Sergeant Johnson looked at his watch one more time and decided that something was not right. He looked into the night in the direction his little detail had gone. "Shit," he muttered and stepped off into the desert. There was a light drizzle falling, nothing like the earlier torrents, but fog was forming in low spots and there was a very low overcast. As he made his way in the darkness, thunder sounded again. It was a long continuous roll of thunder. Johnson had never heard anything like it before. It was more like a freight train. He thought to himself, 'That's not thunder. That's a tornado. They say it sounds like a freight train.'

The drizzle stopped and the wind picked up noticeably. The wind in Johnson's ears made it difficult to hear, but the long rumble definitely continued. There was a sharp single flash of lightning and immediate thunder, but no rain. Johnson instinctively ducked into a crouch at the sound that was so reminiscent of artillery fire. He was about a hundred yards from the barracks when he stumbled and fell. "Well, isn't this a shitting mess," he said aloud.

Ranchers in the area had let their cattle roam the White Sands scrubland, and the army had finally grown tired of negotiating to have the cattle rounded up and removed from the test site. Someone had given the order, and any cows found in the test sight were shot and left in the desert to rot. Johnson had tripped on one of the carcasses that lay rotting in the darkness. Just before his fall, he had been hit by a wall of odor -- the smell of rotting death. And now he had fallen into the decaying goo that had been a cow, then dinner for coyotes and crows. "Goddamn it," he said and then smiled at the thought of reporting to General Groves smelling like rotting flesh.

The armored mercenaries that occupied the barracks area were all above ground now. Three insignificant distractions had been eliminated with some sport. The briefing on the battle capabilities of this time period had indicated only primitive armor and firepower, and that had proved to be the case.

Johnson stood and wiped off something sticky and threw it on the ground. A rabbit in the brush at his feet fled its hiding place and darted toward the barracks. Johnson jumped at the sudden movement from right below his feet. The rabbit set off a chain reaction as it ran through a covey of quail. The quail took flight, their stubby wings making their characteristic roar. Johnson flinched again, then stood completely still, disgusted with himself for his careless night work. "I am a lot better than this," he told himself.

As he stood motionless, looking off at the erratic dashes of the rabbit and the quickly departing quail, he saw something that made his eyes go very wide. The perimeter defense was now above ground and active. Its automatic life-sensing locked onto the carbon-based movement and reacted. The laser bank fired, and the rabbit and fourteen quail turned to smoke.

The mercenary monitoring the perimeter defense glanced at the target data and adjusted the sensitivity so that the machine would not be distracted by every mouse and snake in the area. As he looked at the monitor, he noticed a large carbon-based return 100 meters distant. The defense had already locked on but had not fired because the data were conflicting. The return was carbon-based like the life forms of the planet, but it did not move and its life scan data indicated extensive decay. The mercenary selected cancel. The target in question went off-screen and into a file.

When the lasers took out the rabbit and the quail, Johnson was able to see a large, man-shaped figure, briefly illuminated in red light. He dropped to his stomach beside the carcass. The perimeter defense sensed movement, re-acquired the target, and fired. The ground beneath Johnson shook, and sticky pieces of cow sprayed over him.

The mercenary checked the monitor. Life scan follow-up indicated a hit and disruption of decaying carbon-based flesh. He thumped the computer with his index finger knuckle, "Dumb damn machine. Now it's shooting at stuff that's already dead."

'Moving is not healthy,' Johnson decided and tried not to gag from his newly acquired smell. He crept behind a low dune and slowly raised his head behind a sage plant. Through the low camouflage of the plant, Johnson studied the barracks. It was very hard to see anything. Only occasional movement by several dark shapes that looked like men on patrol. It was not long before the shapes stopped moving. 'Got their positions,' Johnson figured. He could see the empty jeep, and he concluded that his three men were dead or captured. He lowered his head and began a slow stalking crawl along the desert toward the barracks.

The rumble in the sky intensified, and rain began again. Huge drops and small hail began to fall. Lightning flashed and Johnson looked for movement in the compound. There was none. Lightning became frequent. The air went dead still, but the thunder was almost constant. So much so, that the ground beneath the sergeant began to vibrate. Johnson looked up. A loud unfamiliar sound began. It sounded like a ratchet or one of those New Year's noisemakers that twirls around a stick. That noise, but far louder. Then thunder so loud that it hurt Johnson's ears blasted a gust front of air through the barracks compound and continued with 60-mile-an-hour fury to pour over the ground where Johnson lay, carrying the debris of the desert with it.

Johnson pressed his head into the wet sand as the wind blew over him. He sensed light and wondered 'What the hell?' Glancing up he saw a solid wall of lightning hundreds of yards long advancing toward the compound. He had never seen this before -- this lightning curtain. But what really scared him was not the wind, not the furious enigmas of the storm. What scared him the most was what he saw moving toward him.

The lightning curtain parted, and through the gap came a figure. It looked like a man, but it seemed ever so much larger than a man. The curtain closed behind the man and followed him like a troop follows its officer. With the man were two large bears. A crow, jet black with fire in its eyes, glided just over the man's left shoulder, and at his feet snakes, rats, and all the crawling, swarming private-fear vermin of mankind's mind came rolling forward like surf. Suddenly the curtain raised into the storm, all became blackness and wind, and the man and his terrible court vanished. Johnson was left quivering to wonder what he had really seen. A mirage? Hallucination? Or the gates of hell flung open?

The storm threw the perimeter defense screen into a jumble of overload. Carbon units flickered in and out of reality, and the sensors could not distinguish real from false echoes, could not distinguish anything accurately. It gave up and went off-line. Its screen went blank, and the laser bank went dark.

The mercenary spoke on the unit frequency, "All right, girls, all you who were complaining about how boring this has been, now hear this: There is no perimeter defense as of now."

An unidentified mercenary joined in, "He's here."

The commander glanced at the unit activity display that projected inside his helmet visor. There were four active units, and there were supposed to be five. He looked again. Three units active. "You guys, ident!"

Two actives responded.

Sergeant Johnson used the cover of the storm as it passed through the compound. He had gotten under one of the barrack buildings and was preparing to get close enough to one of the dark shapes to find out what he was up against when two of the shapes ran past his hiding place. 'Damn,' he thought, 'for all that armor, those guys can really move.' He inched toward the sitting shape. It sat motionless at its post. 'Vigilant bastard,' Johnson reflected.

The storm was letting up a bit, and Johnson could see the legs of one of the armored men approach the sitting shape. The armored one prodded the sitting one and then he left. Johnson crept closer. He flicked a small stone at the figure before him. It rattled off of the figure's armor, but the figure did not respond. Johnson decided to chance it, drew his knife, and looked for some opening in the armor that would be vulnerable to a thrust. There were some, he concluded. Just like opening a lobster. Except with lobster, if you didn't get it right the first time, you got another chance.

He slowly came out from under the building. Without the flooring above his head, his view increased, and he saw that the seated figure did not have on his helmet. It was upside down in the mud several feet away, as if thrown there. 'The guy's dead,' Johnson reasoned, and he approached more directly. The trouper was clad in impressive armor finished in flat black, and he was wearing what looked like sunglasses. Johnson removed the sunglasses and dropped them in the mud.

"Holy shit," Johnson breathed, and then he crept back into hiding and began another stalk. As he crawled and stopped and crawled, making his way across the compound, Johnson tried to get the image out of his mind. The trooper's face had been frozen in an expression of absolute terror, and blood flowed from his eyes. Sergeant Johnson found two more troopers, both with the most indescribable expressions of fear on their faces, blood running from their eyes. Both dead without a scratch on them. Once more, Johnson faded into the darkness to wait. The two remaining troopers ran by him again. They never suspected his presence. Johnson heard their footsteps splashing across the wet ground. They were firing weapons as they ran. They spread out, and Johnson got a glimpse of their target. It might have been a man -- no armor, just standing there. One of the attackers threw down his weapon and tore off his helmet. He screamed a horrid jarring scream and sank to his knees in the mud. The other trooper fired a long burst of high explosive rounds and fled.

The shadowy figure of the man came toward the kneeling trooper. Johnson could only see part of what was happening, but the man paused directly in front of the trooper and then walked on into the night, passing silently like the Angel of Death. Soon after he passed, the trooper's head exploded. A skull fragment landed next to Johnson.

The mercenary commander now showed one active on his visor monitor. He took off his helmet and waited. The remaining trooper ran up to him and spoke, but without a helmet, the commander did not hear him, so the trooper raised his visor.

His eyes showed that he was extremely frightened. He was about to speak again when the air began to glow. Waves of blue and green began to rotate around the commander and the trooper. The waves continued rapidly to wind around, the way someone might wind a ball of string.

The trooper knew. "You son-of-a-bitch, Mr. James, you didn't tell us we were hunting a bowman!"

"Would you have come if I had?" asked the commander.

"Fuck no."

"I rest my case," the commander said calmly.

The excited trooper asked, "So now what?"

"We set the trap. He walked into it. Now we take him out. Fun and profit, laddie, fun and profit."

The commander dropped his helmet. The trooper watched it fall. It should have hit the ground. In the real world, it would have just made its little hit-the-ground noise and that would have been it. But the helmet fell and continued to fall. The trooper looked -- stability was leaving. The helmet disappeared like a rock falling off a cliff fades into the perspective of the chasm.

"Damn, I hate these Guardian fights." He had seen two others, and the interruption of reality deeply bothered him. He held his weapon tightly, gritted his teeth, and tried to keep his stomach from heaving, as up and down and left and right became meaningless. Light wove an eerie sphere. Flames of electric discharge licked in free play within the enclosure. "I hate Guardian fights. I hate time locks. I wish this shit would stop." But no wishes were being granted this night.

The commander turned, constantly looking for a point of attack. So far, there was only the bluish prison and the Saint Elmo's fire. Then, larger than life -- huge, like a movie screen close-up -- eyes. Two eyes of a demon, piercing into the mind of the trooper. He saw his commander flinch, take a half step backward, and then regain composure. The eyes became a face. The face became a form, and then, with a howling of air and electricity, the form became a man. The man opened his mouth, and a low rumble escaped. Not a roar. Certainly not a shout or scream. But the enclosure shook, and pain shot through the trooper's brain. The trooper was amazed at his commander's attitude. Not calm but definitely still in control.

"Robertson, welcome."

The trooper gave up hope, "Oh Christ, Robertson." For he had heard the legend, and he knew enough to be terrified.

The figure spoke, "So, Christian James. Your momma never knew what she produced when she named you," and the speech echoed in the chamber.

"Thank you for coming, Bob," and the commander's hand formed in the way of Guardian warriors. "We don't have much time for this. They're going to blow the atomic at 0400, and we planted an implosion petard on the tower just to keep things interesting," and a flash of energy flew from his hand.

Robertson raised his own hand with his palm toward the incoming energy, deflected it, and sent it into the recesses of the time lock. The commander's bolt hit something the trooper did not see, did not know existed, and the energy returned at an even greater intensity to explode nearby. "Oh shit," and the trooper closed his eyes. It didn't help. He could still see the duel and the wild unreality of the time lock, and his mind could not rid itself of the images.

The two opponents moved and dodged. They controlled ominous energy force and directed it. The energy in bolts, in constant waves, in the shape of arrows, all flew into the conflict. But the energy weapons were seldom directed at the target. The missiles were sent into the time lock and returned at odd angles to continue the attack from unexpected directions. A strange smell filled the sphere and the trooper gagged. The two warriors continued to move and weave. This was three-dimensional chess for keeps. Fog from the explosions obscured the two figures as they fought. Reflections within the fog produced multiple images. Which was the reflection? Which the target?

A scream of pain.

The fog thinned.

Bolts of energy came from only one source.

They stopped altogether. A few stray incoming remnants were casually deflected by the remaining combatant and sent to explode harmlessly in the depths of the time lock.

The trooper gasped. The standing figure was his commander. "Holy shit, he did it."

As the time lock faded, Robertson sat leaning against the wall of a barracks interior.

The trooper questioned, "How did we get here?" Nobody bothered to answer him.

Robertson was holding his right arm. All that was left was a stump that dangled from his shoulder. Arterial blood pumped from between his fingers as he gripped the stump. He was in great pain. "Good fight, Chris."

Christian James nodded but said nothing.

Robertson looked up at his opponent. His eyes were sad. "Why?"

"Why what?"

"Why all this? Why did we wind up enemies?"

"You really pissed off a lot of folks with that goody-goody lets-stamp-out-corruption-in-the-Force attitude of yours. First of all, the corruption wasn't all that bad. Second, it went very high up. There was plenty for all, and that included you, if you had had any sense. But no, not the 'Great One,' not

Robertson the Pure, Defender of the Balance, and all that bullshit. You were getting too close, Bobby, so that last mission of yours -- it was a set-up the whole way. You were supposed to get dead, and it almost worked out that way. I mean you were in sorry-ass shape when they dragged you back. So they put you on the shelf in Guardian Hall. Life support in perpetuity. And that was politically even better than dead. The hero on display, lots of honors, no investigation. Beautiful."

"Why not just turn off the life support?" Robertson asked weakly. The blood was pooling on the floor beside him.

"What for? You were on the shelf. That project was completed."

"Well, why come hunting for me? I don't give a shit about your corruption problems anymore."

"Oh, I see what you mean. No, this is a whole new project."

"Really?"

"Oh, yeah. And this one pays real good too. You're right. You were no threat. Until you rebuilt. I told them you might. I mean we go way back. I know you. I had to push really hard, but finally they believed me. So we gave you a tracker just in case. Sure enough, you left, and we followed. Very simple, very easy. The only problem, of course, is getting your cooperation about being dead. You are hard to catch, and you are very hard to kill."

"Thank you."

"You're welcome. You're going to make me rich, you know."

Robertson was silent.

"Yep," James continued, "there is a hell of a bounty on you."

"This is all about money?" Robertson asked in disbelief.

James grew somber, "No. It's more. There are pressures you wouldn't understand, all safe and candy-ass retired. You wouldn't have a clue. The sons of bitches. Well, what the fuck, at least I'm gonna be rich."

The trooper interrupted, "Sir, it's getting awfully close to 0400. What do you want to do about the PT-10?"

"Leave it. We'll be gone shortly."

The trooper relaxed slightly. He would have had to retrieve the device, and he knew that if he couldn't get to it in time, he would become expendable while trying.

Robertson asked weakly, "A PT-10? Goddamn, Chris."

"Yeah, I know. But here is the thing. I use the PT-10. If you don't show up here, I leave it, and the planet goes. Eliminate your home, your base. If you win the fight, the PT-10 takes you out anyway."

"Chris, there are only three known oasis planets in the whole universe. You'd risk destroying one of them for a bounty?"

Christian James shrugged, "I like to win."

"You are a sorry shit."

"Ain't that the truth. Don't take this so personal, Bob."

"Well, in the old days, you would never have strangled a dog just to get a little information." Robertson's speech was unsteady.

"What are you talking about?"

"Mose. Good old dog," Robertson said faintly.

"Oh that. That was Peavey, not me. You know how he was always kicking cats and stuff. But who gives a shit anyway."

"Peavey turned too?"

"Yeah. He had some grand scheme, old Peavey did. Took a short squad of pick-up mercenaries and went off to grab your ass. But he must have fucked up, because here you are. Stupid plan of his never was going to work. I told him as much. He figured to go after your family and work some kind of improvisational hostage deal to get you to come to him on his terms. I told him it was stupid, but he wouldn't listen. He's gone worthless now. Mostly sits in bars getting drunk. He did claim a probable kill on your kid, but he didn't bring back any hard physical or DNA, only had his recorded helmet virtual to show, so he just got paid a partial bounty. Still, that made him a very rich drunk . . . a rich, crazy drunk. Come to think of it, everybody I ever saw you deal with wound up crazy. Crazy or dead, of course."

"So, Peavey magged my house."

"Yep. He's the only one that made it back, for some reason he ain't talking about. And he gets real jumpy whenever a new class of cadets forms up. Keeps going up to Guardian Hall and looking them over. My way was better."

"Your way?"

"Oh, yeah. Hell of a plan. I picked some fairly inept shooters and sent them after you. I told them it was going to be a two-sided attack, but I never intended to show up and be the second attack force. They were just supposed to get their asses blown off and provide you with enough hints to bring you here. And here you are. Hell of a plan."

"Congratulations."

"Thank you."

There was a pause. "Peavey and how many others?" Robertson asked.

"Well now, Bob, that's a secret. I could tell you, but then I'd have to kill you." James looked at the bleeding Robertson and laughed. "You are in shitty-dead shape, Bobby. Bobby-wobby," and he laughed again.

"So how many?"

"Thirty. What the hell, I mean you are going down, so what the hell. Ain't a great big secret anyway. There's me and Peavey, except now Peavey is out of it. So then there's Doc and Narley. You remember Doc, right?"

"I remember Doc," Robertson said in a feeble voice.

"So we're the heavy hitters, the bowmen. The rest are rag-ass Guard grunts with big egos and some powder-puff mercenaries. Of course, most who started out are no longer in the hunt. Peavey lost his nine. No surprise there. Stupid-ass Peavey. You took out the six I sent to coax you here plus, it appears, my locals except for Toad here," he said, referring to the trooper still in the room. "So, there's another nine. Doc and Narley wanted to work alone so as not to have to split any bounty. Course with a really good plan, you can use up those who were expecting a piece of the pie and get it all for yourself, anyway."

The trooper now known as Toad did not like the sound of his commander's exposed logic, and he made a note to be extra careful in the future.

"So, of the original thirty, there's not that many left."

"I count twenty-nine," Robertson said.

"Twenty-nine, thirty. Whatever. I never liked math."

"All that, just to come after me?"

"Well, nobody figured you would be all that easy to get to. But the price is out for your whole family, too, and one other old-fart bowman. So don't get a swelled head or anything."

"Who's the other bowman?"

"I ain't telling. I'll get him next. I am going to be one rich motor scooter."

Robertson's eyes grew wide. He smiled slightly. Christian James noticed the changes and looked hard at his opponent. He was certainly near death. Blood continued to flow from between his fingers, and he was becoming very pale. But why the sly smile?

Following Robertson's eyes, James noticed a defect in the flooring below his feet. A large rattlesnake had come out from under the floor, probably from some den below the barracks. The snake was startled, and seeking refuge, it darted into the small gap between James' leg armor and his boot. He could feel the thing writhe inside the armor. James fumbled with the emergency armor release, found it, and his chest armor fell to the floor. He released his sidearm and fired into the armor at his feet. Pieces of snake splattered in the room. "Jesus Christ! I hate those things. Got you, you little bastard."

"Chris," Robertson began in a forced deliberate voice, "you never get all of the snakes."

"Well, I sure got that one."

"Sir," the trooper interrupted again.

"Yeah, I know . . . close to 0400. I'm almost done. You know what I wish? I wish my father could have seen me take you out, Bob. I mean, I did it. I am the best there is. Hell, I am the best there ever fucking was. That would show him."

Robertson smiled faintly, "Chris, your father always thought you were a pussy. Told me to look after you."

"Bullshit. That's bullshit. If he could see this, he'd . . . what are you looking at?" James asked Robertson angrily.

Robertson half-raised a finger to point behind James, "Another snake."

James wheeled around to kill, but there was nothing there. He turned back toward his bleeding victim.

Robertson smiled, silently mouthed the word 'pussy,' closed his eyes, and died.

"Pussy, is it? Well, you're the dead one, Bobby. Not me. And I'll just be taking some of you back with me to prove it. A little bit of hard, goddamn physical stuff." James grabbed Robertson's left hand and stretched the arm toward him. "DNA with fingers." The blade of James' laser knife made a muffled gritty sound as it weaved through the tendons and bones of Robertson's wrist. The arm fell. Blood from the stump oozed onto the floor. "So game, set, match, and good fucking bye to you."

James felt something brush his leg. Snakes filled his mind, and he jerked his leg to one side. There was nothing there. 'You'll never get them all. Goddamn Robertson, anyway,' he thought. James saw the trooper grin. "What's so funny?"

"Nothing, sir."

"Well, you can go to hell." James stuffed the severed hand into his breast pocket and locked the flap. Colors briefly filled the room, and then Christian James was gone, leaving the trooper behind.

The trooper looked at his timer. "Oh, shit," he said, realizing his fate. Glancing up, he saw the body slumped in blood and the debris of battle, an image of defeat that seemed to fit him as well, but the image was fading. As he stared, the blood faded, and he could see the texture of the barracks wall through the slumped figure. The scene was turning to gauze before his eyes, and as he continued to stare into the barracks, he began to see the snakes his commander had feared. The floor rippled with them, and wading forward came a figure of another Robertson. Healthy. Unscathed. The images of two bears and a crow were just fading from his side as he strode into the room. The trooper had heard the legends. Heard barracks stories. Impossible rumors of power. He did not wait for the figure to fully form, but bolted from the barracks in the terrible realization that he was going to die this night a madman.

Robertson rubbed his temples and looked around the room. His head was filled with pain. He was exhausted. The drain of his efforts to control time and the minds of his opponents had been debilitating. 'I guess I'm getting a little long in the tooth for this stuff, too,' he thought. His vision was blurred, but that would be only temporary. The headache, he knew, would last for a long time. And yet, he had to retrieve the PT-10, deal with the remaining trooper, and get back to Margaret. He looked at his watch. He had a little over forty minutes to do it all -- not much time. Forty minutes would be very tight, and with that thought, he strode into the night.

Christian James should have returned to his home time just as he had so often before. There he would have confidently, nonchalantly presented his severed trophy proof and claimed his glory and his bounty. He should have. That was his plan. But somewhere during his travel back, he had felt movement in his breast pocket. Robertson's hand had moved. 'Probably nothing but an involuntary muscle reaction,' he thought. 'Just a twitch. Just a final little twitch of dead fingers.'

He should never have lifted the pocket flap. But he had. And so, he had come home screaming uncontrollably and stabbing and slashing at his chest. Over and over, the five snakes formed and re-formed in his shredded pocket. One after the other they emerged, crawled over his bloody chest, wrapped around his arm, and slithered up toward his face.

One after the other. He would never be able to make them stop.

The night air was cool. The time storm that Robertson had used in his attack was breaking up, but it continued to rumble. There was occasional lightning. A light mist held in the air. He sat on the top stair and loosened the straps on his backpack. He rubbed his temples, sat in pain, and let time flow by.

Finally, he got to his feet and went down the three remaining stairs and stepped into the mud below. He entered the shadows at the corner of the building and his foot hit something. He looked down. Sprawled face down on the ground was the trooper. Blood was seeping from the back of his head just under his helmet. Robertson knelt and felt the trooper's wound. The spinal cord was cleanly severed at the base of the skull. Somebody lucky or somebody very good had been at work.

"Don't make any sudden moves." The voice was deep and quiet and authoritative. "Now just step around the side here."

"I don't have a lot of time for this," Robertson said as he moved slowly in the darkness.

"Who are you?" the voice asked.

Robertson demanded, "Did you do this?" and he pointed to the dead trooper.

"Answer my question," the voice replied.

"God damn it, you son-of-a-bitch, did you do this?" Robertson roared.

"Yeah," was the quiet reply. "I took out a guy who shouldn't be here, and I'm pointing a .45 Colt at another one. So who the fuck are you?"

"Who do you think I am?"

"I think you are a foreign fucking spy, that's who."

"It's a good thing I speak English then, isn't it?" Robertson was trying to locate where the voice was coming from.

"You'd be a dumb-ass spy if you couldn't speak English. So just what are you doing down here by the gadget?"

"Actually, I am deciding whether or not to kill you." Robertson's casual tone put Johnson on edge.

"I don't think you'd be the one doing any killing. Matter of fact, you are just one .45 slug away from dead right now."

Johnson was moving silently after each time he spoke. Robertson could not pinpoint where he was and thought to himself, 'This guy is good.' "If you have a gun, let me hear you cock it."

"You don't do much of this, do you, Jack? It don't do piss-all to cover a guy with a gun that isn't ready to fire."

"So, how do I know you have a gun?"

"You could try making one of those sudden moves."

Robertson was rapidly running out of time. "Molly, does he have a gun?"

"Yes, Robert. It's in his right hand."

"Who the fuck is that?" Johnson asked in a forced whisper.

"Why don't you pack it for him."

"I don't know, Robert. Is this a riddle?"

"Pack the goddamn gun, Molly."

"Yes, your worship," and the beam flashed outward. Johnson's eyes were wider than they had ever been as his .45 automatic vanished from his hand into a magenta-colored line of light that came from his captive's backpack.

Molly continued, "He also has a knife, Robert."

"Let him keep the knife," Robertson said, and he reached into his pocket and put on night vision glasses. He turned and saw Johnson, crouched with a knife in his hand. "Don't do that," Robertson said in a friendly way, as if talking to a child who was about to eat his mashed potatoes with his hand.

Johnson circled to his right, deeply curious now but still on guard. Robertson slid the glasses down his nose and tried to find his attacker. He raised the glasses back to look through them again. "You are hard to see. And you are very good at what you do. So you did this," Robertson said, gesturing to the body of the dead trooper.

"Yes, I did. You with Special Security?"

Special Security seemed to be a good idea, and Robertson adopted it the way a palm reader expands bits of information to amaze a customer and seem clairvoyant. "Robertson. Special Security, M-5 Branch. Why didn't you kill me when you had the chance?"

"Because you were killing those other bastards, so I thought you might be legit."

"Legit?" Robertson was not sure of this term.

"Yeah," Johnson said without explanation.

"Right. Well, that was good thinking. Who are you?"

"Sergeant Johnson."

"Well, Sergeant, normally if I told you what I am about to tell you, I'd then have to shoot you, but that would be an idiotic field-grade thing to do in this case." Most enlisted men had a prejudice against field grade officers as a class of beings, and Johnson was no exception. He lowered his knife and Robertson continued, "At the top of that tower there is a bomb, an atom bomb. It's the first one ever made, and those . . . infiltrators have placed a PT-10, an implosion petard . . . ," Robertson saw Johnson did not understand. "It's a metal sphere about the size of an orange. It doesn't have to be very big because once you get it ignited, it absorbs all the stuff around it and accelerates it inward, then releases the condensed molecular energy all at once. Takes about a billionth of a second. Probably makes a loud noise. It is designed to initiate by high velocity impact, but they put it up there at the top of the tower to use the atom bomb for an accelerator to set it off, okay?"

"I don't know."

"The bad guys made the earth into a grenade, and the good guys don't know it, but they are going to pull the pin."

"What are you talking about?"

"Bad things. Death . . . destruction. That sort of thing. According to the record, at 0400 the bomb in that tower exploded, and if we don't get the petard away from there, then . . . I don't know . . . a hole the size of Texas, maybe all of the nitrogen in the atmosphere will ignite, dust to block out the sun, and temperatures of 200 below zero. Maybe it would be enough to destabilize the orbit or break the earth in half. I don't know. I just don't know."

Johnson was puzzled. "Why not? Ain't one ever been used before?"

"Oh yeah, they've been used. I saw a virtual of one in action, and believe me they work. I've just never seen one used on a planet before."

"Say, what?" Johnson asked.

"The PT-10 was designed for meteor interception and destruction. Only one has been used that I know of, since a significant space strike doesn't threaten very often. Of course, they have been tested on asteroids and the like. But just the one actual pre-emptive. It worked like a charm. That was World Day. Now it's a worldwide holiday. But if one sets off in that tower this morning, roaches will inherit what's left of the earth."

"Jesus."

"Jesus." Robertson wasn't agreeing with Johnson. He had just looked at his watch. The secondhand was rising past the numeral eight . . . past the numeral nine. In fifteen seconds it would be 4:00 in the morning of July 15, 1945, . . . ten seconds. Robertson looked at the tower one hundred yards away, silhouetted by spotlights, hard and distinct near the ground, then gradually blurring into the illuminated mist until it was no longer distinct at all. "What time do you have?"

Johnson looked at his watch, "Oh shit," and he instinctively dove under the barracks.

Robertson's heart sank. There was no way he could get to the tower, let alone climb to the top and retrieve the PT-10 without a time lock. Five seconds to go. His head throbbed. There was a red hot stiletto that ran from his right temple through the back of both his eyes and exited near his left temple. He couldn't do it. His knees felt weak. Four seconds. His head dropped, and he sank into the desert sand and leaned on one arm.

Nothing.

Johnson poked his head out from under the barracks.

Robertson checked his watch. 0400 and ten seconds more. Twenty. 0401.

Nothing.

"Maybe it didn't work," Johnson said hopefully.

"Oh, no, it worked. Trust me."

"Maybe the storm screwed it up. I know the long-hairs were real nervous about lightning and electrical stuff."

Robertson looked up at the sky. The cloud cover was breaking up, and stars were visible in isolated spaces in the overcast. "Well, it's not raining anymore," and he headed toward the tower. "You know Sergeant, you don't smell that good."

"That's a long story, sir. Hey, wait a minute. They won't set the thing off with Dr. Kisty sitting up there," Johnson said, pointing his thumb at the tower.

"Dr. who?"

"Dr. Kisty, Kistokosky, or Kistiasky or something."

"What are you talking about?"

"General Groves was all afraid about . . . well, I'll be damned. The General, he was afraid of saboteurs. I'll be a son-of-a-bitch . . . how'd he known? And a Jap parachute attack. You don't suppose . . . ?"

"No. There aren't going to be any Japanese here this morning."

"Well, the General has gotten jumpy as a cat about security. Sent us to guard the gadget. That's how I got to be here. So they ain't gonna set it off yet because the doctor is still sitting up there. All we have to do is go up and tell him what's going on, get the what's-it, and get the hell out of here, right?"

"No."

"Why not?"

"Because I don't want anyone to know anything about PT-implosion technology."

"About what?"

"About how to make a hole the size of Texas."

"Oh."

"So we wait."

"Wait!?" The Sergeant did not like that possibility.

"Until the doctor leaves. Then we get the what's-it and get the hell out of here."

"But when the doctor leaves, they'll set off the gadget then for sure."

"Where will they take the doctor when it's time?"

"Probably to S-10,000."

261

"Whatever that is, how long does it take to get from here to there?"

"Who are you?"

"What?"

Johnson looked at Robertson. He thought about his .45 disappearing in a beam of light. "Who the fuck are you? You walk by and guys in armor just die. You got some damn thing on your back that dissolves weapons. You said, 'According to records, the bomb went off,' like it already happened. You don't know about S-10,000, and everybody knows about that bunker, and you wear sunglasses in the night. You and those other guys that took over the tower barracks here, you all wear sunglasses. So who the fuck are you?"

Robertson took off the night glasses and handed them to Johnson, "Here, put them on."

Johnson took the glasses and put them on. His jaw dropped. "I'll be damned. Just like the daytime. I sure could use a pair of these."

"You'll have to give them back. They're classified."

"And you'd have to shoot me," Johnson said as he made a mental note to collect a pair of the glasses from one of the dead stormtroopers.

The early morning darkness was damp and quiet. Robertson and Johnson sat on the steps of the barracks and waited. Johnson had the night vision glasses and was watching the tower for signs of activity. He was worried by a thought, "You don't suppose we missed them leaving. You know, with the fog and all."

Robertson shook his head 'no.' It was a mistake. The motion made his headache worse.

"Right," Johnson muttered. "Are you okay?"

"Yes," Robertson said feebly, "just a headache." And he thought to himself, 'Just a headache, like a bowling alley in my brain.' He concentrated on relaxing, on imagining the blood vessels expanding and flushing away the pain like a cool mountain stream. It helped. A little. Robertson nodded toward the body of the mercenary. "Nice kill."

"Yeah."

"It's not easy taking one of those guys out."

"You didn't seem to have much trouble doing it. What did you use?"

"Well, it's sort of a unique family . . . gift. My grandfather started it. My dad can do it. Probably, my son will find out he can do it, too."

"What are you talking about?"

"I scared them to death."

"Bullshit."

"Are you afraid of something, Sergeant? Some deep terror that you hide even from yourself?" As he spoke, he looked into the sergeant's eyes. Johnson's mind whirled. He felt locked inside a diving suit. The helmet was bolted on and the suit was filling with water. The water was rising up past his chin, past his mouth, covering his nose now. He tried to scream but could only gurgle as death filled his lungs. 'Can't get out. No air.' Then it was all over. He was sitting quietly in the darkness. His companion's eyes had softened and he smiled, "You handle fear very well."

"Shit," Johnson said very softly, "you did that to all of them?"

"Most of them. We all have our own fears. If you keep them bottled up, never meet them, never make friends with them, they can kill you. Some of these guys were afraid of a lot of stuff. Others it didn't work on, so I used a more direct approach."

Johnson did not say anything. He was remembering the trooper's head exploding.

A jeep drove out of the night and stopped at the base of the tower. The driver got out and tapped his bayonet on one of the steel tower legs. He called upward into the foggy darkness, "Dr. Kistiakowsky, sir, they said for you to set your switches and come on back to S-10,000."

From the top of the tower a voice called down, "How long?"

"Half an hour, sir. It's set to fire now at 0530. Metro says the storm is clearing and the weather will hold at least until then."

In the stillness following the storm, the corporal could hear the faint clicking and occasional mutterings as Dr. Kistiakowsky threw the switches that armed the device. "Is everything okay, Doctor?" the corporal asked.

"Oh yes."

"Where are the security people? Sergeant Johnson's people?"

There was no immediate answer, but the familiar metallic sounds of the tower ladder could be heard as Dr. Kistiakowsky and the arming crew descended. The hollow rhythm of shoes on metal rungs transferred from the ladder to the whole tower. In comparison to the previous stillness, it sounded like a bell tolling in the night.

"Are you in the pool?" the doctor asked.

"Well sort of," the assistant answered as the crew continued down the ladder. "I bet a box of cigars with the guys that it would go off, but no specific TNT force or anything. Just that it would go off. I heard you bet Oppie a month's pay against a ten-dollar bill that it would work."

"Oh, it will go off. Of that I am sure," said the scientist. "I am in for 1400 tons. Teller, the optimist, went for 45,000. Now that would be something . . . 45,000 tons of TNT . . . Bang!"

"What did Oppie bet?"

"Two or three hundred tons, I forget. With me, he bet ten dollars that it won't work at all."

The arming crew reached the ground and Dr. Kistiakowsky asked the corporal, "What did you ask us, Sergeant?"

"Corporal, sir."

"Whatever. I do not pay attention. If it is shiny, then I call them Colonel. If it is on the sleeve, I make a Sergeant."

"Where are the security guards that General Groves sent down here with you?" the corporal asked.

"The army comes. The army goes. Blessed be the way of the army," and with that the doctor and his crew boarded their jeep.

One of them continued the conversation, "What does Fermi think?"

The corporal got in his jeep and put it in reverse, "The General is very worried about security, sir."

Kistiakowsky gave a dismissive wave of his hand and said, "It is time to go, Corporal. In half an hour we will not need security here, anyway," and he turned to his fellow scientist assistant. "Fermi thinks that we will set the atmosphere on fire and destroy all life on the planet. But he is also offering special odds on the mere destruction of New Mexico."

"Good God, is that possible, Doctor?"

"Fermi thinks so. I think 1400 tons -- bang! -- and then we all go home." And the last keeper of the bomb headed off toward the bunker at S-10,000.

'So it had been the weather,' Robertson thought. The time storm had held up the countdown. The bomb really had gone off at 4:00 in the morning the first time. Robertson looked at his watch. It was 5:06. He had twenty-four minutes to climb, return, and get back to pick up M'Gee. It would be very close. He asked Sergeant Johnson, "Have you got a jeep? Say yes."

"Yes, sir, I got a jeep."

"Good, you're going to have to haul ass," Robertson said as he got to his feet.

"I'm all for that," Johnson said. "Sir, are you okay?"

"Yeah, why?"

"Well, you got up kinda slow."

"I get stiff when I sit too long," Robertson explained as he twisted and stretched his body to try to make it feel younger. "Now what I want you to do is get up off your butt, find your jeep, and drive southeast from here about two miles. There's this really lovely young lady sitting on a rock out there. She's pregnant with my grandchild, and the two of them are waiting for me to come to get them. Well, you get them for me. You pick her up and get her to a safe area, that S-10,000 or over the ridge, whatever, but get it done."

"What are you going to do?"

Robertson made a theatrical gesture in the air, "I am off to save the world."

"You are a bit tight on time, sir."

"Oh, well . . ."

"Why don't I get the jeep and wait here with it for a bit, in case you make the round trip in time for all of us to ride off into the sunset together?"

"Sergeant, get the jeep, get the girl, get out of Dodge," and the tone left no doubt that the discussion was over. "And tell the little fellow what went on here tonight. If genetics are anything at all, he'll settle the score for me."

"So, how do you know it's a boy, sir?"

"We all have been so far."

"Sir?" Johnson asked, not understanding who Robertson was talking about.

"Go, Sergeant," Robertson said as he began jogging toward the tower.

"Yes, sir," and Johnson headed off to find the jeep.

As Robertson began his climb up the one-hundred-foot tower, Kistiakowsky and the guards were in sight of the bunker S-10,000. Ten thousand yards south of ground zero, inside the bunker, Sam Allison sat facing two microphones. It seemed melodramatic to him, and he was a little self-conscious as he announced, "It is now zero minus twenty minutes." His call went into the night through speakers all over the area. Public address systems and intercoms and FM radios sent the '. . . zero minus twenty minutes deep into the minds of the listeners. General Groves heard it and thought, "This two-billion-dollar firecracker better go bang."

The speaker inside the barracks crackled its hoarse echo of Allison's voice. Sergeant Johnson was startled at the voice coming out of the desert silence. Then he remembered the barracks speaker and relaxed, only to become more tense when the significance of the words sank in. In twenty minutes, a hole as big as Texas. "We're dead," he said to himself.

Robertson, at the top of the tower, was impressed by the view. The sky was clearing and the vast open quiet of the desert below was beautiful even in its starkness. 'Not stark,' he thought, 'simple. There is no excess in the desert. Only efficiency. Or death.'

He looked around the tangle of wires that came from the large round capsule that held so much death. He touched it and found it cold. 'Just you wait,' he thought and continued his search for the PT-10. It wasn't there. There was only the shape of the gadget and the wires and switches that were its web. He looked again. He went down the ladder a little way to see if the PT-10 was suspended from below. It wasn't.

The barracks speaker sounded again. Distant, faint, but coarsely distinct, "It is now zero minus fifteen minutes."

Robertson leaned on the railing and looked back at the gadget. A round hulk of darkness with wires coming out of it. Just a big round . . . "Well shit," he said out loud as he realized where the PT-10 had been all the time. It made sense. Whoever carried it up the ladder had not expected anyone to come and babysit the bomb, let alone anyone to come to look for sabotage. Whoever it had been had just put the PT-10 in the easiest place, and in doing so, had effectively hidden it in plain sight. On top of the bomb was a slight depression, and in the depression was the PT-10, looking for all the world like a simple lump that was a design feature of the bomb's exterior.

Robertson reached up and lifted the sphere. It was lighter than he had expected. He brought it down to his waist level and saw a note attached. It read:

> Bob, if you are reading this, I
> assume that I am the dead one
> today, and you are the big
> winner once again. I always

liked the blue planet and would
hate to see anything too terrible
happen to it. So this is not
really a PT-10. Kinda looks like
one though, and it served its
purpose. It brought you here
beside the world's first atomic
bomb. So, check your watch,
Bobby, I got you anyway. Bang
and fuck you. Love, Chris.

Robertson checked his watch. Minutes. Just some minutes. Not many. Not enough. He dropped the sphere over the edge of the tower railing. It hit the concrete pad below, bounced off of its firm surface, and then rolled toward the barracks.

"It is now zero minus ten minutes."

Johnson found his jeep. He jumped into the driver's seat and turned the engine over. It ground over and over but did not start. The obstinate whirring of the starter became slower.

"Oh fuck," Johnson said, "Come on jeep," and he continued his attempt until the battery died. "Oh fuck!"

There was a dreadful silence as Johnson realized that the jeep would not start ever again. And out of that silence, more startling than a cannon going off, came a metallic clank as something hit the jeep's hood. It was the rotor from the distributor. Johnson recognized it. No rotor, no start. The sound, the object, and the concept held all of the sergeant's attention until he felt something very cold press against his temple.

"Climb out real slow, Blackie."

Inside the S-10,000 bunker, Sam Allison was about to light a cigarette when over the countdown system came the sound of Tchaikovsky's *Nutcracker Suite*. The bunker grew quiet. Looks were exchanged. Some FM station with the same frequency was coming over the wires.

"You know, Sam," one of the scientists said, "the radiation may come over the wires just like the *Nutcracker*, or like lightning . . . just come right into the microphone and . . . ," and he made an explosive motion with his hands.

Allison was not amused. "It is now zero minus five minutes," he said as he stared at the microphones so close to his face and wondered.

Robertson approached the barracks, using the final minutes to confirm that Johnson and his jeep had departed to get Margaret. He saw no one. Good. He would rest briefly and then try to ride the colors to another time before the bomb went off. If he could. He felt utterly drained. Maybe Chris had won this one after all. Something moved in the shadows by the barracks. It came toward him. It was Sergeant Johnson. With his hands on his head.

"Go on over and join the nice man, Blackie," and an armored stormtrooper stepped out of the shadows. His visor was retracted so he could talk in open air. He had Margaret and he had a weapon pressed against her head. "I need a guide, Robertson," the trooper said.

"What's going on?" Robertson asked.

"I got careless," Johnson said dejectedly.

The trooper repeated his demand, "A guide, or I kill Blackie and the girl."

Robertson did not recognize the trooper. 'Shit,' he thought to himself, 'all this way to be taken out by some unknown grunt trooper.' He remembered Christian James' math. 'So there were thirty after all. And so runs the Whim of the Universe.' Then to the trooper he said, "So why should I help you just because you picked up some broad?"

"Because when I caught up to this broad, she said all sweet-like, 'Is that you, Mister Robertson?' That's why."

"If you kill her, I am for sure not going to help you."

From the barracks speaker, "It is now zero minus three minutes."

Johnson asked, "What the hell is going on?"

Robertson said, "Oh this bozo wants me to help him escape."

"Escape!?" Johnson exclaimed. "Zero minus three minutes and he thinks we can escape? Fat fucking chance!"

"So, you and Blackie here really are in this together. I figured as much. A guide, that's all," the trooper insisted. "Just a guide back to The Present."

Robertson said quietly without moving his lips, "Sarge, are you a very good shot?"

Johnson whispered back, "Best ever."

"Good. Want your gun back?"

"Uh-huh," Johnson muttered softly.

"Good." And then to the trooper, "If you kill her, I don't help you. If you let her go, I don't help you. So what are you bargaining with?"

"You are going to take me back so I can collect the bounty on your head," the trooper said smiling. "Because I am going to put a round into her where she'll need some real special medical attention. And if she gets it, then she won't die. And I figure you know how to get us there."

"It is now zero minus one minute."

Johnson breathed, "Oh shit."

Robertson said calmly, "You know they're going to set off an atomic in another minute?"

"Don't give you much time to make up your mind then does it, Robertson?"

Under his breath, Robertson said, "Molly, don't answer, but in ten seconds give the Sergeant back his gun. On my mark. If you are able, give a little wiggle." The backpack vibrated quietly. It actually felt good. "Well, if I am going to guide you, what's your name?" and then under his breath, not listening to the answer, "Sarge, open your right hand."

Johnson turned his hands so that his right hand was open. Still, both hands were on the top of his head, but a subtle smirk on the sergeant's lips indicated that he would not be a good little prisoner very much longer.

A loudspeaker crackled, "Zero minus twenty . . . nineteen . . . eighteen . . ."

Robertson stepped slowly toward the trooper. There were ten yards to cover.

"What about the black guy?" the trooper asked.

"Forget about him," Robertson said. The trooper did not realize that as Robertson approached, he was actually opening a firing lane for Sergeant Johnson.

". . . thirteen . . . twelve . . ."

"Molly, mark," Robertson whispered as he approached.

". . . nine . . . eight . . . seven . . . six . . ."

Robertson was very close. The trooper repositioned his weapon to focus it on Robertson, "No funny stuff, now."

In the S-10,000 bunker everyone was frozen. Only the *Nutcracker* haunting the background of Allison's count.

Robertson reached 'zero' and lunged to his right and dove for the desert floor. The trooper fired at where Robertson had been. The round hit in the distant darkness and whined off into the desert.

The MollyPAC had difficulty stabilizing as Robertson lunged, but even so, the sergeant felt the cold firmness of his weapon fill his right hand. He leveled the .45 and squeezed the trigger. The Colt fired. A dark dot appeared between the trooper's eyes. The back of the trooper's head exploded and bone and brain tissue repelled by the back of his helmet sprayed forward into the night. He dropped like a rock into the sand.

". . . five . . . four . . ."

"Nice shot, Sergeant," then Robertson continued, "Get your ass over here now! M'Gee, hold my hand."

"Where are we going, Robert?"

Johnson was amazed, "Going? Are you crazy?"

"I'm going to find my lady and my son. Then Fear and I are going hunting. And then I am going to goddamn retire! Want to come?"

" . . . three . . . two . . ."

Johnson was frantic, "Can't you hear the count? Don't you understand? We're dead!"

"Yes," replied Robertson, "won't that be useful?"

It was 0529. The sound of Allison's last count came over the barracks speaker, " . . . one . . . ZERO . . . ," and then it went dead.

Johnson screamed, "We're out of time!"

Robertson laughed, "Then we'll find some more."

There was no sound. No explosion. Only deep quiet and undulating color. In the bunker, eyes darted from scientist to scientist. Groves looked hard at Oppenheimer. He glared at the thought of two billion dollars spent and the damn thing didn't work.

Robertson held out his hand, "Well, are you coming, Sergeant?"

"No, I thought I'd just sit here and watch the bomb go off."

Margaret advised, "Hold on, Sergeant, this is not going to make any sense to you."

"Do you guys do this often?" Johnson's words made no sound as the colors engulfed the little group of travelers.

At 0529 and 45 seconds, the colors vanished and the night became day. The desert grass vaporized, a fireball 10,000 times hotter than the sun rose into the sky, and its violent wind roared past S-10,000.

Oppenheimer recalled a line from the *Bhagavad Gita*, "I am become Death, the shatterer of worlds," but he couldn't know how close he had breathed to the truth.

"Did you notice that rainbow-looking effect just before the big blast?" one of them asked.

"No. Just a hell of a light. A hell of a light."

'At least we won't have to climb the tower to see why it didn't work,' Ken Bainbridge thought to himself. It would have been his job. He shook Oppenheimer's hand, "Oppie, now we're all sons-of-bitches."

The last passage
----- O. C., The mansion, Killdeer, North Dakota -----

Far to the north of the White Sands desert, the fading light of evening made for difficult reading, and Quigley Bates closed the small leather-bound book and brought his tilted porch chair down to rest on all four legs. He re-lived the last passage. Saw it in his mind. His image was interrupted by a slurping sound, and he looked down at the tawny flap-eared puppy drinking from a bowl that recently had held the ice that cooled his beer.

"Well, Old Lion Heart Wolf Fang, Robert, Bob-For-Short, you may get to meet one of the Robertsons, you know that? Mind your manners when you do. It says here in this book that Robertsons are some awesome sons-of-bitches, and that, Bob dog, is a fact," and Quigley looked to his right at the last porch column and thought, just for an instant, that he saw an arrow embedded there holding an old gray tennis ball.

All of Grandpa's stories
----- The Present, Guardian Hall -----

The old Guardian addressed the new class of cadets with the same words he had used for so many other classes, "Welcome to Guardian Hall . . . I am then either the guard, the curator, the librarian, or the Fiend . . . As you approach Commitment Day . . . And so we tour."

He thought as he spoke, 'It was all rote. The same words. I am losing the fire. But these babies they are sending me now . . . how can I ever be expected to make Guardians out of this lot, let alone ever find bowmen. Oh well, babies, welcome to your first taste of war. Let me show you where to puke,' and he followed the last of the line of cadets into the Hall.

". . . longing to be other men who, safe in ignorance's quiet fort, shun the heaving ground of thought . . ." That line of poetry had circled in the Guardian's mind, for what . . . an hour now? Ten minutes? He did not know. 'You're drifting,' he told himself. That was a bad sign.

The door to the museum opened. A figure entered and tension flowed into the room like fog on the water. Long ago this man may have been a small boy who played and laughed and sang, who cried when puppies died. But the boy had smothered under battle scars. He began to move about the room, glaring into the eyes of the cadets. Demanding names.

The old Guardian's voice was deep. It wasn't loud, but it filled the room. "John Peavey, you are out of line." Cadets' heads turned. Their kindly white-haired Guardian had become something else. Taller, straighter, younger. Their librarian could be dangerous. "This is Guardian Hall. Not your private little inquisition."

"Well, golly gosh, I am so intimidated."

"You are not intimidated, John, you are drunk. Go home."

"I ain't done hunting grubs."

"Perhaps you would like to join your friend, Chris James."

"Chris is in a padded cell screaming about snakes."

"Yes, I know."

There was a frozen moment, and then Peavey laughed. Louder than was appropriate for the museum atmosphere. "That's a good one, Gunny. I tell you what . . . since I have killed my quota for today, I will leave. But fuck you anyway, old man." He paused at the door and addressed the cadets, "Have a nice day, ladies." Then he was gone.

The Guardian spoke, "Gentlemen, I am sorry for that. He has . . . bad memories. Please excuse the interruption and return to your studies."

The Guardian looked about the room. Most of the cadets were still uneasy. One was standing in the back of the room, his face just enough in shadow to be hidden without being obvious about it. Jones. The Guardian liked this cadet but could not decide whether he was shy and a weakling or just so confident of his inner self that he did not need to demonstrate his abilities. He was always quiet. He knew a surprising number of very dirty songs. He was not physically impressive. No one ever picked on him. He never really took charge. Others asked for his advice. He never really followed. He just consented to join in.

The Guardian had discussed Jones with some of the other drill instructors, and in their vernacular, 'Jones either really had his shit together, or he couldn't put it in a bag if you gave him one.' He was just part of the background blur of training. Unnoticed. But was he unnoticed like the grass that is walked on, or was he unnoticed like the snake that is hunting the rat? The Guardian could not decide.   And now, during the interruption, had Jones been hiding or stalking?

"So, what do you think, Mr. Jones?"

"About what, sir?"

"About John Peavey."

"I think I shall remember his face."   Jones approached the vacated exhibit.

The Guardian asked, "Do you have any questions?"

"Did you know him?"

"Oh yes, I knew him."

Jones indicated the deed record. "All of this is accurate? He really did all of those things?"

"Yes," the old Guardian said, "all of that and more."

Another cadet asked, "Do you know where he is now?"

"Peacefully retired, I imagine. I hope he is well."

Jones looked into the vacant exhibit chamber.   He looked at the handwritten words, "Come take my place . . ." The signature, "Robertson."

"I'll be damned," Jones muttered to himself.   "All of Grandpa's stories were true."

The Guardian Night

Siren lights in emptiness
Call to men, 'Come take my place'.
Lovers pause below to kiss
And join the twinkling dots of light
With thoughts and wild imaginings
Into beasts and giants' themes.
Truth is conjured in the mind
And rests upon the beach of Time.
Guardians walk those fickle sands
Longing to be other men
Who safe in ignorance' quiet fort
Shun the heaving ground of thought
And revel in their lovers' dreams
Of twinkling lights and giant themes.
In among the twinkling lights
Come
Travel if you dare,
But know it's here that Duty lurks
With Glory in her snare
And never joy nor peace nor love
Will ever find you there.
Let lovers kiss beneath the stars
And bless their gentle light.
They are the fires of Hell, my friend
These sirens of the night.

Made in the USA
Middletown, DE
17 February 2025

71391406R00166